Dorothy B. Hughes and The Murder Room

>>> This title is part of The Murder Room, our series dedicated to making available out-of-print or hard-to-find titles by classic crime writers.

Crime fiction has always held up a mirror to society. The Victorians were fascinated by sensational murder and the emerging science of detection; now we are obsessed with the forensic detail of violent death. And no other genre has so captivated and enthralled readers.

Vast troves of classic crime writing have for a long time been unavailable to all but the most dedicated frequenters of second-hand bookshops. The advent of digital publishing means that we are now able to bring you the backlists of a huge range of titles by classic and contemporary crime writers, some of which have been out of print for decades.

From the genteel amateur private eyes of the Golden Age and the femmes fatales of pulp fiction, to the morally ambiguous hard-boiled detectives of mid twentieth-century America and their descendants who walk our twenty-first century streets, The Murder Room has it all. **>>>**

The Murder Room
Where Criminal Minds Meet

themurderroom.com

Dorothy B. Hughes (1904–1993)

Dorothy B. Hughes was an acclaimed crime novelist and literary critic, her style falling into the hard-boiled and noir genres of mystery writing. Born in Kansas City, she studied journalism at the University of Missouri, and her initial literary output consisted of collections of poetry. Hughes' first mystery novel, *The So Blue Marble*, was published in 1940 and was hailed as the arrival of a great new talent in the field. Her writing proved to be both critically and commercially successful, and three of her novels – *The Fallen Sparrow, Ride the Pink Horse* and *In a Lonely Place* – were made into major films. Hughes' taught, suspenseful detective novels are reminiscent of the work of Elisabeth Sanxay Holding and fellow Murder Room author Margaret Millar. In 1951, Hughes was awarded an Edgar award for Outstanding Mystery Criticism and, in 1978, she received the Grand Master award from the Mystery Writers of America. She died in Oregon in 1993.

By Dorothy B. Hughes
(Select bibliography of titles published in The Murder Room)

The So Blue Marble (1940)
The Cross-Eyed Bear Murders (1940)
The Bamboo Blonde (1941)
The Fallen Sparrow (1942)
The Delicate Ape (1944)
Johnnie (1944)
Dread Journey (1945)
Ride the Pink Horse (1946)
The Candy Kid (1950)
The Davidian Report (1952)

The Candy Kid

Dorothy B. Hughes

An Orion book

Copyright © Dorothy B. Hughes 1950

This edition published by
The Orion Publishing Group Ltd
Orion House
5 Upper St Martin's Lane
London WC2H 9EA

An Hachette UK company
A CIP catalogue record for this book is available from the British Library

ISBN 978 1 4719 1743 1

www.orionbooks.co.uk

For Betty and Holm Bursum – and Juarez

ONE

HE WAS LEANING AGAINST THE FRONT OF THE Chenoweth Hotel waiting for Beach when the girl came by. He smelled as if he'd been out herding steers for two weeks, which was a fact. He didn't look as if his blue shirt and faded levis had been clean this morning, which was also a fact. He was sweaty and he looked it, he could feel the little trickles of it running down behind his ears into his neck. An August morning in El Paso didn't do much for that Man of Distinction appearance, and chaperoning stock didn't exactly perfume a guy. He pushed his battered brown hat further back on his head for coolness. The shade of the hotel was almost as insufferable as the sun of the streets. He wished to God that Beach would hurry and get over here. If they were going to stay all night he'd have a shower before lunch, if they could get a room. He didn't expect any particular trouble on the room, the Chenoweth would always take care of him if they had any space at all. Yet you never knew when some convention would be taking up that last midge of space.

He wasn't having much luck rolling a cigarette, his hands were too sweaty. Just as he was thinking that he'd better go in and buy a pack, wait for Beach in the air-cooled coffee shop, the girl came around the corner. She was tall, almost as tall as he, but he took a quick look at the pavement and saw that she was propped on heels. That made him feel more male. She had a million-dollar figure in a neat blue-and-white checkered suit, pin checks; the shoes were blue-and-white spectators. She

1

wasn't wearing a hat; her blond and brown hair, cut short, was like a cap on her head. She didn't look like Texas, not even like Dallas. She looked like turista from the East, New York or Philadelphia; or turista from the West, not Hollywood Boulevard but Wilshire; Beverly Hills, Romanoffs, the Bel-Air Bay club. She was upper-level stuff.

She glanced at him, the way a girl does at a man standing around doing nothing, and he saw she had a clean-cut, sunbrowned face, with eyes that matched her hair, gold and brown. Cold sober, high noon in summer-drenched El Paso, he described her eyes thus romantically, gold and brown.

He let the cigarette dribble to the pavement. It hadn't been much good anyway. And he let his eyes rest on the girl with pure pleasure. It wasn't often, no matter what street corner you were standing on, that you got a look at something this good. Of course it had to be then, at that very moment, that the Fernandez brothers rattled by in their old truck.

Ignacio, ignoring the fact that he was at the wheel, leaned out of the cab to yell, *"Que hay, Santa Fe!* How's tricks, kid?" It was pure exuberance on Ignacio's part, being released from the bondage of herding cattle, for a day and night in the border town. He and Jose had parted not more than thirty minutes ago at the yards.

But during the diversion, the girl's heels tapped on into the hotel; when the truck had gone by, so had the girl. Jose came to a definite conclusion. To wait outside the hotel in the heat was plain nuts. To go inside was the way of wisdom. And to follow the girl inside was the will of the Lord, else why had she been sent to tempt him? If you didn't wrassle with temptation when you were tempted, how could you call yourself a godly man? You couldn't, not in his book. You were just a damned sissy who ran away instead of facing up to good and evil, making a choice. Jose laughed at himself for conducting a private theological debate just because a slick dame had passed by. But he would go on in the Chenoweth to wait for Beach.

He needed a cigarette, and if he just happened to run into the girl again, that was pure luck. Nothing angled for.

Having made the decision, he pushed himself away from the plate-glass window, resettled his hat, and started toward the hotel door. He hadn't taken more than a stride when the door revolved and deposited the same girl outside again. She headed directly toward him. He wasn't dreaming. He knew she could have been heading in this direction to pass him and go on about her business. But she'd bump into him in a minute if she didn't stop moving. The clincher was that her eyes were on his face, not in a careless onceover but in a prying fashion, as if she were trying to get into his mind. It was quick, she hadn't time for more. He'd been right about her eyes, they were gold and brown.

She stopped cold just before she bumped. "Senor?" she began.

"*Si?*" If she was going in for Spanish-speaking, he'd play along. Some of the turistas couldn't resist going native in a big way.

But he wanted to laugh when she continued, "You want to make a little money, maybe? *Un pequeno dinero?* A little job, a little money, *si?*" She'd taken him for a bum, a border Mexican living off odd jobs for the turistas, the one hundred per cent Anglo-Saxon, gringo tourists. Well, he looked like a bum. And smelled like one. The hail from the Fernandez boys and their dirty truck had helped out the disguise.

Because it was funny, he played along. He could do the pidgin Mex better than she. "What you want, Maam?"

She studied his face, and then her eyes slanted quickly through the windows into the hotel lobby. What she saw there, he didn't know. What he saw was a scattering of the kind of old codgers who sit around in hotel lobbies. He also saw that Lou Chenoweth was at the desk which meant he and Beach could stay all night even if the hotel was sleeping guests in the boiler room. Lou had more than once shared her own apartment with the Aragon boys.

3

The girl faced him again. As cool as if it weren't ninety-nine in the shade. But she didn't say what she wanted. She continued to sell the job quite as if he had shrugged off her initial offer. "It's very simple. It won't take much of your time. A little job. *Por favor.*" In her kindergarten Spanish she seemed to think that amusing. *"Por dinero,"* she corrected herself.

Jose thought it was a laugh too. If only Beach wouldn't come barging up and spoil it. If only Beach had run into some of the Socorro gang and was sitting in a nice air-cooled bar over a cold beer. Which was what Jose had been suspecting with increasing ire for some time, while he sweat it out in front of the Chenoweth.

"No mas dinero," said Jose firmly. "Dol-lars. American dollars."

"Si," the girl said quickly. "I'll pay in dollars. Dollars not pesos."

He simulated thinking it over. "O-kay," he agreed without much interest. The act must be good or she was an awfully green gringo because she didn't doubt it. She relaxed at his agreement. "What you want me to do?" he asked with the proper accent and intonation.

She was still reluctant to come out with it. She took another quick glimmer at the lobby and made up her mind. "It's a package. I want you to get it for me."

"O-kay," he agreed. "I get the package for you. Where is it?" He was pretty sure what the answer would be and then he'd play indignant and turn the whole job down. She'd think she'd run into an honest bum. Until she ran into him later coming out of Lou's suite and realized it had been a gag. He hoped she'd think it funny then. He knew he shouldn't have carried it this far but it was so easy. And a new way to get acquainted with a new babe.

"I don't want you to get it now." She was talking rapidly. "I want you to come to the desk here at six o'clock. Exactly six o'clock," she stressed.

Indeed she was green. Expecting a Mexican to be anywhere on the dot.

"There'll be an envelope for you at the desk. The address where you're to go will be in it. You'll give that envelope to" —she retained that information—"to the man whose name will be on the paper and he'll give you a package. Then you bring it back to the desk and you'll get another envelope. In it will be ten dollars, American. For your trouble. Do you understand?" She'd increased the speed of her words until she was out of breath. She'd also increased the frequency of her flickers through the window.

Jose acted dumb. "The clerk—how does he know these envelopes they are for me?"

She said impatiently, "Your name is on them. What's your name?"

"Jose Aragon."

She'd never heard of him. He was right; she was from outside. "Your name will be on both envelopes."

He had to force information now, in order to get out from under. "But where is it I go?" he persisted in his newly adopted dialect. "I got no car. I cannot—"

"Juarez, of course."

He began edging. "No, Miss. I cannot do this thing. The police, they are very careful—"

"You're not smuggling anything," she snapped. "I've paid the duty. It's just that—be at the desk at six," she concluded and walked away fast.

He didn't get it; there wasn't a soul in sight. But she must have developed a sixth sense against interruption. For he could still hear the receding heels when the door emitted one of the lobby loungers. Certainly not anyone to get excited about, just an ordinary middle-aged guy with jowls and a reddened face that began to get redder the minute he hit the outdoor heat. A guy with a paunch, a sagging seersucker suit, and a sweat-stained panama. A guy who could have been Kansas or Illinois or any middle-western spot between.

He went on by without glancing twice at Jose. He walked in the same direction as the girl but in no hurry. Jose waited until he'd passed and then he himself entered the hotel. As he crossed the lobby he let his eyes wander over the inmates. They weren't any different here inside from what they had been through the window. A more harmless-looking crew he'd never seen. They were of varying heights and widths and age, but outside of that they all looked like the one who'd just gone out. The girl couldn't have been nervous about anyone here.

Jose saw two familiar shapes sitting together over by the muraled wall and lifted a hand and smiled in greeting. You always ran into Santa Feans in El Paso. The two gestured in return. They'd be down to hurry electrical or plumbing shipments. Jose continued on to the desk.

Lou saw him coming and her round pretty face, squared with a curly gray bob, waggled at him. "Where have you been?"

"Has Beach been around?"

"No. But he's been calling for an hour."

"For an hour I've been standing in front of your gracious hostelry," Jose interrupted with a ferocious scowl, "waiting for that lame-brain cousin of mine."

"He ran into Adam—" Without being aware, her voice made the name special.

"Oh-oh," Jose interjected softly.

"—and they're having a beer at the Blue Label. They want you to join them."

"Look, Chiquita," Jose leaned over the counter and gave her his best smile, "do I resemble a man who wants to go out again into that devastating heat for a beer when I can have the same served me in the shower of one of your finest air-cooled rooms?"

Lou's chin set. "No, you look, Jo Aragon, you know just as well as I do that I wrote you and Beach two weeks ago that with the summer tours I couldn't put you up unless you reserved in advance."

"But, Carita—"

"The name is Lou."

"Carita, Losita, what's in a name? Look at me. Smell me." He pulled at the sticky shirt. "Steers. And El Paso sunshine. Do you want your darling Jose to stink like a Tejano?"

"Mind your tongue. I'm a Tejano myself."

"But not in the heart. Nor in the church records. Darling Lou, I am on my knees."

"You're not on your knees and you know it. You wouldn't get on your knees for La Guadalupe in person, you might spoil the starch of your pants."

"Look at them," he wailed.

She loved him and she loved Beach. The Aragon kids, they were still grimy little kids to Lou. And she loved the game they played. In a minute she'd offer him her guest room because he was too well-bred to ask for it. Spanish well-bred, when you did not ask a favor of one too ill-bred to offer it. She said, "You'd put me out of my own room for your own pleasure."

"But my lovely one, you know better!" He exaggerated indignation. "I would sleep in the gutter, bathe in the Rio Grande, yes, under the International Bridge—" Both of their noses wrinkled simultaneously. "—before I would cause you the least trouble."

"You've always caused me trouble. You and Beach, both of you. The only peace I've ever had was when you two were overseas." She tinkled the desk bell. A young dark face, impenetrable, ambled to answer. "Pablo, take Mr. Aragon up to my apartment." She handed the key to the boy. "And get him two cold beers. I don't suppose you have any bags." She pushed the register to Jose. He signed for himself and for Beach.

"You're wrong. We have bags and bags. We're on our way home from the ranch—"

"The long way," Lou commented dryly.

"Business," he bowed gravely. "Darling Lou, you will call

7

Beach and tell him we're here and to bring the bags over at once?"

"Why don't you call him?"

"Because I'm lazy," he grinned. "And because I'm not speaking to him. Or his beer-guzzling companion. When did Adam get in?"

She shook her head. "Don't know. I haven't seen him. He hasn't a reservation either." But he'd get one. She'd throw out the Governor of Texas or the Aragon boys for her precious Adam. And the big lug didn't know it. Another thing, what was Adam doing in El Paso? He wasn't supposed to come back from Mexico for another month.

Jose turned to follow Pablo, not that he needed the kid to show him upstairs. But that was Lou, a hotel woman with routine in her mind even when her heart was going soft. Then he swung quickly back again. "Lou!"

"What now?" She pretended exasperation.

"Who's the blonde staying here?"

"Do you think I can tell you the name of all the guests? The blonde! Dozens of blondes."

He used gesture to describe her. "The tall, beautiful brown-blonde?" His face took on a mimicry of the girl's, that Anglo sure-of-itself expression.

Lou's eyebrows beetled at him. "You spot them, don't you, Don Juan?"

"Can I help it if I have the eye of an artist?"

"The eye of an old goat." Only she didn't say old goat. What she said was *cabron*.

"I will ignore the insult to the Aragon family. The name, please."

"She calls herself Dulcinda Farrar."

"Where's she from? Is she with her husband or her papa or, may I be forgiven the thought, a boy friend?"

"Jose," said Lou firmly, "I give you shelter. I even give you beer. But you'll darn well have to do your romancing without my help. Now get out of here before I change my mind and send you packing."

He departed. One thing he knew. Dulcinda wasn't a recent arrival, Lou hadn't had to refer to the register for her name. And she wasn't with a husband or Papa or boy friend or Lou would have said so. What was a girl of her class doing hanging around El Paso in the heat of August? The town wasn't a summer resort. It would be full of passing-through transients this month, and the tours that stopped for a day, and men having to come down on business. But why a Dulcinda Farrar who could be at some fashionable and cool resort?

The kid, Pablo, was hanging around the elevator, waiting with the mestizo patience which negated time. Jose came up to him and flipped the key from his hand. "You rustle the beer, chico, and I'll go up. I know the way. I'm thirsty." He stepped in the elevator, informed Pablo's twin, "Six," and began the quick ascent. The Chenoweth was modern and efficient; it had to be with Lou at the helm.

He could have told Lou about his derring-do with Dulcinda Farrar. They'd have had a big laugh over it. But deliberately, he'd kept quiet. Perhaps instinctively; that warning red light of instinct derived from experience. For the way the girl had kept peering around, the way she'd talked, fast and quiet, wasn't the way of an American girl on the noon-day street of an American town. It was the sort of thing he'd run into in Germany, first behind the lines, and later in occupation. And in certain other border states. He hadn't said anything to Lou because this might be more than a simple case of hiring a Mexican loafer to smuggle something over the border. He didn't believe for a moment that Dulcinda had paid duty on whatever the package held, not unless duty was the least important part of this.

"Six," the elevator boy said in his accent.

How long the cage had been stopped at the floor, Jose didn't know. He snapped out of his wondering. "Thanks, chum," he

smiled. He went along the corridor to the front, used the key
to enter Lou's place. She had a nice-sized sitting room; some
good, brilliantly splashed Mexican paintings and rugs; some
good American furniture covered in dusty white upholstery.
She also had two bedrooms, her own and one for her guests,
a bath for each. He pocketed the key, left the door ajar for
Pablo, and headed for the familiar guest room. He stripped
fast, letting his clothes drop to the floor. He couldn't insult the
sun-yellow chairs or bedspreads with their stink. He hoped
Beach would rush the bags over. And Adam with them. He
hadn't seen Adam for months. It was a futile hope, that those
beery companions would show speed, but he could hope that
they would have had enough before he finished his shower.
There were certain restrictions as to what a man could accom-
plish garbed in a bath towel.

He started the shower blending. He didn't want the girl to
turn out to be anything but a sweet kid trying to bring across
more perfume than she could use. He'd had enough international experience ever to want to return to such complications.
Automatically he picked up his levis and emptied the pockets. And not so automatically, he dropped his wallet and loose
change and keys into the top bureau drawer, closed it. He left
a quarter on the scarf for the boy.

He walked into the shower, leaving the bathroom door open
so he could listen for Pablo. You couldn't actually hear with
water pouring over your head, drizzling into your ears. You
had to count on recognizing an intrusion without hearing it.
And he did. Because he'd had to develop that super-sensory
quality or he wouldn't be here today waiting for his *cerveza*.

He stuck his head out from the shower curtain and yelled,
"Put it on the bureau." He couldn't see the boy but he heard
the murmured response, "Awright."

It wasn't right. It wasn't Pablo's voice, and it wasn't the
word the boy would have spoken. He grabbed a towel to wrap
around him as he dripped fast to the door. No, it wasn't Pablo.
It was an ordinary man in a wrinkled seersucker suit, a man

10

who might have just finished dropping Jose's dirty levis back to the floor. The man wasn't frightened when he saw Jose, but he began backing toward the door. "Guess I'm in the wrong pew," he offered.

"Yeah." Jose looked him over thoroughly. "This is Miss Chenoweth's apartment." He punched it. "It's her hotel, too." You couldn't mistake Lou's apartment for any other room in the hotel. You'd stop in the sitting room and know your error.

The man didn't bat an eye. "Mistakes will happen." He'd backed into the doorway by now. And behind him, Jose saw the blue smock of Pablo. When he saw that Jose was gazing beyond his shoulder, a quiver of apprehension went over the man's face. He swung around and it could have been the narrow doorway that swung his hand toward his armpit. At any rate the hand dropped immediately.

"Here's a boy for you," the man said. "Sorry I interrupted." He noticed the two beers; he'd notice details. Maybe he thought Jose had a friend in the shower.

Jose waited until he heard the man go out and close the door. Then he said to Pablo, "Bring the tray in here. On the bureau." Pablo moved with slow deliberation. "The quarter's for you. I'll sign for the beers."

"Miss Chenoweth, she sign for this."

"On the house? Dream girl." The water was still roaring down in the shower. No one outside could hear what he asked. "Who was that guy?"

"I do not know what you say."

"That guy who was in here. Who is he?"

"He is your friend."

"I never laid eyes on him before." This wasn't exactly accurate. But the idea was. "Said he got into the wrong room."

"Your door, she was open. It is a mistake."

"Are there any rooms in the hotel that look like Miss Chenoweth's?"

Pablo understood. "They are not."

"That's right."

11

But Pablo didn't know who the man was, no use keeping him here any longer.

"Be sure you pull the door tight when you leave."

"I will do that."

Jose tilted a bottle to his lips. But he didn't return to the shower until the door slammed after the boy. Mistakes will happen, the seersucker suit had said. But the mistake was that Jose had caught him in the room. Mr. Seersucker hadn't made a mistake, he'd come for a purpose. There was only one reason for him to come. Because Jose had been talking to the girl and the man knew it. Between the girl and the man there was something. And that something wasn't accidental.

Well, the guy had made one big mistake. Because Jose was picking up that envelope labeled Jose Aragon at six sharp. And not out of idle curiosity. He resented a stranger pawing through his things. In El Paso you didn't expect Balkan tricks.

He finally had enough of the shower. Maybe because he was thirsty for a second beer. He turned off the faucets, rubbed himself damp dry, and took a clean towel for a wraparound. The beer was still plenty cold. He jerked open the bureau drawer; no, the prowler hadn't got there before he was interrupted. Jose's stuff was just the way he'd tossed it in.

If the guy had been reaching for his armpit and if he'd wanted to start something, Jose had been in a pretty pickle. Standing there clutching a wet bath towel around his middle. He was sick of the guy sloshing around his head. He went into the living room where it was cooler, picked up the phone. He was dry enough to stretch out in the easy chair. The desk answered.

"Miss Chenoweth still there?"

She came on after a moment.

"Lou, what about Beach?"

"He's coming."

"When? I'm trapped here stark naked. Except for one of your best towels."

Lou gurgled. "You can't be chasing blondes, can you? If it's essential, you can help yourself to a bathrobe from my closet."

"Won't I look pretty!"

"Don't be so vain, chico. How's the beer holding out?"

"It's almost gone. When's Beach going to get here?"

"He said he'd be over pretty soon. He was surprised you'd decided to stay all night. Said you wanted to get back to Santa Fe. I didn't tell him about the blonde, thought you'd like to surprise him."

Jose said patiently, "Look, my little dove, give me the number and I'll call Beach myself. And Lou, how about sending up a salad, shrimp, a lot of them, and some more beer? And also, Lou, *gracias,* but this tab I'll sign. You're not giving a party."

"It'll be on your bill." Her voice trickled off and then on again with the requested number.

He said, "Thanks," grinned into the phone, "If the blonde asks for me, send her up."

Lou made a noise and rang off. He waited a moment and re-lifted the phone, repeated the number Lou had given. It took a bit of ringing before a voice shouted, "Hello."

"Is Beach Aragon still there?"

"Hold it, I'll see." He could hear the man yell, "Beach Aragon here?" and then the voice returned, "Just left."

Jose didn't believe a word of it. "Let me talk to Adam."

"Wait a minute." The voice changed to Adam's warm bass, "Hello, Lou."

"This isn't Lou. It's Jo."

"Why don't you get over here?" Adam rumbled. "We've been waiting for you."

"Look, I can't get over. Incidentally, welcome home and all the trimmings. Let me talk to Beach. I know he's there."

"Bright boy," Adam jeered gently.

He held on until Beach drawled, "What gives?"

"Listen, Beach, Lou is letting us stay with her tonight."

"She told me."

"Okay. She also told you to bring the bags over, didn't she?

13

I'm sitting here in a bath towel waiting. I can't join you and Adam because I haven't anything to wear but those stinking things I took off and I'm damn sure not going to put them back on. Come on, be a pal. Besides Lou might like to see the old Adam, no?"

"Will do," Beach agreed. A touch of romance could usually bring him around. The blonde would have brought him faster but the blonde was a business proposition, Jose's business.

Jose urged, "Don't stall any longer. I'm getting claustrophobia shut up here by myself." He replaced the phone. They might come and they might not. Adam might meet twelve other guys he wanted to gab with before they made it.

Jose paddled into Lou's room and surveyed the robe situation. There was a terry cloth which wasn't fancy. It was short in the skirt and the sleeves, tight in the shoulders, but in a pinch it would cover him. He carried it back to the living room where it would be handy. Because he didn't want to think he turned on the radio and found afternoon music. The knock on the door made him start. It wasn't his cousin and Adam, they'd approach with noise.

He called out, "Who is it?"

"The lunch."

The accent was right. He put on the robe, feeling all arms and legs, and opened the door an inch. It was the lunch all right, another twin of Pablo's in another sloppy blue smock. "On the table." The boy struggled the tray to the low carved table. Jose remembered that he wasn't wearing pockets with pants. He went into the bedroom, found a quarter, and brought it back to the boy. No use making him wait for it, once the beerdrinkers arrived lunch would stretch on to dinnertime.

The boy took the quarter and pocketed it. "Pablo he say Tosteen."

He didn't get it. "What's that?"

The boy repeated the exact words. "Pablo he say Tosteen."

Pablo, he knew. Tosteen had no significance. And then it

did. *"Mister* Tosteen?" What other message had Pablo to send but the name of a man?

The boy shrugged. "He say Tosteen."

"Okay." The hunch must be right. "What's your name, fellow?"

"Jaime."

"Jaime, you say to Pablo, *mil gracias.*"

"I will say it." The boy pulled the door tight after him.

So Pablo had found out the guy's name. Because of a quarter tip? Uh-uh. Because it was Aragon against Tosteen; the gringo didn't have a chance. Jose peeled off the skimpy robe, the towel was more comfortable, then removed the white tablecloth from the tray. The shrimp salad was a special, not what you'd get if you ordered it on the menu in the coffee shop. The rye bread was cold and firm. And the bottle of beer had five brothers. Lou must have believed Jose's phone call to the Blue Label would bring results. He put the five in the ice box behind her portable bar and fell to. He was plenty hungry. It had been a long time since that six o'clock breakfast on the ranch.

You could hear Beach and Adam from the time they got off the elevator. Their laughter cross-boomed against the corridor walls. He held the door open for them. "High time. Look at me!"

"You ain't so pretty," Adam allowed. Laughter rolled over his face, opened his mouth, shook his big frame. Adam was the biggest man that had walked the earth since Paul Bunyan. The biggest man who'd ever walked the Rio Grande valley. Jose was only an inch under six foot himself; beside Adam he stood like a schoolboy. So did Beach's full six feet.

Jaime was like a toy. He trailed after them, carrying the three bags. His polished black eyes ignored Jose's loincloth. Beach and Adam were loaded, both arms, with enormous paper sacks. More beer. Beach tipped Jaime and pushed the door to a loud shut. Adam was already at the shrimp bowl.

"Get out of there," Jose warned. "Order your own."

Adam swallowed the shrimp he'd filched and licked his fingers. He was a sight for sore eyes, pleasantly beery, dirty and sweaty and wonderfully normal.

"You didn't lose any weight on your tour," Jose remarked pointedly.

"What are you talking about? I lost fifteen pounds. So help me, I tip the scales at only two hundred and thirty this minute —full of beer though I be. Want proof?"

"I'll take your word," Jose said hastily. "You don't want to break Lou's scale. Sit yourself down—away from my lunch— and I'll see what I can do for your emaciation." He lifted the phone. "Send up two more big shrimp salads. This is Jose Aragon." He cradled it, tucked the towel more safely about him as he returned to the couch, and resumed eating.

Beach said, "You could have knocked me over with a blunderbuss when I saw Adam going into 'The Blue Label.'"

"A man can't have his morning beer without being caught at it," Adam decided.

"When did you get in?" Jose garbled with full mouth.

"S'morning."

"How was the trip?"

"Pretty good. Mexico City's always good. But the beans and *pan* got pretty monotonous in those hinterland dumps. That's how I lost all those pounds."

Adam had come to the Rio Grande valley in the thirties. But he wasn't like most of the refugees from the East, well-heeled, looking for a place to sit out the coming holocaust. A guy that big couldn't be satisfied twiddling his thumbs at parties. He'd started trading in less than a year. The war had skipped him, a lot of too big fellows had something wrong. Adam Adamsson, trader, was about the smartest importer in the state, maybe the Southwest, by now. Jose loved him like a brother. Everybody loved him.

Adam rubbed his big hand over his stubbled chin. "Got a razor, Jo? If I'm going to eat in Lou's apartment, I got to be fancier than this."

"Help yourself."

Beach stretched. "You shave, Adam, I'll shower. Put the beer on ice, Jo. What made you change your mind?"

"What do you mean change my mind?"

"You were hell-bent to get back to Santa Fe tonight."

"I wasn't hell-bent. I was indeterminate. It was hot."

"Still hot," Beach argued.

"I'm cooled off. We can get an early start in the morning when it's fresh."

Adam lifted the bags as if they were filled with cotton puffs. "I got to start back tonight." He returned for a parcel, stripped off the paper, and revealed a clean shirt, socks, and shorts. He traveled light.

"What for?"

"Business."

"Another day won't hurt," Jose urged. "Call your office. Tell them you're with the Aragons." He'd finished the last shrimp; he was pleasantly stuffed.

"I've got better sense," Adam grinned slowly. He went back into the bedroom. Jose helped himself to a cigarette from Lou's box and followed. He'd forgotten to buy that pack. The shower was pouring. Adam had all the bags open and was rummaging.

"In that one," Jose pointed. "What's another day?"

"I've got to be in Santa Fe in the morning. Shipment coming in."

Jose stretched out on the bed which had the least junk on it. "Stay for dinner anyhow. We'll go across the bridge. To Herrera's." It wasn't that he wanted Adam's bulk behind him on his junket. It was the fun the big guy put into any gathering.

"Sure I'll stay for dinner. What about lunch first?"

"It'll be along." Jose put on clean shorts, the buzz of the razor joined the shower downpour, conversation was stymied. He unpacked his white linen suit. Not the sort of thing you carried to a ranch for the cattle, but he'd had El Paso in mind when they started out. And there were always parties in

El Paso if you wanted them. The suit needed pressing, he'd send it out when lunch showed up. The others might guy him about being so fancy for dinner in Juarez, but he didn't have to explain why. He couldn't explain too well, it had something to do with a gorgeous gal seeing him at his worst and maybe he'd run into her again at his best.

It was Jaime who brought the lunch. And with great pleasure, a message. "Pablo say it is *Mister* Tosteen."

Jose was gravely courteous. *"Mil gracias* to Pablo and to you, Jaime." Closing the door on the boy, he yelled into the bedroom, "Chow," and sidestepped the stampede.

Lou joined them around five. They hadn't dressed yet, none of them. It was comfortable to be shirtless, sitting around gabbing about nothing. Nothing that was actually on your mind. They hadn't been bothered by the remains of lunch and the empty bottles until they saw through her eyes.

"P-uu." She picked up the phone. "Send up a boy, Clark."

One big stride took Beach to the table. He began gathering the remains and hiding them under the white napery. "Honey," he said in that sweet voice which got them whether they were seven or seventy, "we're awful sorry we made such a mess." He gave her the sweet smile which melted them like maple sugar. "And you so good to us." He was six foot, yellow-haired and blue-eyed; he had the face of an angelic child and he was a brat. He was the only Aragon who resembled the old Spain side of the family, seven generations back. But he was wasting the charm on Lou. There was nobody for Lou but Adam, that's the way it had been for twelve or fourteen years now. If Adam weren't so damn in love with Mexico, maybe he'd see what he was missing. For a warm guy, he was a cold fish.

Lou dismissed Beach. "Go put your pants on." She surveyed his bright pink nylon shorts with distrust. "You too, Jose. Adam, you can open a beer for me if you pigs left any."

Jose's shorts were candy-cane-striped. "I can't. My suit isn't back yet. Throw me a robe, Beach. The lady resents our peacock feathers. We're going to dinner at Herrera's. Join us, Lou?"

"And a glass," she instructed Adam. "I'm a lady. Broke a tooth on a bottle once. I can't, Jose. There's a banquet of the dear old Rose Club and I have to be around. You boys may each bring me a jug of rum, white. I have to give a party sometime this fall, a pay-back one, and I'm stocking up."

There was no delay on a boy when Miss Chenoweth requested. The discreet rap was Pablo this trip. He shouldered the tray but he delayed his return to the door. Jose realized the little fellow was trying to attract his attention. He sidled over to him.

"That Jaime he tell you what I say?"

Jose lowered his own voice to match Pablo's. "He did."

"He is so dumb that Jaime, I do not know if he tell you right."

Jose said, "He did. Thanks."

Pablo continued to stand there, gazing into Jose's face with his polished eyes. Waiting for another tip. And Jose still without his pants. Then he realized that wasn't it; Pablo wanted to say something and the other three weren't even making polite sounds to cover this private conversation. They were all peeling their ears. Jose stepped in closer.

"That Mister Tosteen he want to know what is your name."

Jose kept his face without expression. "He asked you?"

"He ask it of me and Jaime and Garcia, who runs the elevator."

"And you told him what?"

"We do not know." With the weight of the tray on his shoulders, he still managed to give the impression of a shrug. Somewhere behind the graven face lurked a smile. "Even that dumb Jaime, he understand he does not know."

"See you later, Pablo." Their eyes understood what he meant. *"Mil gracias."*

"Es nada."

He leaned himself against the closed door. Now he had to

face the gang. They were waiting all right, ready to jump him.

Adam jumped first. "Now, what's that all about?"

"It couldn't be a blonde?" Lou queried dryly.

"A blonde?" Beach sparkled.

"You mean he hasn't told you about her?"

Adam growled, "Not one lousy word."

"A bastard," said Beach softly. "So that's why we're staying all night in El Paso."

"Slow up," Jose advised. How much to tell them—and in that instant, he resolved to tell them nothing. If this was a shady deal, he wasn't going to have them involved in it. If it weren't, the story would be better when it was embellished by further developments. "What Pablo and I were discussing, *amigos,* had nothing to do with any female." He reached. "It had to do with his *domb primo,* Jaime. And if you doubt me, ask Pablo."

"After you've got him on your side," Beach complained. "What's with the blonde?"

Jose reclined in a chair. "She is so beautiful," he embroidered, "she is like the morning star caught in the leaves of a tall aspen." The more he said of her, the more they would believe there was nothing to this but Jose trying to pick up another dame. "She is a knockout, a dream a man dreams around a lonely campfire when the cows are bawling. The tawdry rhymes of a jukebox love song become honest because the heart yearns for her beauty. . . ."

Adam grunted. Insultingly.

"Who is she?" Beach demanded. "Where can I find her?"

"One, I don't know. Two, lay off, she's a lady. I've never met her, all I did was ask Lou who she was because she caught my eye."

"Lou?" Beach queried.

"What difference does it make to you, love?" Lou asked lazily. "Jose saw her first."

"I have no loyalty."

"All of you hombres ought to get married. You'd stop thinking girls were trees or cows bawling, you'd know they were women." Lou didn't look at Adam.

Adam said, "If I ever meet one who can cook better than I do, I'll remember what you said. Until then I'll be a no good like the Aragon boys, ogling blondes."

It was all nice and normal, just like old times. Just as if Jose's blonde were an ordinary doll, not one mixed up with an inquisitive man in a seersucker suit.

II

Jose refused to trust his pristine white linen to Adam's truck.

"All right," Adam grudged. "We'll take Lou's car. But if you guys aren't ready to come back after dinner, you'll have to ride the trolley. I'm not going to hang around Juarez all night."

It would have been funny, he was always the one who delayed the crowd, he knew everyone from Chihuahua to Mesa Verde. But nothing was funny now. Not even the gags about Jose's first communion suit; Beach with an out-of-joint nose because there wasn't time to get his whites pressed once he found out what Jose was up to.

Nothing was funny because of a slip of paper in an envelope. On the paper was penned a name, Senor Praxiteles; an address, Calle de la Burrita. The envelope was in Jose's white pocket, where his right hand could brush casually against it. On the front of the envelope was his name, Jose Aragon.

He'd never met Praxiteles, Senor el Greco, but he'd heard enough to recognize the old man if they met in the dark. And he didn't want to meet him in the dark. He didn't want to go on with this. He was retired from violence, he was a part-time peaceful ranchero of Socorro county and the rest of the time a gay caballero of the royal city of Santa Fe.

He didn't believe that the name Jose Aragon would have a special pertinence for Senor el Greco. But he couldn't be sure. Because the web in which Praxiteles sat like an evil black spider had tendrils on every border all over the world. You could never be sure how much the wily spiders knew about those who had tried to sweep out their murky corners.

But he was done with that, Jose reassured himself with more aplomb than he possessed at this given moment. Even if el Greco did recognize the name of one small twig from a great war-time forest, it wouldn't matter. The war was quits. Certainly there could be no violence involved in doing a favor for a pretty girl.

Yet the moment he opened the envelope and read the name of the man, Jose knew that he'd been right to put a guard on his tongue. This was not something in which he could involve Adam, tired out from three months' trading through Mexico. Much less could he mention it to Beach who'd be determined to flail in with his usual daring. Beach had been spoiling for a ruckus since they'd taken his fighter planes away from him. And there was Jose again, thinking of it as violent. It wasn't going to be. But an early ,idea he'd had to send Pablo to fetch the package died fast when he read that name. This job was his, he'd let himself in for it.

It was true that he didn't have to do anything about it. He could simply ignore the whole thing. Or he could leave a little note for the young lady, explaining the comedy of errors. A note which might lead to some violence on her part but no knife in the back. And certainly and inevitably would lead to the acquaintance which he'd had in mind from the start. He had no intention of pulling out. Not since learning that Senor Praxiteles was involved.

One small advantage was his. The man in the seersucker suit was curious about the girl's activities. Curious enough to invade the apartment of the hostess of the Chenoweth Hotel, although, conceivably, Tosteen might not have known it was her apartment. Curious enough to care about a poor Mexican to whom the blond girl might have spoken on the street. To go further, to seek the name of the Mexican. But the man didn't know that the girl had sent a message to that fellow. Thanks to

Pablo putting his protection on Jose, he hadn't had to pick up the envelope himself. Pablo brought it up with the linen suit and with the information, "A lady leave this at the desk for you." Pablo was keeping his black eyes open and his ears pricked.

The suit arrived just before six, the envelope had just been handed over by the lady. "I tell Mister Clark I will bring it to you. The lady she is gone. She say give it to you at the desk but Mister Clark he say I should bring it to you." If anyone was watching to see who picked up the envelope, he would be disappointed. There would be no significance attached to Clark handing Pablo an envelope to deliver. If anyone was watching, he'd have a long, feckless watch.

The only one who could possibly connect Jose Aragon with the blond girl would be the seersucker man. He might have been able to get the name from sources other than the three mum boys. Not from Clark, though, should he breeze up to ask who was in Lou Chenoweth's room. Clark had worshiped Lou too long to allow anyone to question her business. Jose did not believe that Tosteen knew the Mexican was actually Jose y Maria Angelico Aragon y Vaca, a don by right of inheritance. And he was quite certain that the man would not connect the slim, elegant, white-linened Jose Aragon with either the sweaty Mexican of the noon street or the dripping guy behind a bath towel in Lou's room. Not at first sight. The three were three different men.

Adam drove. As if he didn't trust either of the Aragons at the wheel. He turned into the wide street leading to the bridge, a dark street bisected with trolley tracks, flanked by dark warehouses, shabby with unclean hotels before the lights of the bridge approached. They parked on the American side out of custom, in turn out of the wisdom of experience. Adam picked the best-lighted lot, not that it was too good. It was a small one, set between two scabrous buildings, littered with dirty blown papers and melon rinds, peach pits, corn cobs sucked dry. Adam locked the car and put the keys in his own pocket.

"Don't forget, kids. After dinner, we head right back to El Paso."

"If you were a gentleman," Beach mused, "you would give the keys to me or to Jo. There's two of us, you should take the cab to the Chenoweth."

"If you were a scholar," Adam rumbled back at him, "you'd know that two in a cab are safer than one in this part of town."

"Not two borrachos."

"I hope you've got sense enough not to get drunk across the bridge. Not both of you at once."

They were crossing the street, headed toward the bridge. Jose stayed out of the conversation. He focused all his nerve centers on possible danger—smell, sight, sound. The smell was sour, but that was normal. The sound too was normal, the drift of babble and music from the garish lights beyond. As for sight, there wasn't anyone who appeared suspicious around here. The faces of those who worked in this neighborhood were no more sinister, and no less, than the faces of Pablo and Jaime. Beach led across the narrow bridge walk to the customs gate, Jose managed to be next, with Adam as rear guard. Caution over valor. Below was the sluggish, murky trickle of the Rio Grande, protected by mid-high, dark, cindery banks.

And then they were at the double barrier. On this side uniformed officials, matter-of-fact, recognizing the look of men such as Adam and Beach and Jose, average fellows out for an evening's fun. Inspection was perfunctory. With it there may have been an unspoken cynical hope that the three make no trouble for official United States while across the border. The uniforms on the other side of the barrier were quieter and even less concerned. They mumbled their few words, that was all. North American business was the life blood of Juarez. Their hope would be more pious, that no international incident come of the Norte Americanos, so often bad-mannered and always uncivilized drinkers.

The crossing of the barrier was always quiet this way, as if it were set up to offer contrast to the blare of color and sound and smell that smote you as you stepped off the bridge. No matter how many times you crossed the bridge, it was the same. The quickening of the pulse to meet the lively Latino tempo. The watering of the mouth at the spice of garlic and roasting ears and chestnuts and chile scenting the air. The scent covered the less enticing odors of unwashed flesh, cheap powder and paint, and beer and whiskey and rum and gin and tequila and pulque and other temptations to turista palates. The toes danced to the American music, played badly, pouring from cafe loud-speakers, and to the dainty pluck of strings, played well, by the dirty fingers of strolling musicos. It was always bad and always good; the odor of evil ever-present beneath the spangled perfume. It wasn't Mexico; it was border. And borders were ever venal because they catered to venality. This one was no different from any other.

The turistas looked exactly what they were, middle-westerners, Texans and New Mexicans, passing through El Paso on their summer vacations, staying overnight for a whirl at Juarez. Middle-aged couples for the most part, strolling the few blocks of border Juarez; loitering in the open curio shops, pricing, buying French perfume cheaper than in the States; buying booze cheaper, if the laws of their own state permitted them to carry it across the border; buying knickknacks, straw dolls, painted pigs, souvenir sombreros, postal cards. Only the bold walked the length of Avenida Juarez and found their way to the Mercado. The turistas did not feel exactly safe surrounded by strange faces and a strange tongue. They pushed together near the reassurance of the bridge.

A scattering of young couples from El Paso promenaded with more assurance, with less interest in the shops, with no undercurrent of strangeness to bother them. They came here often, as in another town they'd go to the lake or the dance hall for an evening out. And the natives tended their shops and tended their sidewalk stalls; the former with the dignity of *ricos*, the latter with noisy chant to lure the tourist dollars. Only in this way could they too have fine shops *manana*. This was border Juarez, turista Juarez, ignorant of the pleasant city of homes and families that lay away from the river; ignorant of the perversions of the cribs that were a hidden sore in the darkness beyond; ignorant of the twisted byways where men could buy any furtive evil, even ugly death, for dollars. One of these back streets would be called La Calle de la Burrita.

Jose managed to retain the center place as they ambled up the Avenida. Beach's heels were light; his nose twitched to the delectable Mexican smells. "We needn't eat yet, need we?" He didn't want to leave the embrace of color and lights and movement.

"Yeah, we eat first," Adam decreed.

Beach coaxed, "Jo, my intimate one, my own primo hermano, you will decide."

Jose was watching eyes as he walked along. Not Mexican eyes alone, more especially the turistas, the innocent-appearing turistas. Those who resembled the man in the seersucker suit and the other men who sat in the Chenoweth lobby. He had to think what Beach had said before he answered, "Let's eat." Once they got Adam into the Senora's he'd simmer down. And a big leisurely dinner would somewhere along the way afford an opportunity for Jose to slip out to the Street of the Little Female Burro.

Before Beach could object further, Jose winked at him. "Adam and I are hungry. I can smell that Gallino Mole. After dinner, we'll make the rounds." Quickly he diverted Adam. "We've got to get the rum for Lou, don't we? We won't stay long."

They turned off the Avenue at the second block. The side street, Calle Herrera, was brief as all the side streets which wandered off the Avenue. It was also dead end. But it was not perilous. Senora Herrera had a magnificent sign in red and green and orange lights hung crookedly over her gate, spelling out *Cafe Herrera*. When she'd first started to cook for discriminating tourists, a small, carved, wooden plaque had been the only guidepost.

The walls of her garden stood flush to the street. A door in the wall opened, with a jangling bell, into a patio lit with pink paper lanterns. There were wicker chairs in which to recline. A tiny plashing fountain was ringed with geraniums in yellow lard cans. Great wooden tubs of oleanders decorated the whole with lacy shadows. The patio was traditional; the cafe had been the Herrera *casa* before the border was given over to American aliens and their money. Across the flagstones were the amber windows of the cafe. Through them came the hum of satisfied diners, good food smells, the strum of music and plaint of Mexican song.

The Senora was older but there was no gray in her ebony braids; she might have been plumper but she was more the brisk, efficient business woman then ever. She and Adam were familiar friends, business brought him so often to the border. But without any prodding she recalled the Aragon boys who hadn't been here for so many years. She accepted their compliments as renewal of friendship. "Your table, it is waiting for you. Senorita Chenoweth telephoned to say you were coming here."

There was nothing wrong with the table except that it wasn't backed by a wall. You learned in the business Jose had been in that it was wise to have a wall behind you. He circled the neighboring tables with his eyes before seating himself. There was no sign of Tosteen or of Dulcinda Farrar. Or of anyone particularly interested in him. Yet he appreciated the reassurance of Adam speaking to a table here and a table there, an El Paso group, another from Carlsbad. He could relax.

Jose insisted upon ordering highballs all around, they hadn't had a stiff drink all day. He'd have to put a couple under Adam's belt to have time to make his side trip. He also insisted upon ordering a dinner of some length and great perfection. Tempting Adam and Beach, each of whom succumbed to his palate. His stomach was too nervous to eat half what he was ordering. He hadn't expected it to be this way and he tried to tell himself, *This is nonsense. A simple little favor for a sweet blond number.* But the abracadabra failed to take. Because he had knowledge of the evil which seeped like dirty mist through the city.

The Senora's cafe was as good as he'd remembered, the flower murals as exciting, the girls as pretty—they'd be Herrera granddaughters not daughters now. There were twin guitarists who were hot enough for the Mocambo or the Starlight Room. There was everything, including a white suit, to give to a man a feeling that he was a man of culture, even of elegance, not a nursemaid to cows. The only thing wrong was the feel of an envelope in his right-hand pocket.

The time to go was after the enchiladas and before the chicken mole. There'd be a wait in service, Senora Herrera was too intelligent to pull away an empty plate and plunk down a full one without affording one a respite in which to savor and digest the preceding dish. Or to tempt the taste buds anew with exquisite sips of wine. His leaving was made easy. Adam had wandered to the Carlsbad table. Beach had his eye on a dame who might be with her father if it wasn't her husband. Jose sauntered toward the cigarette trays by the outer door. He was unobserved; he had only to open the door and walk out. Yet he lingered there with no stomach for this errand. He half determined to return to the table and tell the others he was stepping out on a bit of business. In order that if he weren't back soon enough, they'd come looking for him.

He was deterred only because he knew Beach would be sure it was a rendezvous with the blonde and insist on sharing. He'd like Beach along, together they could make an amusing adventure out of this, the way it had begun. But Beach had been trained for four years in power tactics, smash, thunder, annihilate. He didn't know how to walk softly, speak gently, for a more permanent end result. As for taking big Adam along, that would make a coward of Jose. He was no coward. He might not be brave, but his trouble was his own.

His hand had curved on the latch, when behind his shoulder

the question was asked in heavy accent, "You wish to buy the cigarette?"

If he hadn't been jumpy, he wouldn't have darted around at her. He'd have realized it was a girl speaking quite harmlessly. But he'd walked past the cigarette trays; it was evident that he wasn't waiting to buy cigarettes, but was a man bent on leaving the cafe. And he was jumpy.

She was so small she could have bumped her forehead against the top button of his jacket. He had thought that all the Herrera granddaughters, who flirted their bright full peasant skirts from table to table, were indistinguishable one from the other. He had captured in his mind their round pretty faces and round fringed eyes of chocolate brown, their shining hair which rippled like clean black water below their shoulders, and the coffee-and-cream, plump shoulders rising above the bright embroidery of Mexican blouses. He had captured in his ears the laughter of their rich, red lips.

This one was a maverick. Her face was small and square, her lozenge eyes black as stones. Her hair was straight and stiff, banged above her straight black brows, hanging behind her ears, chopped off halfway down her back. Her ears were small and square like her face, thin Mexican silver earrings pierced them, a tiny silver heart dangling from each ring. She was thin, undeveloped as a child, she was the youngest of the girls here. And she wasn't a Herrera.

It could have been that the Senora had given the cigarettes into her care; it could have been that she thought he was stepping out to buy some on the Avenida, being neglected here. But she didn't move over to the tray to supply him, she stood there in front of him, silent, like a field servant brought to the house in the days of the great rancheros.

He shook his head, giving her a pleasant smile for reassurance. "No, small one, I have pockets full of cigarettes." He turned back to the door but she moved more softly and more quickly than he, and again she stood in front of him, blocking his path.

"You do not go? Your dinner, it is ready."

She hadn't asked if he were going; she'd said he wasn't going. Her interception wasn't accidental. Again his eyes swiftly circled the room. But there wasn't anyone paying attention to him. Beach and Adam were still occupied; Beach by now had moved over to the table of the girl with the husband or father or rich *patron*. Beach was getting along swell. Adam was having a drink with Carlsbad.

Jose returned his attention to the girl. She hadn't budged. There was no more expression to her face than to the face of an Aztec carved in stone. Somehow she knew about him, and although it was incomprehensible, knew what he was about. Whether she belonged to the seersucker man or to Dulcinda Farrar or to Praxiteles or to a yet unknown didn't bother him particularly. What did was that she was wasting his time, and he hadn't much time to pull this stunt.

He leaned closer to her and invented. "There is a beautiful lady I must see for a moment, and alone." Romance should be the best appeal to a thin, young girl who so far could have known nothing but dreams. He indicated his companions. "They must not know or they too would wish to see this beautiful lady of whom I have spoken and I would be unable to whisper to her the words in my heart. For there are men who laugh at the anguish of love—"

She was listening to him. Whether she was believing him was something else again. But if she was in on the other business, her knowledge would be slight. She was too young to be trusted with conspiracy; she wouldn't be told why she was to detain him. It was up to him to sow doubts that he was the man she had been asked to watch for, this caballero with love, not intrigue, in his heart.

He spoke rapidly. "If my friends inquire, I will be back so soon. They must wait for me. You understand, they must wait for me. But say nothing unless they inquire or unless they would go." He set her aside, his hand on her thin shoulder, a shoulder deeper brown than that of the other girls here. She was not of Spanish roots as were the others, hers were more ancient in this country. What was Spanish in her would have been by right of conquest a brief three centuries ago. The conqueror blood, despised and hated, burned out in smoldering centuries, until there remained a breed more pure for its defilement.

In no way did she give indication that she accepted what he said. She had been bred by countless ancestors to wear the stone mask. She might be thinking, "These crazy Norte Americanos are crazy." She might be thinking, "I spit on this man whose fathers brought blood and fire to mine." She might even be wishing she were the beautiful lady he was going to meet, or she might be wishing he'd buy a pack of cigarettes. But her face, including the polished black eyes, was blank.

He stopped thinking about her as soon as he stepped into the pink glow of the patio. The oleanders patterned the flagstones, the lanterns quivered in the motionless heat of the night, but he shied at no shadows. There was no one visible in the patio and he crossed it swiftly and silently. As he reached the gate, he remembered the jangling its movement set up. He could have scaled the wall, it was rough adobe, but there was no necessity for such antics. He was permitted to come and go from the cafe as he desired; he was an American tourist who visited Juarez as did any tourist, to glimpse a foreign land.

The Mexican police were very careful that the North Americans should be safe here. The men of business of Juarez would permit no incident which might upset the flow of dollars. If there were little puffs of trouble now and again, it was because the visitors had left behind their manners or their judgment, and the pobrecitos, God pity them, were tempted beyond the guardian of their consciences. The little puffs would wisp into nothingness in the sobriety of daylight, with profuse apologies from the Mexicano officials and acceptance of these by the Americanos. After a night in the Juarez juzgado, transgressors were inclined to be gracious beyond their wont. That there were uglier things which occurred, things which could not be erased by apology or dollars, was known on both sides of the border. Of these things one did not speak, Mexico and the United States being good neighbors now, and both north and south of the border there being a will to prolong this happy state. As an Americano, Jose was as safe as on the streets of any village, safer than on the streets of some cities. The Norte Americano prestige was a golden halo gracing his head; the envy and greed with which it might be observed was held in check by men of policy.

The only actual danger he faced was that of being overtaken by his cousin. Adam wouldn't follow, not surrounded by that good food. As yet the cafe door had not reopened; Beach hadn't missed him. He had this much head start. He needed more. Therefore, he eased the gate ajar, the bells merely tinkling, and he slid quickly through the small aperture into the pool of red and green and orange light.

The narrow street would have slept in darkness but for the sign. On either side of the road the walled houses, old houses, once fine homes of fine families of Juarez, were an unbroken shadow. Jose stepped out of the colored light and turned toward the Avenida. There were no walks, Calle Herrera was laid with uneven bricks. The street itself was scarcely wider than the pavement in front of the Chenoweth where he'd been standing at noon minding his own business. If he had any mistaken idea that it was the tilt of the walls which narrowed the street, it was dispelled when the egress to the Avenue suddenly closed. In a simple fashion. A man stepped into the frame, blotting out the brightness beyond. The man could have been a tourist, standing there to get his bearings or to rest his feet. Gazing out at the kaleidoscope of Avenida Juarez. He wasn't. He was a big shapeless man in a seersucker suit.

His back was given to this small street of the Cafe Herrera. It would seem that he didn't know Jose was approaching his seemingly defenseless rear. But Jose had no illusions in this respect. Mr. Tosteen was there with intent.

Jose walked quietly, decreasing his pace for thinking time.

He couldn't hear his own steps and was conscious for the first time of the rubber-soled shoes he'd worn tonight. He was as pleased upon the realization as if he'd chosen them deliberately for this purpose. The white suit was not such a careful choice, in the dark he would have the luminosity of a ghost. So much for his vanity.

The man hadn't moved. His big frame, in the loosely draped, wrinkled coat and wilted, sagging trousers, had the implacability of a cop on the beat. The comparison struck Jose like a snapping whip. This man wasn't necessarily the enemy. He might well be the law. It was Jose who was dabbling outside the pale of respectability. Whoever he was he wouldn't have declared his shoulder holster at the border.

Jose moved the last few paces with additional silence and with speed. He spoke the moment he was behind the big shoulders, "Your pardon, Senor."

The man swiveled ponderously. He didn't unblock the exit, he merely reversed his position. Jose was wired for quick movement, to dodge away, to duck through the opening into the safety of the Avenue. But there was no opening. Tosteen stood where he was; nothing moved but his pale blue eyes. They were photographing the size and shape and features of Jose Aragon. He gave no indication that he'd ever run into Jose before. He might have been observing a complete stranger.

Jose repeated, gesturing toward the street, "Your pardon, Senor." And out of whim, surely for no other reason, he converted to the Spanish tongue. "Step aside, you great mountain of warm chicken fat," he directed. "Allow a true gentleman to pass beyond the stench of your uncleanliness." All of this he spoke in gentlest fashion, smiling courteously the while, bowing in compliment.

The man gave no indication that he understood. Not one of his sparse eyelids twitched. He did stand aside, but only as if it had just permeated his thick brain that Jose wanted to go by. He said nothing at all, not so much as a grunt of apology.

Jose passed, murmuring, *"Mil gracias."* He turned left, he

had no idea where lay the street of the Female Burro but it wouldn't be to the right, the bridge lay to the right. Tourists were coming across it in a constant trickling line by now. The time by his watch was eight-twenty. He would not inquire directions as yet; if he went as far as the Plaza it would be no more than a brief and entertaining walk. A man might need a breath of fresh air and moonlight away from this perfumed section of town. There were shops on the Plaza, shops that did not depend on Americanos, where he might make his inquiries with more discretion.

By this hour the pavements were crowded. He threaded his way through those men who would sell and those who might buy. The din of those who cried their wares, and those who babbled of the heat and the smell and the prices and the postcards they must send to the folks back home, the added blare from the loud-speakers of the big cafes across the street, did not permit a man to speak to himself of precaution. The large woman in the damp print dress, the large man with wet circles under his arms, a wet swathe across his shoulders, did speak a warning. The same kind of jostling might remove an envelope from a pocket. Jose slid his hand into his pocket and kept it there. Without the envelope, he could not receive the package from Senor Praxiteles.

He had moved one block only when his path was again barred. And again it was deliberate. But this time it was not because of the envelope he carried. The barrier was a small staunch man, incredibly dirty from his shapeless straw sombrero to the gunny sacking laced about his feet. Not because shoes were difficult to steal, from a borracho it was nothing, but because shoes hurt the man's toes. Hung from his neck was a battered accordion, an equally battered cornet, a flute which had once been polished, and two small brassy cymbals. He clanked when he moved, he had clanked from the doorway of a liquor store just before Jose approached. He was called Canario.

He swept his dirty hat from his dirty head and he bowed with a renewed clanking before Jose. "It gives me pleasure," he pronounced in Spanish, "to make music for you, Don Jose."

Jose had not expected the old brigand to remember him after so long an absence. It was true that Canario had helped him and a couple of fraternity brothers escape the police on a night out in long ago college days. But the memory was as far away as childhood to him. How Canario could carry one face in memory, out of the hundreds he saw come and go on the bridge, was little short of incredible.

Jose gave him bow for bow before apologizing, "Later, my good friend. I am in haste at the moment."

He might as well have saved breath. Already the flute tootled from Canario's lips, his elbows squeezed the accordion, a string wound about his tapping foot clanged the cymbals.

"Later," Jose repeated impatiently, meanwhile attempting to crowd by. But Canario would have none of it. He pulled away the flute and began to sing in cracked falsetto. It was a moment before Jose listened to the words:

> *"Take care when you walk the Avenida Juarez,*
> *Take care, take care, my old friend;*
> *There are girls who will wink at you,*
> *There are men a little drunk,*
> *There are men who follow you. . . ."*

It was the last line which stung Jose's ears to attention. When the nut-brown eyes in the wrinkled monkey face observed the attention, he broke off the song, snapped the cornet to his lips and blared a brassy grin.

Jose said, "I would hear the song again." As soon as Canario began inventing a new chorus, he spoke softly. "Perhaps it would give you pleasure to make music for the man who comes behind me? It is possible?"

"It is possible," sang Canario, "that the band will play when the man walks down the street—"

Jose tossed a silver dollar into the cup as Canario shuffled by. He himself slid ahead of two stolid couples who were stacking Juarez up against Alton, Illinois, to the detriment of Juarez. A fresh cacophony from the Canary's band gave him courage to twist his head about. Tosteen was blocked by music.

Jose moved on quickly. He did not believe that Canario could delay the seersucker man for long. The musico was not brawny enough for that. Jose wasn't particularly surprised that Tosteen would follow him, obviously he had blocked the exit from Calle Herrera for a purpose, and also obviously it hadn't been to stop Jose from proceeding on his errand. Jose could have eliminated the pursuer after he knew where he was going. Until then the chase would be an aimless one guaranteed to tire the wilted man. Nevertheless, he was grateful for Canario's assistance. If he could get away now, all the better. And it looked as if he were going to make it. The music had halted in the middle of a phrase, an altercation was ensuing. Not a quiet one, an uproar. From a jewelry stall, sly comment was offered, "Canario performs again."

There was going to be a chance to duck across the street under cover of a trolley trundling bridgeward. Jose timed it. As he darted out, he managed to glimpse the distant hubbub. Tosteen wasn't watching him. He was surrounded by a pawing, gesturing, gabbling throng. If the man actually had no Spanish, it would take the police to straighten out the affair. By then Canario would be so innocent of starting trouble and Tosteen so impatient of delay, the matter would be dropped. By then, Jose hoped to have executed his mission with success.

The opposite side of the street was not crowded. There were dark houses to pass, the shops were soon left behind. It didn't take long to reach the Plaza.

Neon was not the decoration here. There was moonlight instead. On the steps of the old church, a few old men rested, a few women wandered inside, and a few women wandered out. There were children everywhere, babies in arms, little boys running after each other in shrill games, little girls rubbing against the protective black skirts of their mothers. The movie theatre was a bright spot; there was a double feature, Maria Felix in one offering, Cantinflas in another. Lads lingered under the marquee, waiting for their particular *carita*, or for any *carita*.

Jose walked close to the darkened shop windows. There was no one following him. There would be as soon as Tosteen could proceed. He must move fast, he was too easy to follow, the white suit was a glimmering beacon. He could ask anyone on the street the way and be directed to Calle de la Burrita. He could ask the way to Senor el Greco's but that would be less circumspect; the reputation which surrounded the Senor's name was not savory. His particular concern at the moment was whether mention of the street would automatically point to the seeking of el Greco's shop. Why else would a fine gentleman wish to be directed away from the bright lights? He would be less suspect if he asked directions to the cribs.

He made a quick decision because he must. He beckoned a street urchin sitting on the curb. The boy, small and cheeky and ragged, came without haste. "Gimme dime." He stuck out a hand encrusted with dried, dirty juice of the watermelon. "Gimme cigarette."

Jose measured the boy with his eyes. "Chico!" he commanded.

The boy dropped his hand. Suspicion clouded his eyes.

Jose spoke in the boy's tongue. "I have need of a guide. I will give you a dollar if you will serve me."

The suspicion didn't go away but greed crowded it.

"What do you say?"

The boy muttered. "You will give me a dollar?"

"Yes."

"I cannot go far," the boy hesitated. "The old one, my grandfather, leans on me." Jose followed the gesture to the bent shoulders and gray hair of the man who stood beside the tray of watermelon slices.

"Is the Street of the Little Burro far?" Jose inquired.

"But no." Suspicion vanished in a smile. "He will not know I am gone. Come, Senor."

The boy squirmed away, taking care his grandfather did not observe the departure. Jose followed, cutting across to the opposite corner, in the direction he had come, but not on the Avenue now. Up a darkened side street. They had gone but a brief way before the boy stopped and faced him.

"You will give me the dollar now."

"That I will not do," Jose answered coolly. "If I give you the dollar, you will not lead me to the street of the small she-burro. You will run back to your grandfather."

"If I lead you to the street, you will need me no longer," the boy argued. "You will drive me away without the dollar you have promised."

Jose pushed the boy forward, following behind him. "You do not trust me. And I do not trust you. But because the reward is great, you will show me the way and hope I am an honorable man. Which I am, Chico."

The boy's bare feet dug into the pavement. "If you are an honorable man, give me the dollar now." Jose began to shake his head but the boy's grimy finger pointed. "This is the street you desire."

The words flaked on the wall, Calle de la Burrita. Jose walked quickly to the corner, peered into the narrow passage. "My dollar," the little boy wailed, tugging at Jose's coat.

"Yes." He reached into his pocket, drew forth a silver cartwheel and pressed it into the small hand. The boy's eyes rounded with disbelief. The Senor had been an honorable man. It was not often so in his experience. Jose warned, "Say to no one where you have found this."

The boy clenched his fingers over the prize. "I will tell no one nothing," he gurgled. Jose understood. The *chico* would not risk losing the dollar to someone stronger than he.

Jose turned into the alley. It was as narrow as the street where the Cafe Herrera stood but it was not elegant, not even in a faded fashion. The houses here were not walled, they crumbled on the street without protection. The street was not paved with tipsy bricks; warm dust sifted over the hard-packed dirt. It had one advantage over Calle Herrera, it was not dead end. At the far corner it twisted into another lane, much like the one he had just traveled with the boy.

This byway seemed deserted. It showed no light, it made no sound. The faint echo of the Avenida's merriment whimpered from another world. Jose walked silent as a glimmering ghost, but boldly. If he was under observation from behind dark windows no suspicion should attach to him by reason of his gait. The way seemed to grow darker and more silent, although that was pure nervous stomach and he knew it. He walked the entire length of the narrow lane before coming upon the shop of Senor Praxiteles.

It was a real shop with a large glass window through which tourists might peer before entering. If they should happen to wander this far from the bridge. Jose did not stop to peer through the undisturbed dust which swathed the pane like mist. He merely made note that the darkness was broken by a flicker, dim as a candle, far in the rear of the shop. The light was so small it laid no color on the street. The entrance was on the corner, there were tip-tilted earthen steps leading to a heavy wooden door, so old the iron of the hinges and the latch were worn black and thin. Above the door was a small iron bell, a dirty piece of string hanging limply from it. Jose didn't ring, he was loathe to disturb the absolute soundlessness of the street. He put his hand on the latch. It didn't give. There was nothing to do but ring. Gingerly he took the soiled string between thumb and forefinger; he pulled. The clang was faint, but he could hear it echoing within the shop, attached to another bell inside. When it died away, silence lay more heavily. He could make out the tinkle of the Beer Barrel Polka from the Avenue, and it seemed he could hear the one man band and Canario's singing whine.

Nothing happened after the bell. He stood there waiting, wondering. He might be too late but the blond girl hadn't set any particular time for him to pick up the package. Perhaps she'd taken it for granted he would rush with the envelope from the desk to the Senor's. The sooner to enjoy his pay. He wasn't wondering so much about the delay as about the number of people who seemed to be in on this business. Canario couldn't have remembered him from more than five years ago, the musico was a part of this thing. It was not accident that Canario had waylaid him, he had been watching for Jose's appearance. The girl at Herrera's was a part of it. And the seersucker man. As was the blonde who'd known when she hired the Mexican lout that it wasn't a cinch job.

The door opened so softly, he was taken unawares. There'd been no warning creak, those ancient hinges were well-oiled. Someone was peering out at him but his eyes were unable to penetrate the blackness inside. The door was open but a crack. Through the aperture a voice whispered dustily, "It is too late. Return tomorrow."

Jose rebelled. He'd be damned if he were going through this again. And he'd be damned if he were going to give up now after the trouble it had been to reach here safely, trouble to his nerves if naught else. He was missing the best chicken mole on the border, he might be missing a safe ride back to El Paso; he would not depart empty-handed.

He edged one white buckskin toe against the crack. He announced, "I won't be here tomorrow." The words sounded too loud in the empty night. And prophetic in an unpleasant way.

The croaking whisper didn't care. "The shop of Senor el Greco is open only by day. El Greco is a poor man—*el pobrecito*—he does not have the lights *electrico* to shine upon his poor treasures—*el pobrecito*—" The voice was so old it was without cadence, there were accents laid upon accents in it.

Jose realized two things. He'd been peering at eye level for the figure, he sensed now that it huddled no taller than the latch. The other thing was that the Senor wasn't interested in anyone without an envelope. He said, almost whispering himself, "I bring this to you." He took the envelope from his pocket, held it to the crack in the door.

A claw snatched it. Again Jose waited. The door pushed against his foot but it didn't close because his foot was there. Why didn't the old buzzard let him inside? His nerves were quivering anew, expecting at any moment that Senor Tosteen would round the corner.

And then the door gave. "Come inside," the whisper invited.

Now that the invitation had come, Jose didn't think much of the idea. Yet sinister as the place appeared, and sinister as he knew Senor Praxiteles' reputation to be, there should be no danger attached to picking up a package. He wasn't here officially as he once might have been. He stepped in, blinded by the dark as the door was shut to the street. He didn't know where the old one was standing until the whisper came from behind him, "Go straight ahead."

He moved cautiously and perceived after a step that a heavy curtain separated this vestibule from the shop, creating the blackout. It explained how the old man had been able to study the envelope. Jose reached out and spread the curtains. The shop was dark but not black, the globule of flame at the rear conjured enormous grotesqueries of shadow which clawed the walls. The room seemed to be empty. There was no way to be sure. There were hiding places in the black of shadow, in giant ollas and mammoth woven baskets. El Greco's poor treasures were ancient with dust, they might be ancient with value as well. It was a motley collection, the cheap clay trinkets and inevitable straw dolls on horseback mixed indiscriminately with what might be museum pieces. There was a stone altarpiece which could be Mayan.

However, Jose hadn't come to appraise el Greco's collection. He was no expert. The old man followed him into the room. He was as old as his voice, old and withered and dusty, yellowed like vellum with age. He would never have been tall; bent now with the years, he was no larger than a child, no larger than the *sorbita* who had barred Jose's path at the cafe.

He was dressed as if he had been expecting company other than a messenger boy. He wore a frock coat, too large for him and green at the seams; the shirt front was a warped dicky, the string tie had been fumbled into an unpracticed effort at a bow. His trousers were stained with splotches, from wine dribbled down them long ago, but they were once fine broadcloth. The faded grandeur ended at the ankles. On the old man's feet were carpet slippers, made of pieces of discarded carpet; Jose remembered once as a boy finding a like pair in the old stable at home. Perhaps, like Canario, shoes hurt the old one's feet.

It was Senor Praxiteles, it could be no other, yet Jose asked the question. "Senor Praxiteles?"

The man did not answer. He stood there, his eyes fastened on Jose. He had eyes like a lizard, hooded, unblinking. The hand which clutched the envelope lifted slightly. "Your name is . . . ?"

"I am Jose Aragon," Jose repeated. "You are Senor Praxiteles?"

"Yes."

There was again the silence, the lizard study of Jose. Perhaps the wonder why a gentleman had come for the package. There was even the possibility that the earlier Jose had been described. Jose was ready to get things into action when the Senor questioned again. "Why do you come here?"

"I come for a package."

"Who has sent you?"

He was not supposed to know her name. He shrugged. "I am earning an honest dollar, Senor. A lady has hired me to come for her purchase."

Evidently what he said was acceptable. Senor Praxiteles dropped the questioning. He began to shuffle slowly to the rear of the shop. Jose followed. It wasn't a candle that led them; it was a lamp, the wick turned low to save oil. It stood on a high-built desk, out of another century. It was whispered that the old miser was the richest man in Juarez, that he owned

42

the Avenida Juarez from the bridge to the Plaza, that he even owned the bank.

Praxiteles shuffled around to the back of the desk, his head alone visible above it. He climbed onto the high stool as if he were climbing a ladder, rung by rung. His ledgers lay open in front of him, a stubby pen rested on a pen wiper fashioned of yellow and white felt into the shape of a daisy. The white petals were smeared with dried ink. A tall brown bottle and a tumbler dregged with red-brown smelled of wine.

Impatience grew in Jose. "The package," he reminded.

The lidded eyes lifted. "Yes," said Praxiteles. His hand reached under the desk.

Jose had stood like this before and had a gun drawn on him. With el Greco it would be a knife. All Jose had was two empty hands and the instinct when to drop. But what the old man brought forth was a package, wrapped in green paper like that used by druggists in the States, tied with thin brown cord. It was about the size of a book but of uneven bulk, not the rigid oblong lines of a book. What it was, was perfume; you could smell it all the way to the Plaza.

Jose's relief came out between his lips. As if the expelled breath had chilled him, the old man hunched his shoulders higher. "There it is," he croaked. He seemed in a hurry for Jose to take it and be gone.

"The papers," Jose demanded. "I am no smuggler, Senor. The lady assured me the papers were correct."

Praxiteles' head swiveled in the direction of the window. Swiftly Jose's eyes followed. But there was nothing to be seen outside, nothing at all to be seen but the dust fingering the glass.

"The papers," Jose repeated. He had not touched the package.

The yellow claws rummaged under the ledgers. They brought forth a receipt book. Praxiteles dipped the pen into an encrusted glass well. His fingers squeezed the wooden holder and he scrawled the necessary forms. Again he rooted, found an ink-scrolled blotter, blotted. Carefully he wiped the pen on the daisy before pushing the receipts across the desk. "This satisfies you?"

Jose took time to scan the scrawl. There didn't seem anything wrong; the wording was standard. He folded his slip, placed it into the inner pocket of his coat. The unblinking eyes watched as carefully as if it were a wad of bills Jose placed there. When the receipt was stached, Praxiteles was holding out the package. Jose accepted it as if it were nothing, as if there were no blond girl and no man in a seersucker suit.

He said briefly, "Thank you, Senor."

The withered hand edged toward the wine bottle. "I may offer you refreshment?"

He might have accepted as a gracious gesture, a pretense that between them there was friendship. But the hooded lids lifted too soon. Evil glittered across the saurian eyes.

"To my regret, I must refuse, Senor," Jose said. "I am in haste."

It was well. The old man's mouth would have been sour on the glass.

III

Jose took a deep breath when he stood outside the door again. To expel the odor of mold which had seeped from the old man. The smell of the perfume he couldn't escape. It wasted its cheap headiness on the still, dusty air of the mean little street, the fragrance seeping through the heavy green paper. His hands would be stained with it. Tosteen would have no difficulty following him now no matter what back streets Jose covered.

It was the thought of Tosteen which held him to the protection of the doorway for that long minute. Whether it was better to retrace the length of the street or to round the corner here. The lay of the street was visible; what he would find around the corner was problematical. As far as he knew, no one was aware he had come to Praxiteles, much less why. Except for the blonde. The trouble was he didn't know very much.

Out of past experience, remembering other murky alleys, Jose hushed the rise and fall of his breath to listen. Where before the drift of metallic music from the street of the turistas had been ephemeral, it now rattled with perverse frenzy. Drowning out any faint footfall, obliterating the heartbeat, the muted breath, the trickle of blood through veins. The spoor of those who lurked in dark places. Yet without eyes and without ears, he knew. He was no longer alone on the little burro's street.

The darkness stirred, a waver of dark against dark in the doorway of the house next door. Even as his eyes distinguished this, his nose sniffed through the reek of perfume another odor. The sweet cigar smell of a Mexican cigarillo. Around the corner.

He was caught then, between a cigarette and a shadow. It was up to him to choose. Or to step out boldly and let the choice be theirs. If it weren't for the damn package, he'd take a chance on either one. If it weren't for the damn package, he reflected wryly, he wouldn't be here. The perfume was too bulky to push into his coat pocket, one hand must be engaged with hanging on to it. He wasn't accustomed to arguing with just one hand. But if he set it down it would be the last time he'd have possession of it. By now he wasn't doubting that someone wanted that package like crazy. Someone other than the blond dame.

He hadn't any idea what he was going to do but he moved. Moved before Senor el Greco brought up the rear.

The whisper was softer than breath. "Senor!"

He stopped, balancing on the teetering step.

"Senor!" The sound, if you could call it a sound, came from the doorway of the next house. The shadow stepped away from the shadow and was a little thing, a *sorbita*. He didn't believe it but he was off the steps, against Senor Praxiteles' wall, and edging toward her.

"For the mercy of God," he breathed. It was the girl, the sloe-eyed child, got up in a mourning shawl that covered her long black hair and most of her face, all but the eyes; that also covered her brown shoulders and thin white blouse, hanging down over her red flowered skirt. In the dark the skirt was black.

She said, "There is no time. Give to me the package."

With his free hand he shoved her back into the doorway, flattened himself beside her. "What package?"

"The one you carry." Her thin little hand reached for it.

He closed his free hand over hers. "Listen to me, Sorbita. I have here perfume for my girl, get it? I'm not giving it to you or anyone."

She was breathing soundlessly but too fast. He realized all at once that she was terribly frightened. Her hand, despite the firmness of his clutch, was trembling.

"You will not return to your friends with that package. You will not be permitted. Give it to me and I will bring it to you safely. I swear by Jesus, Mary, and Joseph."

He didn't believe her. He wasn't expected to believe her but it was a brave try. He played along out of pity for her inexperience in these matters. "How is it you can carry it safely?"

"No one will see." He could feel the trembling all over her fragile body. "Beneath my shawl."

"Each man has a nose."

One small flicker of amusement lifted her voice. "I will smell only like a girl of Juarez."

He wanted to help her, to warn her to get out of this tumble; whatever it was, it wasn't for a kid. Also he wanted to find out what she knew about it. If the unknown who smoked should peer around a corner, he would see only a man with a girl, eluding the watchful eyes of those who had forgotten what it was to be sick with love and separation. This close they stood together in the doorway.

At his silence, a sudden bleak anger was in her. "I will not steal it. I have sworn to you." Her hand touched the package.

He held on. "What's so important about it?"

The waft of smoke seemed sharper as he spoke. She twisted the package out of his hands.

"Sorbita!" He exclaimed aloud in his anger, reaching out for her but this soon she had melted away. He could hear no disappearing footsteps. The anger rose up hot in him and then burned out. There was nothing he could do now. He wouldn't know which way to start out chasing her through the labyrinth of dark streets. He could only hope hopelessly that she had meant what she said. If not he'd find her even if he had to put the seersucker man on the job.

Right now he was free to investigate the cigarillo. And incidentally give her time to get safely away. He whistled as he rounded the corner, making sure his approach was announced. Nor did his step falter when he discerned not one but two men leaning against the side wall of the Praxiteles tienda. He walked directly up to them. "Hey, Bud," he used American, "which way to the market?" He put a cigarette in his own mouth, struck a match.

They were Mexicans, hirelings. Not good Mexicans, youths corrupted by the evil that washed back and forth over the bridge. They wore like suits, bluish purple in this unlight, pinched at the waist, sharp-lapeled. Their shirts and ties were garish in pinks and greens, their dark homburgs shaded their faces. Jose shook out the match and pitched it to the ground. Their shoes were narrow and pointed, patent leather.

"El Mercado?" one said.

Jose was not the man they were waiting for. He carried no box of perfume.

"You go this way," a thumb jerked in the direction he was headed. The accent continued, "Then you go this way and then you follow the signs."

The other said, suspicious, not certain of Jose, "The market she is not open this late."

"You sure of that? They told me—" He slid his sleeve, looked at his watch. "Yeah, you're right. It's after nine, closes at nine." They might jump him for his wristwatch and his possible wallet. He had a cigarette for weapon. "Then how do I get back to the main drag?"

Directions were reversed. The opposite direction, follow the curve of the street at the next corner.

"Okay, thanks, Mac."

He made a wide wheel before putting his back to them. And he walked off with the cigarette glowing, slanting across to the opposite side once he'd passed the entrance of the burro's street. From his sidelong glance, there was no sign of the small girl. If she were there, she wouldn't let herself be visible.

Once he was out of the hirelings' sight, he walked fast. Putting as much space as possible between them before they got new orders or started thinking. It wasn't their job to think. The music was increasing in volume and he could see the lights ahead now. After a short block, the side-street shops, lighted ones, let him catch his breath. But not until he was again on the Avenida did he actually slow down. He cut across it and was inconspicuous among other white suits and light suits and seersucker suits.

Calle Herrera wasn't deserted. Looking down it he could see two couples emerging through the garden door. He passed them midway. He walked by but was stopped by the "Hey, Jo," called after him. He hadn't noticed in his hurried passing; it was the two business men from Santa Fe with two fairly good-looking Texas dames. "Did your friend catch you?" the plump one asked. He was Wade, Wade's Plumbing Fixtures.

"Friend? What friend?"

"Some guy at the hotel. Just missed you. He was asking the bellhop where you were. I just happened to be standing there."

"So you made yourself useful."

"I asked Lou. She told me to try Herrera's. She thought I was looking for you, see?"

Jose swallowed the words gagging him. He asked patiently, "Who was he? What was the name?"

"I don't know." Wade might have had more to say but the babe was dragging at his arm. Wanting some Paris perfume out of him while he was still feeling good. His wife would get some too, solving the conscience problem.

"Thanks, pal." Jose lifted his hand, made it fast to the gate while the guys and their one-nighters were sauntering away. He didn't care about the warning bells now. Nor about the shadows of the patio. As a matter of fact, there were couples in the patio, loud-talking ones. ". . . don't see why we couldn't string up lanterns around our barbecue . . . they're so . . ." and the inevitable *"quaint."*

Most of the tables were empty, the dinner hour was over. A scattering of late-comers and wine-bibbers lingered. Neither Adam's massive shoulders nor Beach's taffy head was among those present.

Jose went to Senora Herrera, following her until she put away the silver she was carrying. When she saw him, her black eyebrows sailed high. "Where have you been, Don Jose? You did not finish the dinner you ordered."

He gave her the smile with which Beach charmed the older generation. "I had a small errand . . . and was delayed." He pushed the smile harder. "Now I am hungry. You will serve me?" He had to wait around for the girl.

"You think my chicken mole will keep while you run yourself all over the town? I do not serve food which is so cold I must wear a shawl to carry it." But she would bring him fresh food out of cook's pride.

"What happened to the other fellows, Senora?" The small girl was to have held them here, instead she'd come running after him.

"Senor Adam has returned to El Paso."

Jose groaned. Adam had meant it.

"Senor Beach is out looking for you."

In the bars. He knew what that meant. Following the elusive cousin from spot to spot, always one jump behind him. A night of it. And him hanging on to a smelly package which advertised itself to the ones who were after it. But first he had to get the package.

The Senora herself brought the chicken. "I'm keeping you late," Jose apologized.

She shrugged. "I do not close when there are customers." Her eyes measured those who remained. "Sometimes it is very late before they will all go home. If it is difficult, my son Marcelino is firm."

"You won't have to throw me out," he promised. "Did Beach say he'd look in here again?"

She was dubious. "He say he will find you," her mouth pursed, "—and a beautiful blonde." She began to gurgle, tapping Jose's shoulder. "The blonde was otherwise engaged, no?" Jose, his mouth melting with mole, permitted himself to wink at her.

He finished the dinner, finished two cups of coffee, finished the sweet, and knew comfort of body but disturbance of soul. The small girl hadn't shown. He'd delayed as long as possible; it was past ten o'clock.

The Herrera girls had gone, there was no one left but two dallying tables, the Senora and himself. He went to the desk where she tallied the day's accounts. He was reluctant to question, knowing the curiosity it would prod in the woman, the questioning of the girl which would later ensue. The *sorbita* was too young to stand up to the iron of the Senora. While he pulled out his wallet to pay, he tried to make it sound unimportant. "Where did the small one disappear to?" Senora Herrera didn't understand and he had to describe further, "The cigarette girl. The one with the straight hair."

"Francisca," the Senora identified. Her lips set narrowly.

He was gallant. "I noticed her because she seemed not of your family, Senora. The Herrera beauty was not there."

She muttered. "Francisca. I give her a job because I am so sorry for her, half-starved little rabbit. And what occurs? She is so ill! While we are most busy, she must go home right away."

"And she went home?" His stomach, well-filled though it was, suddenly appeared to have a big hole in it. "Like that?"

The head nodded direly. "Like that, she goes. Running. So fast one would consider the devil himself is on her heels. She can be trusted no more than her *abuelo*."

His mouth hung open. Warily he repeated, "Her grandfather?" He wanted to wad cotton in his ears. He wanted to kick himself in the seat of his white linen pants.

She wasn't waiting for his reaction. Fire waved from her nostrils. "That wicked old one. It is he who sent her here, to run my business that he may put a mortgage on the name of Herrera." Her hands beat the air. "And I, a woman of charity, have pity for her, so hungry-looking, so sorry that he beats her, that she is afraid of worse things he will force on her. I say to her—"

He broke in, refusing to believe his belief, insisting it be said, "Senor el Greco is her *abuelo*?"

"Of whom am I speaking but that foul spawn of the evil one and the lies he has put into her mouth to ruin a hard-working lady of family—"

Again Jose broke her words. With demand. "When did she begin to work for you?"

"But I have told you. It is this evening she comes to me and she tells me—"

He wasn't listening. And he'd hesitated to inquire about the girl, fearing she would suffer from the Senora's wrath. The dirty little liar.

TWO

THE AVENIDA DINNED HIS EARS. BUT NOT AS
raspingly as the names he was calling himself. The bright guy.
The kid with the medals. The prize package of the cloak-and-
dagger boys. So he stood there and handed the package over
to the old man's granddaughter. Whoever didn't want that
package delivered didn't need to strongarm Jose Aragon. No,
sir! All he had to do was ask for it. The girl wasn't even a babe.

He went into the Paris to waste time. Their perfumes were
Parisienne, he smelled a case full of amber bottles and they all
smelled luxurious. For Miss Haughty Paris's trouble, he bought
the Chanel she recommended. If Lou was overstocked, she
could give it as a door prize at her party. This bottle was lost
in his pockets; his ideas and that of the lady tourists on the bargain price of perfume didn't jibe. He'd have had to sell an acre
of the ranch to buy Chanel of the size of Praxiteles' bottle.
It could be the lost bottle was important just in itself. It might
be better to give up right now, to find the blonde and confess
all. Only he wasn't going to do it. Whatever it cost, he was
going to keep her lulled until he could find the *sorbita* again.

Having so decided, all he had to do was drop in at every
perfume shop on the street. And to long for the cool, clean
smell of beer. You couldn't fool a dame on perfume. Why the
blonde wanted such blatant-smelling stuff wasn't his business.
Her package was going to contain the right one if he had to
sample every bottle in Juarez. The small matter of locating

Beach would have to wait until this mission was completed. There was no sense in wasting his strength combining the two; the shops were laid like dominoes on this side of the street, the big saloons were on the opposite side.

He tried two more shops without any luck. In the third, which was given over to guaraches and sombreros and glittering Chino Poblano skirts, his spirits soared. The girl who flirted over to assist him reeked of the right stuff. She was too plump for her flimsy blouse and teetering red heels, too old for the flower, artificial, stuck in her thick black hair. Her hair was oily, it smelled dirty. Her red lips breathed garlic. But the overall smell was the perfume.

His manners were those of a gentleman, he tempered enthusiasm with courteous dignity. "Would you be so kind, Senorita, as to tell me the name of the perfume you wear?"

The question surprised her. Certainly no turista had asked this before and no one of Juarez would inquire, they would know. Her mouth opened, emitting garlic more strongly. "It is La Rosa." She tilted her head flirtatiously. "La Rosa del Amor."

"I wish a bottle."

She shook her head. "We do not sell it here. We do not sell the perfumes."

"Where can I find it?"

"Any place," she shrugged.

"Not at the Paris."

"The Paris!" She sniffed. "You can buy it any place on the street, I think, not at the Paris." The Paris was for *los ricos*.

He thanked her and hurried out. He found what he wanted at one of the open booths. La Rosa del Amor. He bought the big bottle in its cheap cardboard box, a bright pink rose decorating the label, the name wiggling around in gold letters. Made in Mexico. Made for the Five and Ten. It cost five pesos, possibly because he was North American. About a dollar. He insisted on having it wrapped, brown paper for this one. And dirty white string. Dulcinda Farrar wouldn't know about the wrapping; she'd know only she had the perfume she was expecting. Her nose would know.

He carried it openly, there was nothing else he could do. Now he could take up the problem of Beach. It would be a problem to get his charming primo-hermano steered back to El Paso. Yet unless he wanted to leave Beach on the loose here, which would mean they wouldn't get started home in the morning, he'd have to cozen him into calling it a day. You'd think Beach would want to call it a day. The six o'clock start from the ranch this morning was too long ago. With the strain of this night piled atop it, Jose was ready to flop.

He cut across the street, making his way in and out of the noisy palaces and their reek of music, booze, and jabber. He didn't stop for a drink at any of them, a drink would make him fall on his face the way that the weariness was eating through him. He wasn't discouraged. The Cock and the Central were just ahead, the biggest and best. Beach was a true Aragon; he preferred the best.

Jose was leaving the Caballo when he ran smack up against Tosteen. He could have said, "Excuse me," and gone around him, the man wouldn't start anything in a crowd. But Jose didn't. By then he was sick of the sight of anyone connected with Senor el Greco. This time he blocked Tosteen and with mocking courtesy said, "I keep running into you, Senor." Out of contempt for the man, he put on a Mexican accent.

The big, sagging man looked twice as tired as Jose. He also looked startled, as if the last person he expected to run into was the man he'd been following, Jose Aragon. Or Jose Aragon carrying a bottle of rose perfume.

"Or is it you seem to keep running into me, Senor?" Jose showed his nice white teeth. "I do not like it. I do not like you. Remove yourself."

He might not have been so bold in a dark alley but here in the safe din of the Caballo with the police only the roar of a fight away, he swaggered. Tosteen didn't say a word. He didn't move his hand to his armpit. He wasn't interested in Jose, only in the package Jose carried. His eyes were damp on it. Almost eagerly he stepped aside.

The encounter had revived Jose. He strode next door to the Cock. The old Cock had been a small place, away from the hurly-burly, a favorite spot. The new one was as popular, it coined money enough to live up to its name, but it was a Christmas tree not a comfortable beer parlor. Through the rhythmic shoulders of the rumba dancers he found the one head he was seeking. He started directly for it, gesturing aside the waiters who would have led him. It wasn't until he reached the other side of the dance floor that he saw what ringside party Beach had joined. Actually he saw only one member of the party, Dulcinda Farrar. Beach wasn't there by accident.

It was too late to retreat. Beach was calling across the intervening space, *"Mira,* Jose! I found your blonde!" With a firm hold on the brown-paper parcel, Jose reluctantly put one foot in front of the other until he reached the table.

After what had been transpiring, he was more critical in his study of the blonde than he had been in the gay noon-day sun. But she was just as lovely as she'd been then, the patrician face wasn't marred by the rigors of a night in Juarez, the eyes were as golden-brown, the mouth as bold. She was wearing something filmy in gray, something that dived daringly when you stood, as he did, above her. The mist color accentuated her suntan and she wasn't wearing La Rosa. There was something about her that stirred his pulses, something that made the poetry he'd woven about her earlier no longer a joke. And it wasn't the provocative dress.

Her glance flecked over Jose as it would over any stranger. Beach made offhand introductions, "My cousin, Jo. Dulcy Farrar, Tim Farrar, Rags . . . ?"

"The name is Harvey Ragsdale."

"Jose Aragon," Beach concluded. "Pull up a chair, Jo. Where have you been?"

Dulcy continued to appraise Jo as if she'd not seen him before. "Your cousin has been searching everywhere for you," she commented with faint amusement.

A scrawny waiter had brought up another chair, inserting it between Beach and the girl. While Beach was ordering a new round, Jose slipped into it. "Make mine beer," he put in. He set the package on the table, keeping it near hand touch. "I know," he told Dulcy. "He has searched in every glass and in the eyes of every pretty girl. And he couldn't find me."

Beach was sailing high and would be happy to soar higher. If he'd been drunk, Jose could have walked him out of here; if he'd been sober, a word under the breath would have been enough. Unfortunately, being neither flesh nor fowl, it would take some figuring. Unless Jose could procure allies. The two men with Dulcinda weren't happy about the Aragon cousins.

Tim Farrar must have been a younger brother. His face was very young, what he hadn't buried in a yellow-brown beard. His features were hers but the supercilious sneer descending the slender nose, burying itself in the beard, was his own.

Ragsdale was a big brute and he didn't need to get to his feet to prove it. No fat, brawn and muscles; Tim was a match-stick stacked beside him. A Tim would need a Rags. Ragsdale's window dressing was okay, the right clothes and the right crop to his curly hair, dark as Jose's own, but he was out of his class. He belonged in the ring or in the oil fields or on the docks, not with the Farrars. Nor the Aragons.

Beach, the order given, demanded cheerfully, "Where did you disappear to, Jo? All of a sudden, you're gone. Without a trace. Adam went on home."

"I ran into some old friends," Jose explained easily. "I left a message, didn't you get it?"

"No messages."

"You probably didn't miss me until that senorita ran you off. Or was it she had a husband who objected?" He told Dulcinda, "My cousin was very busy with a young lady when I left him."

Beach managed to glare. "Don't you believe anything he says, Dulcy. He has a pretty, lying tongue, beware of it."

The three of them might have been doing a scene on a stage with Tim's sneer and Ragsdale's square blank face for audience. Dulcinda's companions were that interested and that disinterested. Rags was drinking tequila straight, out of a tumbler. Unless it was pulque. His tastes would have developed before he latched onto the Farrars.

Dulcinda tilted her eyes at Jose. "Why has your cousin insisted that I am your blonde? I've told him we never met, can you convince him?" There was no hidden message in those clear eyes; she was clever.

"Convince me," Beach grinned. "If she's not your blonde, she's mine."

"Perhaps then I do not wish to convince him," Jose said softly to her. He didn't like it that he could have meant what he was saying.

"But he has a blonde stached out somewhere," Beach warned. "That's why we're not in Santa Fe tonight."

"You are from Santa Fe?"

Jose said, "I am. Beach is the California branch."

"We're headed for Santa Fe," Dulcinda said casually. "Perhaps we'll run into each other up there."

"We will." He looked deep into her golden eyes, as if he were just another guy bowled over by her fascinations. Not one who didn't intend to be. As if he didn't know that she'd known where he was from and that somehow it was important to her. It was after the Fernandez brothers had yelled their nickname that she'd returned to hire him.

"I'm warning you to pay no heed to him," Beach insisted. "You can't trust this *burlero*. Women have learned that to their sorrow from Cape to lonely Cape. Isthmus to Isthmus. Peninsula to Peninsula." He was enjoying his tongue trouble with the words.

Jose lighted her cigarette. It was natural to bend his head to hers. "Perhaps we will run into each other before then?"

She smiled. "Quien sabe?" It must have been her special smile. Despite decision, Jose's heart or whatever it was in the mid-hollow gave a special bump. Dulcinda could be dangerous.

Beach was paying off the waiter. Neither Farrar nor Ragsdale had made a pass at their wallets or said thanks for the drinks. Jose told him, "Drink up, chum. We've got to get back to the hotel."

Beach opened his eyes boy-wide. "What's your hurry? The night hasn't begun." He ogled Dulcinda pleasantly.

"It's ended for me. I'm out on my feet." He didn't have to strive for a convincing sigh.

The beard murmured, "Don't let us detain you."

Beach hadn't noticed or he was used to Tim's distaste. "Run along," he told Jose. "I've got work to do."

"No." He was firm. "Your sainted mother told me to watch over you. Besides we're taking off early for Socorro and I don't intend to drive it alone."

"Socorro?" Dulcinda's eyebrows were curious, too curious. "Not Santa Fe?"

He outlined it. "We return a truck to the ranch. We pick up my car—and then homeward bound." He promised, "Where we will meet."

She gave him a hint of the smile again. Just enough to keep him hopeful. If she'd been an innocent, she wouldn't have spent it on him. Not with Beach around. It was Beach the dames went for. For tonight he'd had enough of Dulcinda's game, whatever it was. He set to work on Beach, a stubborn Beach.

The only interruption was from Tim Farrar. "Perhaps if we were to leave," he suggested in a thin, cold voice, "you would have no trouble."

Dulcinda warned her brother sharply, "Don't be ridiculous."

It looked to Jose as if he'd have to give up. It looked as if Dulcinda Farrar preferred him to go over the bridge alone. It wasn't too farfetched, not with all the other oddities he'd run into tonight. Because he was too weary to think straight, it took far too long to think up a way to convince Beach. When actually it was so simple. Beach was an Aragon, the Aragons were gentlemen. He whispered, "Lou expected us to return after dinner for a visit with her. She is our hostess. . . ."

Beach sighed to Dulcinda, "We must go." He sighed again. "He's right. Usually he's wrong but this time he's right."

If she were disappointed, she didn't let it show. She didn't even display curiosity. She said, "Until we meet again?" She said it to Jose not Beach.

"Until Santa Fe," Jose replied. He tugged Beach's arm. "Come on, amigo."

Reluctantly Beach got on his long legs. From under the table he pulled out two jugs of rum. "Bet you thought I'd forget," he told Jose. He made a teetering bow to Dulcinda, "Until Santa Fe." Dulcinda's escorts had nothing to say, not even goodbye.

"Wait," Dulcinda called to Jose. "You're forgetting your package." She didn't touch it.

He'd left it there deliberately, it seemed an easier way to make delivery than hocus-pocus at the Chenoweth desk. It seemed however that she wanted it her way. He said, "Oh?" and "Thanks." He picked it up as if it weren't important and hurried after the weaving Beach.

As they made their way to the door, Jose returned his glance to the table. None of the three had moved. He couldn't help wondering who or what they were waiting for. Certainly they weren't enjoying each other's company. They were three empty shells.

The exit doorway was always cluttered but as they reached it now, it was barred. Clanking his band, gesticulating vociferously, and cursing with imagination and bile was Canario. He broke off when he spied Jose. "Senor Aragon," he doffed his dirty hat and bowed metallically, "it is a pleasure to see you once more." He didn't say if it was a surprise, but returned to his tirade. "They are so fine here. They will not let a poor man enter their doors. Come, throw me out!" He yelled, "Come!"

Beach was crying out in tipsy pleasure, "Look who's here! Good old Canario. Give us a tune, Canario!"

Canario's bird-bright eyes cocked a villainous scowl at the manager. The manager did not budge. Canario decided against complying with Beach's request. "Come to my cafe and I will play for you. *Una linda piada!*" He backed out of the entrance, allowing Jose and Beach to follow.

His cafe was the street. He struck up his discordant jangle the moment they were outside. It wasn't possible to accuse him of detaining them, Beach was too eager an audience for that. Yet they were being held here, held just as securely as if he were still blocking their path. They were held by his desire to entertain them, held because a gentleman would be as particular regarding the artistic pride of a street musician as of the merits of a concert master. No song of warning was sung although Jose waited for it. Canario seemed to have no purpose in making music this time beyond the pesos which would be reward. Nor did those who gathered about him from the cafe and the street seem to have any purpose but to listen to the *piada*.

He completed the number with a grand flourish, acknowledged the pesos with another wide sweep of the dirty hat. But this was not enough. As Jose led Beach away, Canario followed, clanging and squeezing and tootling a merry march. He followed them to the customs barrier. He and a parade of dirty-faced little boys with their incessant gimme a penny or a dime or a cigarette.

La Piada was in the background as the Aragons walked across the bridge. It echoed with a ridiculous clarity while Jose declared his Chanel and his Rosa del Amor, while both declared the jugs of rum. For once there was a taxi waiting; it was just pulling out of the dirty lot where earlier Adam had parked the car. Jose hailed it, pushed Beach inside, clambered after him. "The Chenoweth," he sighed.

The cab made a tired noise and chugged forward.

Beach nudged Jose. "We've got company!" he declared happily.

II

Jose hadn't noticed that there was another occupant when he piled the two of them in. But it wasn't unusual to share a cab at this hour.

"Drunk," Beach stage-whispered.

"Good, he won't mind you," Jose returned without sympathy. Only then did he glance across Beach at their companion. The man was Mr. Tosteen.

There was nothing to fear from Tosteen at the moment. He had succumbed to his long day, he slept, his mouth open, his head riding the bumps against the leprous upholstery of the seat. Jose slid the package out of sight against his thigh, keeping his hand tight on it. The driver careened up the street, empty at this hour, vacuum-silent after the dissonances of Juarez. The cab aerialed around corners, it pulled up at the Chenoweth in ten minutes flat. The driver might have been in a hurry to get home, more likely he was in a hurry to return for more drunks.

Jose piled out fast, clutching his package. Beach followed swinging the jugs. Jose said, "Take the loot in. I'll pay the guy." As Beach ambled off with the rum, Jose spoke to the driver. "Hold it a minute." He didn't want to get back into the cab. "I dropped something." He stuck his head and shoulders in but that wasn't enough. He had to lean across to where Tosteen slept. Quickly he retreated, slammed the door, shoved the fare at the front seat.

The driver had a narrow face and yellow teeth. His cap was greasy, his cheap knit shirt was sweaty, his breath was garlic. "This other one—"

"Don't know him," Jose said briefly. "He's passed out. Take him back where you found him." He was half into the revolving door before he finished speaking. He didn't know whether the taximan was in on it or not. He wasn't waiting to find out. He wasn't going to be stuck with anything more.

In Jose's ears echoed Canario's band playing them across to a conveniently waiting cab. Beach leaned just inside the whirl of the door. He whistled, "What a ride! Enough to wake the dead."

Jose answered him silently: *No, the dead do not wake.* Aloud he said, "I'll get the key."

Beach started to tag along like a kid tied to Daddy's coat tails. Jose suggested, "You hold the elevator."

The night clerk was an unknown, an aging man, colorless, gray-haired. Jose set the package on the desk. "Jose Aragon," he said.

"Yes. Miss Chenoweth left a key." He handed it across, with it an envelope with Jose's name on it. The envelope would contain one ten-dollar bill. He didn't touch the wrapped perfume.

Jose had to request, "You'll take care of this?"

The gray man said, "Oh, yes," as if some memory stirred. Jose left him smelling the package, trying to remember what he was to do with it.

The elevator operator was a sleepy boy. He rode them up without interest. In the empty corridor Jose warned, "Lou's probably asleep by now so keep quiet. You can apologize in the morning for being so late."

"Look," Beach protested cheerfully, insistently cheerful. "Don't be blaming me because we're late. What happened to you?"

Jose put the key in the door, swung it open before entering. It swung noiselessly, the lamps were lit, the room was empty. Only when he was sure did he enter. Beach hadn't noticed.

He couldn't tell Beach tonight. Beach would think he was kidding. The irrepressible one was making a great array of the jugs on Lou's threshold. Jose went casually to the front windows. It was safe to lean out, just enough to peer ten stories down to the street. To see if a cab lingered. The marquee hid the cab if it were still there. It didn't hide two men under the street lamp on the corner. Two whose suits glowed purple even this far away. Two who were waiting for something, or someone.

From behind him, Beach commented, "Show-off."

Jose pulled himself in. "Can't a fellow smell some fresh air?" He moved on to the bedroom. The yellow coverlets were turned back, the bed lamp glimmered. It all looked comfortable and hotel-safe and normal. As if there were no evil, no death, no cheap perfume.

He and Beach could leave in the morning. He didn't have to stick around and look for the answers. What was it to him that there was a lying kid whose *abuelo* was called Senor el Greco? Who cared if Dulcinda Farrar's perfume came from el Greco or from some Juan with a sidewalk stall? Who cared what happened to the first bottle or why? Or why Canario baited his traps with music. Jose had plenty of questions, no answers, and he didn't want any. Not even why he had been bundled into a cab with the body of a man called Tosteen. He didn't want trouble. He wanted to go home and enjoy a well-earned vacation.

Beach came yawning. "Whyn't you get ready for bed? How early are we going to leave? About noon?"

Jose unknotted his tie. "About sun-up."

"You're kidding."

"Wake me and find out." The phone between the twin beds dinged. He grabbed it before Beach could. "Hello." He'd had a hunch.

She was talking quiet and fast, as if she expected to be both overheard and interrupted. "Jose Aragon?"

"Speaking."

"I must see you."

"In the morning."

Beach wandered on into the bathroom. He'd lost interest in the conversation. A guy didn't use brusque talk to a blonde.

"Tonight," she said. "I'm leaving in the morning."

Beach was brushing his teeth with fervor. It was a trap; Jose was sure of it. But because he was too curious, he asked, "What's your room number?"

There was quick reaction. "No. No, not here."

"You're not alone?"

She was hesitant. "I might not be. I'll come to your room."

"I've got a roommate. Make it the lobby."

Again came that quick reaction. "No." Almost as if she were frightened. She didn't have anything to be scared about. Purple-suits wouldn't bother her. She had a nasty brother and a big baboon for bodyguards.

Beach returned, began pulling down the covers on his bed.

"Why not? There's no one down there."

"No." It was firm. And her plea was almost desperate. "I must see you."

Beach was sighing into the bed. It shouldn't take him long to get to sleep. Jose could hear the whisper of her breath at the other end of the line. He'd give a peso for a glimpse of her room right this minute. He had a picture of it, Tim sneering in one corner, Rags flexing his muscles in another, Dulcinda—but imagination stopped there. She could be smiling over her abilities as an actress; she could be truly troubled. He was less sure about the trap. He'd offered to bait it.

He said, "In fifteen minutes."

"Up there?"

"Yeah." He didn't say goodbye. He hung up.

"Now what?" Beach didn't care very much. He was comfortable.

"Unfinished business," Jose growled.

"What's it all about? Dames?"

"I said business," Jose stressed. "To me dames are a pleasure."

It was at the moment of speaking one whale of a big lie.

Dames were poison, blondes or brunettes, Norte Americanos or Mexicanos, strictly poison. He didn't bother to put his tie back on. He clicked off the lights, left Beach to heavy breathing. The door he closed carefully behind him. By the reflection from the street, he steered across Lou's sitting room and made a light here. He didn't have to be nervous, Dulcinda and her pals couldn't be planning any mayhem with Lou asleep in one bedroom, Beach soon to be in the other. Nevertheless, he helped himself to a stiff drink, straight, from Lou's scotch.

The faint tap came before the fifteen-minute deadline. He opened the door an inch until he saw it was she and that she was alone. As he admitted her, he warned, "Keep quiet. Everyone's asleep."

She nodded. Her eyes were taking in the room, including the two closed bedroom doors. Without invitation she went to the couch and sank to it. She had a trained grace, she could even sit down and make artistry of it. She said, of the room, "This is nice."

In case she didn't know, he made it plain. For whatever protection it afforded. "This is Lou Chenoweth's suite. She and her brothers own the Chenoweth hotels." He didn't offer a drink or a cigarette or any hospitality. She was a lovely thing but he didn't want her here. He didn't want any more to do with her. There were plenty of women who could quicken your heart by their very presence. All he had to do was look for them. And why had he let her come up tonight? That was one question he could answer. Because somehow she was connected with a dead man. And through her, he too was connected. "Well?" he demanded.

"I want to ask another favor of you."

He didn't say a word. He stood on his two feet and let his expression show what he thought of that one.

She ignored it. "It is very simple. You are going to Santa Fe in the morning." It was a statement.

"Yes."

"You picked up the package."

"Didn't you get it? I left it at the desk."

"Will you carry it to Santa Fe for me?"

He wanted to shout laughter. But it might wake Lou or Beach. And his curiosity was greater than his wish to show contempt. "Why?" he asked.

She had better make it good. She twisted one finger around another as if trying to figure out what to say. "I will pay you well," she began. But she knew as soon as she said it that it was the wrong approach. Knew from the curl of his smile.

"Ten dollars American?"

Her cheeks colored faintly. "I didn't know this morning that you were. . . ."

"Who am I?"

"Jose Aragon."

"I told you I was."

"I didn't know. . . ." He didn't help her and she let it trail away. She lifted her enormous eyes, pleading, "Will you?"

"Why?" he demanded more harshly.

She gave all the outward appearances of being desperate. "Because I'm afraid I can't get it there safely."

"I don't like a knife in my back any more than you do."

"I didn't mean that," she breathed. "I mean—I'm afraid it will be taken away from me."

"Stolen?"

She didn't answer save by a nod. She was watching the way her hands moved. As if they weren't hers.

"What if it's stolen from me?"

"It wouldn't be." Up came the eyes and the attempt to convince him. Hoping. "No one would know you were carrying it. No one would know you knew anything about it."

He could ask her what it was and let her think up an answer. But he already knew. He could ask her why it was important to carry a bottle of cheap perfume to Santa Fe. And get a tall tale for his pains. He could tell her everything that had happened today since she spoke to him on the street. He could even tell her that the man who threatened her was dead. He could, and that would start something, tell her that her precious packet had already been stolen. But he didn't tell her a thing.

"How much would you pay?"

Hope glistened. "Fifty dollars?"

He waited.

"How much do you want?" She was slightly wary.

"Fifty will do. And an answer."

The wariness stiffened. "Yes?"

"Would you have asked the noon Jose Aragon to do this job?"

Relief became a trickle of laughter. She lied well. "No, Senor." She rose in one fluid movement.

"Just a minute. Where do you want it delivered? And when?"

"We're leaving tomorrow. We'll be at La Fonda. Will you drop it off at the desk there? You know where that is?"

That was a funny one. There was only one La Fonda. Quite evidently she'd never been to Santa Fe. "Yes, I do," he said gravely. "And how do I get the package again? From the desk here, I mean. It was left for you, wasn't it?"

"Don't worry. It will be there for you in the morning." She skirted by him to the door. But he was quicker than she; he'd handle the exit. He gave it the usual inch. No patent-leather toe was stuck into the crack.

She said, "Thank you."

He wanted to touch her. It was almost a compulsion. She looked so fragile, as if she were a small girl, not one tall and proud. She looked as if she needed his comfort more than she needed his help. He kept his hands dug in his pockets. *"Por nada,"* he shrugged. Then he grinned, "Thank you. Those ten bucks will come in handy. With the fifty, I'll buy another ranch. Or a night on the town." He was even more impudent. "With you?"

Her cheeks colored again and she slipped away. He didn't watch her disappear up the corridor. He closed the self-lock-ing door fast. And again he shrugged. He didn't want anything more to do with her so he'd taken on another assignment. No one could call him a sissy. He was going out of his way to hang on to temptation. Whether he was winning the wrassle was a different question. If Lilith had the indescribable something which Dulcinda had, it was a wonder he was here at all.

He put out the light, joined the sleeping Beach in the bedroom. In the dark he undressed, fell into the other bed. But sleep didn't come easy. It didn't come until he'd figured out the next move.

Sleep lasted longer than he'd expected. It was after nine when he opened his eyes. Beach was still snoring cheerfully, his covers draped on the floor. It was a pity to wake the kid. He wouldn't feel so cheerful after the load he'd hoisted last night.

The sun was cauldron bright against the open window. This would be another killer. Jose wanted to go home, to mountain coolness, to swimming pools and tennis courts and La Fonda Cantina for cocktails at five. To pretty, safe girls summering in the little Spanish town, appreciative of Aragon attention.

"Are you going to sleep all day?" he inquired loudly.

It didn't make a dent on Beach's honking.

He gathered the covers from the floor, dumped them on the sleeping beauty. "Come on, come on—"

Beach made sounds, bleared his eyes. He recognized Jose and growled, "For God's sake, go away."

"It's morning, primo. Time to go home. Snap out of it."

Beach buried his head under the pillow.

"I'm going to shower. Start pulling yourself together." It took a little time for a man to come to after a bar tour of Juarez. But by the time Jose finished showering, Beach's first fogginess should have worn off. By the time Beach finished his shower, Jose could start talking to him.

He didn't know just how to start on it. He waited until both of them had their shirts buttoned, their sleeves rolled, their levis snug about their lean hips. The tough part was that he could give Beach neither the whole picture nor a little part of it. He could do nothing but ram the decision down Beach's throat.

Beach opened. "Aren't you going to pack?"

Jose didn't ease into it. He said flatly, "No."

"What's the idea?"

He sat down on the rumple of his unmade bed, lighted a cigarette with deliberation. "I'm not starting back this morning."

"For . . . God's . . . sake!" Beach tossed the clothes he was folding in two directions. "I was sleeping peacefully. You woke me, you insisted I get up and get going. For what?"

"You're leaving," Jose said.

Beach eyed him as if he were nuts. Well, he was. "And you aren't?"

"That's correct."

"What's the clue?"

He had to be cautious. Otherwise he'd have Beach along and it would probably be Beach who'd get the knife. Beach was only a year younger but he'd always been like a kid brother. Maybe because Jose would have liked a kid brother along with a sister. Maybe because when the California relatives came to New Mexico in the summer, they always turned Cousin Beach over to Cousin Jose to take care of.

You didn't get out of the habit of taking care of someone. Even when you knew they'd grown up, piloted fighters all over the Pacific, while you were stupidly pretending to be a peasant behind the enemy lines. Beach would get a kick out of going along on this ride but it was no deal. He had to protect the kid brother. This was the easiest way. There was nothing dangerous about the phony package. Thanks to it, he could keep both Beach and Dulcy out of his way.

"Unfinished business." He tried to make it sound not very important.

Beach eyed him shrewdly. "The same as last night?"

"Somewhat the same."

"And you're not talking."

"I'll tell you later." When it was safe.

Beach sighed. "Call down for some breakfast, double order coffee. I don't know whether it's you or Juarez firewater but my head is whirligigging."

Jose reached for the phone while Beach continued his oration, "Why do I have to start back? I'm in no hurry. How long is this business of yours going to take anyway?"

Jose concluded the order before he replied, "I don't know. I hope I can hop a ride this evening. There's always someone driving up to Santa Fe."

"I don't get it. Why shouldn't I hang around and we'll start back tonight instead of this morning? What's my rush?"

"The truck. They need it at the ranch. That's why." Actually it would make little difference whether the truck was returned this afternoon or tonight. Beach would point that out as soon as it clicked. "The other reason is that I promised to deliver a package to Santa Fe today. I can't make it and I'm asking you to do it for me."

It was too much to hope that Beach would ask no questions, although he was beginning to sense that Jose didn't have any ordinary unfinished business to dispose of. Beach wasn't one to sniff and circle a problem. He'd ask outright; if he weren't answered he'd find out another way. He asked, "Promised whom?"

Jose revolved the answer on the spit of his mind.

"Why can't we put this package on the next bus? What's so important you deliver it? Or me? Who's the package for?"

He'd have to open up a little or Beach wouldn't cooperate. "I promised Dulcinda Farrar," he said.

Beach's eyes were bigger than harvest moons.

"I don't know why it's so important to her but it must be. She's made it plain that her brother and that gorilla friend of his aren't to know about it. Or anyone else." If he could say: one man who knew too much, who wanted to know more, died last night. But that would have Beach in the thick of it. "All you have to do is take it to the desk at La Fonda and leave it there."

Beach accepted it without more palaver. He returned to his packing. "Your business must be *muy importante,* boy, to give up a date with Dulcy. After the way you doted on her last night."

"Don't get any ideas. I'll be there soon," Jose warned. Beach had enough girls without getting mixed up with this one. He added a more serious warning, "You don't take the package to her, you take it to the desk. You don't mention it to her!" His emphasis was too heavy.

Beach was careful. "She was your blonde. I don't get it."

Jose was saved by the door buzzer. As if he weren't in a hurry, he ambled to answer.

Pablo was bright as the new day. "Good morning, Senor Aragon." There was no indication that he knew anything about trouble last night. He carried the large tray to the table, set it down, went out again without further conversation.

Unasked, he'd brought along the morning paper. Chenoweth service. Jose snatched it with the closing of the door. There was no murder on the front page. He was opening the sheet as Beach appeared. He couldn't appear anxious now. A casual scanning showed nothing. If Tosteen had been found, he wasn't news.

Beach began eating hearty. "Have you told Lou?"

"Not yet. I haven't seen her. I'm leaving the hotel with you, just as if—"

Beach poised a forkful of ham and eggs in midair. "What is up?" Worry pricked his voice. "You're not in trouble?"

"No." Not yet. Jose appealed to him, "I can't tell you yet, Beach. Like I said, it's unfinished business. As quick as I can settle it, I'll give you a full report. It'll hand you a laugh."

"I'll bet," Beach said wryly.

"You'll lose. But I don't want anyone at the hotel to know I'm not leaving. I'll tell Lou later on."

"What about Dulcy?"

"Particularly I don't want her to know."

She wasn't around to know. When they went down to the desk, the lobby was the everyday thing, tourists waiting around for wives or husbands or the kids, and middle-aged business men in the big leather chairs, half of whom could have doubled for Tosteen. No one who looked any more suspicious than Tosteen had. Jose's goodbye and thank you to Lou was as convincing as Beach's.

She might not know for a couple of days she wasn't rid of him, unless he returned to tell her. The maid would make the room neat. It wouldn't occur to her to say anything about the guest's clothes even if no guest were around. An employe didn't display curiosity about the boss's friends.

Clark made the package deal easy. "I believe you left this last night." The same brown paper and dirty string. The same sweet stink. One thing different. A name penciled on the wrapping: Jose Aragon. Jose hadn't put it there.

The sun was climbing higher, no silver cool of morning remained in it. Today would be worse to endure than yesterday. A short walk took them to the garage where their truck was parked. No one stopped them on the walk, no one noticed them. Beach pitched his bag into the cab, climbed under the wheel. "Get in," he ordered.

When Jose started to demur, Beach repeated, "Get in."

He obeyed. Beach started the motor and rolled into traffic. "I'll give you a lift to the bridge." His eyes slid to Jose. "That's where you're headed?"

Jose nodded. The truck was too noisy for conversation. But Beach continued, "I wouldn't start anything over there, if I were you. It mightn't be healthy."

Jose nodded again. When Beach let him out, the bottle of perfume remained on the seat where he'd left it.

III

Crossing the bridge was easy. Like always, you simply walked across, paying your pennies, mumbling your citizenship declaration. Neither the Americanos nor the Mejicanos gave a second glance to a dark young guy in levis and blue shirt, a dusty hat keeping sunstroke off his head.

He didn't know exactly where he was going or what he was going to do when he got there. He was hunting a small girl who'd stolen a package, snatched it right out of his hands. But he wasn't headed for Senor el Greco's to find her, not yet. That was the way not to find her, unless it was to the Senor's advantage that she face up to the man she'd gypped. And in that event, it would not be to the advantage of Jose Aragon.

Someone had murdered Tosteen. He didn't doubt that it was murder any more than he doubted that Tosteen was marked for it. Any more than he doubted it had happened in Juarez and the body taxied to the other side. How the dead man had passed customs was something else again but it wouldn't be too tough, a drunken companion declaring for his passed-out friend. Drunks were a dime a dozen on the border any summer night.

He had to start somewhere. He glanced down the Calle Herrera carelessly as he passed. The street was as deserted as it had been when he left the cafe last night. Walls made shadows where the sun slanted into the narrow street. The neon sign slept. The cafe didn't open until five, not even the workers would be there at this hour. The *sorbita* would never be there again.

Jose let his steps lead him on, along the Avenue of the shops. Quiet, disinterested shops. The sidewalk vendors, too, were somnolent. Only the greenest gringos dared the blaze of noon. Those with pesos to toss away came later in the afternoon.

As he wandered along, he watched for one face. The one

with whom he must begin. One particular brown face among many, a wrinkled face whose monkey grin was a mask to cover too much knowledge of the border. Jose came to the intersection without spotting the one he sought. He could follow the arrows to the Mercado or he could join the hum of the Plaza. He chose to walk aimlessly into the thicket of native life. He might have been one of them; they didn't know him, but he wasn't alien as he leaned against a dirty wall rolling a limp brown cigarette. He leaned there with others as aimless as himself, listening to the phrases they spoke to each other, nothing more important than the heat of the day, the tempting plumpness of a woman lagging by, the opportunities of the lottery. They knew a Norte Americano had been killed in Juarez last night. They were wary, they were watching and listening as carefully as he. If the subject was not worthy of phrases, it was because one they didn't know stood among them, or because they'd talked too much of it before he arrived. When a policeman swanked by, there was a quivering silence among these men and women and children.

Because he was attuned to listening, Jose caught the boast of a ragged kid, "I saw him." It was muted braggadocio, with an eye poked toward the disappearing uniform of the police. It spilled out because the excitement was too great to be subdued for long. "He was bloody all over. . . ."

Another kid, equally ragged, equally thin, brown, and big-eyed, said with hushed vehemence, "You are a dirty, God-damn liar. There was no blood. He was in the river, all over with mud. . . ."

The kid broke off as a gnarled woman cuffed him, demanding silence. "You talk of what you do not know. You talk too much." The cluster of boys eased across the street, only the smaller ones whipping their eyes to the wall Jose leaned against. He knew then the silence was demanded because he was unknown. Not because he was Norte Americano, that they didn't know. Because he might be a police spy.

He lingered a little, then drifted away from the wall, careful

74

to move in a direction opposite to the one the boys had taken. He knew where to find out just a little more. The street boys would tell him, a few pesos would wag their tongues. But he'd have to wait until the suspicion had lulled, until others had leaned on the wall and smoked a cigarette, until his face was forgotten.

He moved on, crossing at the corner, continuing up the street deeper into the native city. His shirt was sticky against his back, his hat clung wet to his temples, his throat was dry as the dust of the street. He chose a bar no tourist would dare enter, a bar belonging to the men of Juarez. Bartolomeo's bar. It was, if possible, hotter within its walls than in the outside sun. A lazy overhead fan did no more than stir the heat and the smell of beer and the stench of sweating flesh.

The bar wasn't crowded, no more than half a dozen men gathered about it. The loudness of their voices diminished when Jose came in. It wasn't that he looked any different but he smelled different; he hadn't been long enough in the sun to overcome that. He shouldn't have showered this morning, he should have chewed garlic for breakfast, but even then they would have known. They didn't resent him but they didn't know him. They were careful men.

He didn't care. The keg beer was cold and the beer came first. The thick glass mug might not be sterile but it had been rinsed out, better than some joints he'd invaded. The man behind the bar was squat, his face pocked. The butcher's apron wrapped across his jeans was patterned intricately with dark beery finger streaks. Jose downed half his mugful before he spoke. He might have been muttering to himself but he made sure the others heard him.

"A stranger is not welcome in the city of Juarez." He spoke as a native, his accent was not theirs but it was not the accent of the ricos either. "It does not matter that he is a good man who attends the early mass on his saint's day. It is not important that he is a devoted son to his angel mother or that he works very hard to bring home to her a few pesos with which she may buy for herself a new shawl. In the city of Juarez he becomes a mongrel dog." He finished the beer and the muttering without glancing at any of them. He knew they had listened to his words and that some of them were ashamed. "Senor," he addressed the bartender, "if you please, another beer."

The half-dozen men were muttering together, their black-brown eyes observing him. He was not meant to hear or to notice the observation. Opinion was divided as to whether the stranger should be greeted or continue to be ignored. One fellow, he was called Salvador, was not to be convinced. His phrases were for Jose to hear. "It is not healthy to be a stranger," and "The wise man does not speak with strangers." He might be a type easily made apprehensive by ill events but he didn't look it. His teeth were bad, his chest was narrow. He looked as Jose might have had he been born to Mexican peons instead of Spanish-American hidalgos. He was not a fellow you'd want to meet with at night in an alley.

Again Jose spoke to his beer. "A man is lonely when he is without friends."

He had finally evoked a *"Com'sta?"* From a little old fellow in whose worn face there was no malice. "I do not believe I have seen you before."

"I am a stranger," Jose stated, ignoring in proper fashion what had gone before. All of them were willing to speak now that there had been a beginning of social exchange, all but Salvador who maintained his voluble distrust.

"From what part of the country do you come?"

He saw no reason to tamper with the truth any more than was necessary. "From Santa Fe," he told them. He allowed the calloused palms of his hands to be seen, grateful for the results of cowpunching.

"And where is Santa Fe?"

He weighed the answer. "It is north. In New Mexico."

The others gabbled, "My brother, he has been to New Mexico." "My mother, she has a cousin who has been to the city of Silver." "We have been to the beet fields of Colorado."

Until the surly question broke from Salvador, "Why do you come here?"

Jose shrugged gracefully. "My cousin and myself, we have worked on a ranch in Socorro county. Only yesterday we have brought to market the cows. For this we receive money. He now has returned but to me there is the consideration, perhaps I can earn more money. It may well be that someone wishes a strong young man to deliver some cows to the north. It is possible."

"You will find in Barto's no men who own cows," Salvador grunted. "For these you must go to the Chenoweth Hotel." His example could have been El Paso, to narrow it to the Chenoweth was deliberate.

Deliberately Jose said in return, "Only a rich man can visit the Hotel Chenoweth. I am a poor man who wishes to earn his way home." He measured the faces carefully while he took a full drink from his mug. They were off guard now, all but Salvador, and this one had dared him. He dried his upper lip with his forefinger. "I have heard there is a man who at times is in need of a delivery boy. He is called"—he paused as if trying to remember the name—"el Greco."

Their faces closed as he spoke. They didn't answer him in words, only in caution. One murmured, "I have heard the name." They wanted no more of Jose because he spoke of Senor Praxiteles.

Boldly, Jose continued it, asking, "Do you know where I can find this Senor el Greco?"

The sequence of sounds did not become a phrase this time. The men edged farther away.

"Perhaps you would know, Senor," Jose addressed the bartender.

"I do not know this man," Barto denied flatly. He kept his eyes on Jose.

Jose drained the mug. "Someone must know. I have heard of him." He set the mug hard on the bar. As it thudded, the little men shrank. Not Salvador or the bartender. "I will find someone who knows him," Jose said boldly, and he walked out of the saloon. He didn't walk far; he leaned in a shop doorway until he saw Salvador emerge.

He put his back to the street then, examining the shoddy shoes in the shop window. Until the fellow had passed. He figured it would happen this way. Salvador was moving with a purpose, much too energetically for the hour and for a fellow who had been enjoying his beer. Whether Salvador was headed to inform the police of a stranger's interest in el Greco or whether he was going to el Greco himself was what Jose intended to find out.

He left just enough space between them, his own stride was apparently purposeless, but he knew how to lengthen without hurrying it. It wouldn't have been easy to follow Salvador on a crowded street, the jeans, the sweaty shirt, and the straw hat burned saffron were uniform. But the street was uncrowded. Trailing was too easy; it wasn't safe. If Salvador were to glance over his shoulder, he would behold Jose.

He was right, it was too easy; something had to spoil it. As Salvador waited to cross at the first intersection, Jose's eyes slipped by him to the opposite corner. To Canario.

It took him a moment to recognize the man. Without his band, Canario was no more than another Mexican sauntering along with his cronies before the hour for work. With recognition, Jose had to decide without delay which man was of more importance. Regretfully, he decided against Salvador. Jose stepped back against the wall of the corner shop and waited.

Canario trotted on with his gesticulating friends. He was almost beside Jose before he saw him. Quite obviously he didn't want to see Jose. Dismay pulled down his lip, skittered his eyes, and he ducked out into the wide street without a thought of the squalling cars. Jose was after him at once. His hand grabbed the small man's shoulder, bringing him to a halt.

"Look where you're going, *amigo,*" Jose warned.

Canario's great friendship had vanished overnight. He spoke

in English even as Jose, although his was spiced with border accent. "What is it you want?" He eyed Jose as a stranger.

Jose kept his hand where it was, drawing the musico back to the curb. "I don't want you run down before I buy you a drink."

"I do not think I care for a drink."

Jose's clutch tightened. "I don't either. But where else can we talk at this hour?"

"What is it you wish to say?"

"Plenty," Jose snapped.

Canario searched for escape. He was an unhappy man, Jose was too big, too young, too determined. Too Norte Americano for a small Mexican street musician.

"I've just had two beers at Bartolomeo's. Shall we return there or you have perhaps a better idea?"

Desperately, Canario's eyes searched the street for assistance. His friends were out of sight.

"Barto's?" Jose repeated.

"No, no. I am a sick man, Senor—"

"The sickness has come on you quickly. Too quickly for my pity. Shall we sit over there in the churchyard?" He began moving Canario in that direction. "If your sickness increases, I can ask the priest to attend you."

It wasn't a bad choice, in the open where none could overhear. There was the usual scattering of sightseeing tourists wandering in and out the tall doors; the usual old women, all in black like crows, the fringe of their shawls rippling as they moved in their little black shoes. And the usual scatter of ragged kids chasing each other in play. That Canario approved the choice was doubtful, he likely hadn't been this near a church in years. Jose guided him to the very steps, pushed him down, and sat beside him. He pulled out his tobacco pouch, his cigarette papers, and offered them first to Canario. The man shook his head.

Jose began to roll one. "Death walked in Juarez last night."

Canario's face was blank. "I do not know what you say."

"There was a man who followed me. He was called Tosteen. You knew him."

"I did not know him," Canario's teeth clicked. "Before God, I know nothing of this man."

"He is dead." He probed Canario's eyes. "You know that."

"No, no." Canario's nostrils quivered.

"In the river. Everyone knows it."

For some reason the fear and tension oozed out of Canario. As if Jose meant nothing personal but was merely repeating street gossip. "It is this one you mean?" He was eager now to please. "I have heard of this one." He could grin. "There is much trouble. Our police and your police must decide on which side of the river he has died. It is most difficult." He shook his head. "Because a man gets drunk and falls into the river. So much trouble!"

"He didn't drown," Jose snapped. Canario blanked again. "There isn't enough water in the Rio Grande to drown a flea from your miserable body. He wasn't drunk, either. He was on a job, a man doesn't drink on that kind of a job, Canario. He was following me. Until you stopped him from following me. What happened after that?"

Canario allowed himself to disbelieve. "It is the same man . . . this one in the river and the other one . . . ?"

"You know damn well it is. He was thrown in the river. After he was dead. What happened—?"

Fright stammered, "I know nothing."

"—when you stopped him?" He waited.

Canario began cautiously, "I give him a fine *piada*. Like I give you." Little drips of sweat rolled from beneath Canario's straw hat. He wanted to be believed.

"He didn't want to hear a *piada*. He was after me."

"Why, Don Jose?" The voice insinuated, "Why was he after you?"

"I don't know," Jose answered bluntly. "I don't know a damn thing about him. All I know is he was following me, and now he is dead. . . .

"I heard the kids talking about it." Jose watched the clumps of children running in the street and the churchyard, sitting on the curbs, pink watermelon juice or cheap pink and green ices dripping from their chins. "Who was he, Canario?"

"I do not know this." That much was spoken honestly, Canario wasn't exaggerating the roll of his shoulders and his eyes. He didn't know.

"How then is it you know he was in the river, dead?"

"Everyone whispers about it, one to another. Until there is no one, not the ninitos nor the deaf abuelitas nor Don Jose, who does not know." Canario smiled with childwise bliss as he explained, "There is not much happens in our little city, Senor. It is not like El Paso and the cities of the United States where always there are so many things happening. Where a man may die, and who is there to care? Here it is most important."

"Yeah." Here it was most important. Because delicate governmental relations between south of the border and north of the border must not be upset. Most important—more important than the death of a sloppy man in a seersucker suit. And how happy Juarez would be when it was decided that Tosteen died on the American side of the river. As it would be decided. "Why did he die?"

Again the shrug, but again the stained rivulets began their flow from the ragged hat brim. "I do not know this thing. He drinks too much, the Norte Americanos all of them drink too much, he falls in the river, he dies. It is sad, may his soul rest."

"He wasn't drunk. I told you he wasn't drunk. After you entertained him with the *piada,* then what? Where did he go?"

"Who knows? He did not remain to hear the Coda. And Senor, he did not give me so much as a *centavo.*" The indignation was honest, more honest than any words he had spoken. "Not one *centavo* when I have play so beautiful for him. He push by me—he push me, Senor—and he walks on very fast." Canario's lips quirked at the corners. "But not very far."

"Someone sticks a knife in him."

"Senor!" Canario gasped. Then he tittered, wiping the sweat from his eyes. "You are making a joke. A gringo joke."

"I'm trying to find out what happened." Jose brought out his pouch and papers again. They were limp with the heat.

This time Canario reached for them. "He does not go very far because he meets with some friends. They are so happy to see him. They say, 'Come, have a drink.'" Reproachfully he inserted, "You see it is true he did have a drink, Senor, then perhaps another, then he forgets how many he has had—"

"Uh-uh, Canario. That's what the newspapers are going to say. But you and I know it isn't true. We know he was on a job. Who were these friends?"

This was safe ground for the musico. He was happy to say he did not know them.

"You saw them. What did they look like?"

"Turistas."

He was beginning to suspect. Or he'd known all along. "A lady, perhaps?"

"Ah, so beautiful a lady!"

Jose said slowly, "A blonde. A beautiful young lady—so tall—" He measured toward the high arch of the church. "Young—"

Canario kept giving little quick nods.

"Who was with her?"

Canario stroked his chin. "La Barba."

"And," Jose grimaced, "El Chongo."

"You know them, Senor!" Canario was pleased.

"No. I saw them later. With my cousin. The dead man was not with them. You had seen them before, Canario?"

"Who knows?" He began to argue. So many turistas, every day, every night. "How can one remember?"

"You'd remember her. She was special."

He snickered. "Special." He rolled the syllables. "Special." He would remember the word.

"How much did they pay you to warn me and to intercept Tosteen?"

Canario was so innocent. He didn't know what Don Jose spoke of.

"How much did they pay you to meet me at the door of the Cock later? To play me across the bridge?"

The innocence was aggravated. "You are my friend, Don Jose. Your father was my friend."

Jose hammered it quietly, "How much?" His eyes crinkled on the protesting face. "I could pay you more."

Canario vowed friendship to all Aragons but the spittle of greed was in his mouth. "It was a joke," he confessed.

"Ha ha," Jose said.

"Yes, Senor. A joke. This man does not know his friends are waiting for him. I must play for him while they watch—"

"You're lying. It isn't even good lying."

"Senor!"

"You have forgotten what happened. You sang to me. Now you remember? You sang to me that I should be careful, a man was following me. You permitted me to pass and you stopped this man so he should not follow me. As I requested. But the turistas had already paid you for this."

"It is very warm," Canario said. Sweat dripped in wider streams. "I must go now."

"Like hell." Jose replaced his hand on the sticky shoulder. "These turistas have gone north. Tosteen is dead. And I'm here. Is that what happened?"

"Quien sabe?" Canario murmured unhappily.

"Where did they take Tosteen?"

"I do not know. I do not see them after this. I play for all the turistas who come over the bridge."

"You saw them again. That stunt at the bridge wasn't your idea." It wasn't theirs until later, when they needed it. "The police could be interested in all of this, Senor Canario. You have told them how you played for the dead man?"

"Senor Aragon!" The old face begged pity. "I am a poor man. A poor *musico*. For pennies I must play every night. When I am so sick I must play." He clutched his belly, writhed with pain. "Do I know this man walks with death? How could I know this thing? I am a poor ignorant fellow—"

"I want to know about the bridge stunt," Jose stated coldly. "Who paid you to do it?" He was impatient. "I am not going to the police. I have no wish to visit your bug-ridden juzgado."

"It was for the lady. The sweet—how you say it—" He tried to soften Jose with a small joke. "The candy kid?"

Dulcy . . . Dulce.

"And it was a joke?"

"Yeah."

"I think," Canario's eyes slid curiously to Jose's grim face, "I think you and the lady have maybe had a little fuss, no? She says to me, 'The great Senor Aragon, the band must play for him when he goes across the bridge.' It is very funny! Like you are the *gobernador* or the *major* of El Paso del Norte maybe?" He tittered, begging Jose to consider it funny.

She hadn't left the table after Jose arrived. And she hadn't fixed it up early in the evening. Tosteen wasn't dead in a cab then. He didn't get it. "What time was all this?"

"What time?" Canario didn't watch clocks. "She is going into the Cock and she sees me and she laughs. 'It is Canario again,' she says, because we have had a joke before this, you understand. And her friend, he comes to me and he tells me this other joke she will play on you."

"A great little joker," Jose said savagely.

"It is very funny." Canario went into his phony laughter again. But he was waiting for a chance to get away. He was edgy.

It didn't seem that Canario had any tie-up with Senor el Greco. What he'd told could have happened just the way he'd said it happened. He didn't invent Dulcy Farrar and her body-guard, hiring Canario to separate Jose from Tosteen early in the evening, hiring him to put them back together after Tosteen died. How did they know Tosteen was going to die? The seersucker man was walking the bars while they were ring-siding it at the Cock. But the Chimp and the Beard and the lovely girl who connived with Death wouldn't have to do the job, not with pesos in their pockets. He recalled the hirelings in the purple suits, smoking their sweet cigarettes against el Greco's wall, shadowed against the Chenoweth lamp post. Canario didn't have to be tied up with el Greco to be involved. Yet Jose felt impelled to mention the Senor, he needed Canario's reaction. Canario wouldn't skip until Jose's hand came out of his pocket.

Jose eyed him. "I'm looking for a girl."

The change of subject suited Canario. "She has gone—"

"Not the Candy Kid. Another girl. Her name is Francisca. Her *abuelo* is called Senor el Greco."

The reaction was the same as it had been in Barto's bar. No one was willing to talk about Praxiteles. "This one I do not know." Canario's fingers plucked at his dirty shirt. There might always be an unhealthy respect when the old man was mentioned. But not always this green look of fear. They knew, somehow all of them knew, that el Greco and the dead man were threaded together. With sticky spider threads.

"You know a young fellow named Salvador?"

"There are many named Salvador."

"This one drinks beer at Barto's."

"There are many who do."

It would be true. Jose dug his hand into his pocket. Five pesos. Not too much, Canario mustn't think Jose was paying for silence. Five was enough. He folded the small bills together. Canario's hand was outthrust. It trembled just a little. Not from eagerness, only to secure his pay and escape.

"*Adios,* Canario," said Jose. "See you around."

"*Si.*" He managed a weak grin but only because he was a showman. "See you around."

He scuttled, out of the churchyard, into the street. He was heading toward Barto's bar. Well, it was the closest and by now Canario's tongue would be parched. One thing was certain;

anything Jose wanted to find out concerning Senor Praxiteles, he would have to find out first hand. He pushed himself up from the low steps, shook out the kinks. It was about time to pay a visit to el Greco.

THREE

JOSE MOVED OPENLY UP THE STREET WHERE THE boy had led him last night. He turned boldly into the alley called Calle de la Burrita. It was no more than a quiet little street made up of shops and houses. A street where men were about their gossip and women their chores, where dogs lay panting in the afternoon heat, and children, too small to wander the Plaza, played with melon rinds in the dust. The tourists, too, were here; they all resembled schoolteachers reaching for their retirement pay, a little too stout or a little too scrawny, quite a bit too warm in their silk prints and white sensible oxfords. Some were armed with cameras, others with pesos alone and the urge for bargains. They wandered in and out of the shops free of the imagination which bred fear. Not one of them would have dared venture here after sunset. Instinct would protect them.

Senor Praxiteles' shop was a busy place. Three printed ladies in rimless eyeglasses, like three stair-steps, were spreading the garish colors of Mexican rugs near the window. Their speech was brisk, they knew exactly what they wanted and would not be hurried until they had weighed well their choice.

A fussy woman, the heat breaking through her makeup, and a portly man, who carried his checkered jacket, were involved with the serapes. The heavy goat's wool they fingered increased their discomfort. The man was complaining, "I will not try one on, Veda. . . ."

At the gimcrack counter, a pretty woman shepherded two

teen-age girls. The girls looked cool enough in their white blouses and full pink-and-blue skirts. Mexican peasant wear was popular this summer on both sides of the border. The mother may have looked smart in her dark chiffon when she bought it in Detroit or Omaha. Right now it clung to her as if she'd been caught in a freshet of rain. She perched on the edge of an old table and was patient.

Senor Praxiteles was dividing his attention between the rug ladies and the serape couple. A young assistant, so young he couldn't have been more than twelve years old, waited with unwavering apathy for the young girls to decide on what they would carry back to their friends at home. It would take a long time, although the mother, panting like the curs in the dust outside, tried wearily to hasten the buying.

The bell tinkled on Jose's entrance, even as it had last night. But the door was unlatched and there were no curtains now dividing the shop from the entry. Praxiteles looked up from the rugs but he didn't advance to Jose. His wrinkled, hairless head, yellowed with years, signaled the young boy. There was little resemblance between the gentleman who had stood in the dim lamplight the night before, and this poor *nativo* who had come in, perhaps for no reason but to cool himself from the heated street outside.

The boy who was *primo* to Jaime or Pablo or the *sorbita* edged from behind the counter. He padded over on his dirty bare feet and stood in front of Jose. He didn't say anything.

Jose put on a native's accent. "I wish to buy me a bottle of perfume."

"No perfume."

He frowned, spoke louder, as if the boy were deaf. "It is the perfume I wish to buy. The perfume you sell here."

He had drawn Praxiteles. With little murmurs of apology to the paying customers, the old one shuffled over and peered up at Jose. He did not recognize this yokel; it was evident in his dismissal. "We do not sell perfume. On the Avenida are the perfume shops. Or at the Mercado."

"I have the money." Jose fished for pesos in his pocket. "I have enough money to buy a bottle of your perfume. A bottle of La Rosa del Amor."

The old man kept shaking his head. He was annoyed at the insistence. He was in a hurry to return to the good money of turistas. "Look about you! There is no perfume. I do not sell perfume." He shuffled off toward the serape couple, mumbling, "No perfume. Go to the market."

Jose didn't go. He followed the boy to the counter. "There is no perfume?" he persisted. The teen-age girls giggled to each other.

Jose slanted over his shoulder at Senor Praxiteles. The old man wasn't free to listen, not if the fussy woman was to be sold the costume she had chosen for her husband. Jose lowered his voice, "Where is Francisca?"

The boy's blank face said something now. It spoke of fear. "Yo no se," he stammered. He did not want any more conversation with Jose. His eyes sought Senor Praxiteles' for help. But his fear was of the old one. He shrank again when the Senor approached the troublous peon.

El Greco's tongue was barbed. "What now is it you want, Senor?" The title was a sneer. "I am a busy man. I have told you there is no perfume to be had here. Go to the Mercado."

"I want to see Francisca."

The girls giggled more shrilly. The fussy woman said loudly, "Well, make up your mind, Horace. The blue or the green," and the schoolteachers conferred, "This one would go well in front of your fireplace, Julia." Praxiteles' silence was the more menacing for these extraneous sounds which dangled from it.

"She is not here," he finally said.

"Where is she? She tells me I can see her. It is for her I wish to buy the perfume."

Praxiteles might believe it, he might not. Francisca wasn't too young to have a fellow seeking her, they started young on the streets of Juarez. "She told you to come here?"

That must be wrong. Jose was belligerent. "You are her

abuelo. Where do I look for her but at the house of her abuelo?"

Senor Praxiteles spat, "You are wasting my time. I am busy." He beamed a wrinkled smile at the arguing couple. *"Un momento, Senora."* From his narrow lips, he ordered Jose, "Get out of here. Go away. If you bother me further I will call the police."

That was a good one. But Jose skirted by the old man as if he were cowed by the threat. He would return later. When el Senor had more time for him. On the broken steps he lingered long enough to roll a cigarette. He rounded the corner where last night two men had waited for him. No one shadowed the sunlight. In the back of his mind, he might have wanted a look at the rear entrance of the Praxiteles tienda. He was not expecting a whisper from the window.

He saw the boy's empty, frightened face. "Francisca, she did not come home last night." The boy was gone that quickly. He must have made some excuse to the gigglers to come into what would have been a stockroom, something which would hold water with the old man, such as fetching more gimcracks.

Jose walked on. Tosteen was dead, Francisca had not come home last night. Francisca had the package Tosteen was after, the package el Greco had turned over to Jose for Dulcy Farrar. The package which was more important than a bottle of cheap perfume should be. He was going to find the *sorbita*. He wouldn't listen to the dreary whisper that she too might have been laid to rest in the river. He would find her alive.

There was one more source of information, an honest one. Senora Herrera wouldn't know anything about what made a perfume bottle important but she could tell him more about Francisca and the spidery old man. Senora Herrera was one person who wasn't afraid to speak out about el Greco. He couldn't call upon the Herreras in his sweaty work clothes. They were gentlefolk. He'd have to return to the hotel and change. It was just as well to report in to Lou before evening. He'd stirred up fuss in enough quarters over here to make a friend essential. He didn't want to be found on the riverbed tomorrow morning.

Instead of returning to the intersection, he cut across side streets to Avenida Juarez. His guardian angel must have been nudging him. Certainly he hadn't thought about trouble waiting at the intersection. The short cut gave him a head start when they spotted him, Salvador and two men in purple-blue suits.

He wouldn't have noticed them if he hadn't short-cut again, slanting across in the direction of customs. Salvador was pointing to him, the men began a slant cross of their own. Jose lengthened his stride, eeling through the clusters of tourists and vendors. He didn't know what the two wanted with him, he wasn't anxious to find out. The men were half-running but he kept ahead of them and, in a last spurt, declared himself quickly to the Mexican officials.

He was midway to the American side when they reached the barrier. Over his shoulder he watched them gesticulating to the officials. They might be accusing him of anything from theft to rape to subversive activity but they weren't permitted to follow. He didn't breathe easy until he had been passed by the American side. Steaming from the heat of the chase. It wasn't the climate for foot races.

He had a natural distaste for the waiting taxis. No telling what you'd find in a border cab. It was safer to be out in the open. His luck held. A slatternly street car was approaching and he waited for it. His pursuers might have been on board but they weren't. The car was sparsely filled at this hour. He rode the short way into the city with Mexicans who were crossing the border for shopping or a job. The El Paso streets were cluttered with safe afternoon crowds. When he swung off the trolley, it wasn't more than a stride to the hotel.

He hadn't eaten since breakfast and he went directly to the coffee shop. The cooling system enhanced appetite; he ordered steak and potatoes and a tomato salad, iced coffee. While he waited, he munched on bread. He sensed rather than saw that someone stood above the table. It was Lou.

"What are you doing here?" She didn't seem pleased about it.

"Sit down." His mouth was full.

She hesitated and then she pulled out the chair across from him. "I thought I spotted you coming in." For Lou the waitress rushed to the table. "Nothing for me, Annie." She waved the girl away. Her frown returned to Jose. "I said you'd checked out."

He was quick. "Who'd you say it to?"

"The police."

They observed each other silently. He asked, still not understanding how or why, "The police were looking for me?"

"Not exactly." There was an ink stain on her forefinger. She rubbed at it. "One of our guests died last night."

"Was killed," he said.

Her eyes jumped to his face. "You know about it!"

"I've been in Juarez. Everyone knows about it." He put butter on another slab of bread. "I don't get why the cops wanted to see me."

"I don't know that they did," Lou said slowly. "Until those friends of yours—"

He waited without expression.

"Jim Wade and Dee Meighan volunteered that Tustin had been looking for you last night."

He began to chomp the crust. Annie was bringing his plate, it gave him time to think about how much he should tell Lou. By the time he'd sampled the steak, he'd decided to open up. About so far.

"I ran into those two in Juarez last night with a couple of bims. They told me someone was looking for me. Not who." He told the truth. "I didn't know Tustin. I didn't know that was his name."

"Why was he looking for you, Jo?"

"I don't know."

"You have an idea."

He'd go a little further. "Listen, Lou. I saw the guy for the first time when I got here yesterday. He was coming out of the hotel as I was going in. I didn't pay any more attention to him than that. And it wasn't an hour later he was in my bedroom—your guest room—going through my things."

Her eyebrows zoomed. "Why?"

"I didn't know then, I don't know now. I caught him at it because I was expecting Pablo with that lunch, remember?"

"What did he say?"

"He apologized for mistaking the room. You don't mistake that apartment of yours for a room, Lou."

"No, you don't," she agreed. Her pretty face was screwed tight with thinking.

"I didn't like it. Pablo arrived about then and the guy took off. Pablo found out his name for me later." *Tosteen*—Tustin.

"Why didn't you tell me about it?"

"What for?"

"We like to keep an eye on irregularities."

"He hadn't taken anything, Lou. He'd apologized."

She pronged a fork on the table cloth. "Did you see him again?"

"In Juarez. We passed each other again, like strangers." He wouldn't mention the later altercation. Maybe no one would remember it.

She frowned. "Then why?" She persisted, "That's all there was to it, Jo?"

"That's all." With reservations.

She said slowly, "I don't understand. I don't understand at all." But she'd lived too long on the border not to be suspicious. Even of Jose Aragon. "There must be more to it, Jo."

"Sure," he agreed. "That much doesn't add. But how are we going to find out the rest of it? Tosteen—Tustin's dead."

"You said killed."

"What do the police say?"

"They think he got drunk, fell into the river, or was rolled.

That's what they say. That he died from the tumble. Not that someone killed him."

"Why are they so interested? Another drunk."

"You know why," she told him impatiently. "Neither side wants any trouble."

"That's what they're saying in Juarez. On which side did it happen? It's safer if he was killed American. Norte-American."

She agreed.

"They're afraid. They don't want to talk about it. They know he was killed even if the cops won't say so. Do you know el Greco, Lou?"

Alarm touched her. "Is he in on it?"

"Do you know him?"

"Everyone knows Senor Praxiteles. He does business both sides of the bridge. He's a bad one, Jo. Where does he come in?"

"I don't know," he began, but at the refusal in her face, he made it stronger. "I honestly don't, Lou. But no one in Juarez wants to talk about him or about Tosteen, your Tustin. It's fifty-fifty on not talking."

She spoke softly. "Why were you asking questions in Juarez?"

"I was trying to get some answers." It sounded flip but he wasn't feeling that way. "I didn't."

"Why did you stay over to ask questions?"

The taxi driver hadn't come forward. He was pretty sure of that. Dirty little guys like the cabbie could get in trouble too easy. Jose Aragon had been the one selected to·take on that trouble but he'd refused. Whether the cabbie was an innocent victim or one of the Praxiteles boys, he'd keep his mouth shut. It could have been he who pushed Tosteen over the embankment to get rid of him. Jose didn't even have to speak up.

He had waited too long to answer her. She went on, "Why did you stay over to ask questions about Tustin? Before the police knew he was dead?"

"I didn't kill him, Lou. For God's sake!"

"I know you didn't," she returned as angrily. "But how did you know?" She was almost fearful. "What have you to do with el Greco?"

"Not a damn thing. Or with Tustin. Believe it or not, but it's God's truth."

"I believe you, Jo," she said but she was still angry. Then she switched emotions. She became shrewd. "Go home, Jo."

"I can't." He'd spoken too quickly.

"Why not?" The two words were bullet hard.

He shouldn't have told her anything. Every little piece led to another little piece. He was exceedingly careful now, choosing each word, weighing it before he gave it to her. "I lost something last night in Juarez. Until I find it, I can't go home."

She didn't ask what; if he'd wanted her to know that he'd have told her. But she reached back and put things in order. "What about Praxiteles?"

He'd be safe telling her the whole story. She could help him, she had an importance, the woman who ran the biggest hotel in El Paso. But the little fellows wouldn't be safe; she wouldn't care about Canario who'd played a joke and was this soon regretting it or of Francisca trembling in the darkness and as yet he didn't know why. Lou would short-cut to take care of Jose Aragon and the hotel; what happened to the others wouldn't matter. She'd been here too long, she'd known too many who deserved their border reputation. She'd tar them all with the brush until they proved otherwise. And they couldn't prove it with two sets of police on their necks; they couldn't prove it with el Greco's threads winding about them.

He had no compunctions about involving the Farrar bunch, but if he did, they'd sail out of it with full white sails. Between the Farrars and a border punk, the punk wouldn't have a chance. He'd save the Farrars for one who saw them without illusions, for himself. He must continue to speak with care. He answered her, therefore, "I don't know yet, Lou. I only know what I've told you, across the bridge the two names are linked. Maybe not by the police. By the people in the Plaza. In the bars."

"It isn't safe to play games with Senor el Greco, Jo."

"I've heard that one before."

"Have you met him?"

He was careful. "I've been in his shop."

"I wouldn't go back. If he knows you've been asking questions about him, and he'll know, I wouldn't go back."

"Thanks, Lou," he said noncommittally.

She said, "You were CIC during the war."

He flared, "You think I'm playing cloak and dagger out of habit? I'm not, Lou. But look at it straight. A guy I don't know follows me around. Before I can find out why, he's dead. Now the police are looking for me. I've got some things to learn."

He'd finished his dinner a long time ago. Annie was hovering but not too close; she could see the boss didn't want an interruption. He beckoned the girl now. "Bring me some peach shortcake and more coffee. How about it, Lou, join me for coffee?"

"I must get back to the desk." When the waitress withdrew, she said, "There's a lot you aren't saying, Jo. I know it. You know it."

He smiled at her fondly. "I'm hoping to get done with it tonight. Maybe I can catch a late ride. If you hear of any, let me know. You think I ought to see the cops before I leave?"

"It isn't exactly the cops. It's Ozzie Harrod. Border patrol. We went to school together."

"You think I should talk to him?"

"Not until you're ready to talk, Jo." She shook her head gravely. "Not while you're covering up this way. He's no dope."

It annoyed him that he was so wide open but he swallowed the rebuke. He said, "Okay."

She pushed away from the table. "You're going across the bridge again tonight." She disapproved.

"I've got to."

"You wouldn't want to take me along?"

"I can't, Lou." He shook his head.

"Be careful." She walked away on efficient heels.

The girl darted forward with the dessert as soon as the boss had gone. "Get me an afternoon paper, will you, Annie?" He smiled at her. She was eaten up with curiosity but the smile would help her to forget. It was his forward-pass smile. One he'd learned from Beach.

The story was on the front page but you had to borrow a microscope to find it. A couple of lines about a man found dead in the Rio Grande near the bridge, identified as H. E. Tustin. Believed to have lost his balance and fallen over the embankment. Suggestion was he'd lurched through too many bars; the reporter didn't have to put that in words. Nothing about who Tustin was or what he was doing wandering on a dark embankment. The police would have been through Tustin's papers, they'd know. It looked as if he'd have to see the police despite Lou's warning.

When he returned to the lobby, he was aware of every face decorating it. Among these would be cops. But no one paid him any special attention and he wasn't able to spot which ones. That was the way they wanted it. He had to go to the desk for a key. Lou ignored him. Clark handed it over without words. Lou may have warned him to keep quiet too.

As Jose turned toward the elevators, he almost bumped into Pablo. The boy said, "Your pardon, Senor," and got himself out of the way. His flat black eyes held on Jose's face. As if he had words on his tongue but there were others heading to the elevators and he withheld them.

The others got off along the way, couples and the usual business men. Jose rode to the top floor. He let himself into Lou's apartment, shoved the door tight after him. He was stopped cold. By a smell. A smell he knew by now. The smell of La Rosa del Amor.

On Lou's cocktail table was the lumpy green-wrapped package. Quickly Jose went into the bedroom, into the bath, out again, and without a halt into Lou's room and bath. He was here alone. He was just reaching for the package when the knock sounded at the door. A knock without any special significance, not Lou's quick rap, or Pablo's hesitant one. A plain knock.

Automatically he hitched up his jeans, rubbed his hands dry. He crossed to the door, opened it as an ordinary guy would to an ordinary knock. He didn't know the man who stood outside but he'd seen him in the elevator. He'd got off on the floor below. A tall, bony man, about Lou's age, a weather-beaten face; a man with the horizon in his intelligent gray eyes, a quiet voice, a pleasant manner. He might have been a rancher. Jose guessed who he was.

"Jose Aragon? My name's Harrod." He held out a small leather folder. Jose took it, glanced at the credentials. "May I come in for a few minutes?"

"Yes. Come in." He was conscious of nothing but that sickly sweet smell, Harrod couldn't miss it. Jose was deferent as a younger man must be to an older, offering the good chair. He himself walked boldly to the couch, sat himself down. He couldn't hide the package; he could make it harmless by making it more conspicuous.

"I was asking Miss Chenoweth about you earlier. She thought you'd checked out this morning."

Lou hadn't sent him up here, Lou didn't want Jose talking with Harrod yet. The chief had other sources of information.

"I intended to," Jose admitted. "But at the last minute I decided to stay over another day."

"For any particular reason?"

He could answer that as he pleased. He knew Lou hadn't talked, there hadn't been time. She wouldn't repeat their conversation no matter how much time there was. His delay in answering Harrod wasn't pointed, it was as if he were considering the question. "No," he finally decided. "I haven't been down this way for years and I thought I'd have another day of it."

"But your cousin left this morning?" Evidently Harrod had been trying to make something of that.

Jose said agreeably, "Yes. Someone had to take the truck back to the ranch." He smiled. "Beach was elected."

Harrod seemed to accept it. He might send someone north to check with Beach but that too was all right. Beach wouldn't know anything. "You know why I'm here, Mr. Aragon."

Jose nodded. "The death of a man named Tustin."

"What can you tell me about him?"

"Not much." He recited the same incidents that he had just given Lou.

"You don't know what he wanted from you? Enough to risk searching your room?"

"I haven't the slightest idea." The package stunk in his nostrils. "Who was Tustin, Captain Harrod? What was his business?"

"We don't know that, yet," Harrod drawled. He had a permanent small frown which drew his eyebrows together. "You were in the late war, Mr. Aragon?" Before Jo could answer, he continued, "In intelligence." Again he continued without waiting for Jose to speak, "From Tustin's papers it would seem that he had traveled considerably. Across Europe to South America. Then north through Panama to Mexico City. Before this jump to El Paso."

As if he were following a trail, or a blonde.

Jose said, "I was in the European theatre most of the war, Captain. I started out in Panama, yes, and I thought it was going to be South America. Because of language. But the brass must have decided that was too pat."

"You didn't run across Mr. Tustin?"

"I'm certain of it," Jose said honestly. Nor had he run into any of the others mixed up with this. He'd take an oath on it. He was in this for one reason only, because he'd stood in the

noon sun of El Paso looking like any Mexican lout wanting
to earn a couple of easy bucks. He asked a question of his own.
"It's your opinion this is more than just a drunk falling in the
river?"

"What do you think?" The gray eyes were shrewd, the
mouth was straight.

He couldn't play it too innocent. He said, "The first time
I saw the man I thought he was a traveling salesman from
Albuquerque or Dallas or Fort Worth. When I caught him
with my pants, I thought he was a sneak thief. Though he
looked a hell of a lot more prosperous than I. But then, I figured maybe the word had eased around that we'd sold a big
shipment of cattle and we'd trucked the two prize bulls down
in person, so that maybe he'd think we were paid off in cash
like in the old Westerns, not by check. Last night—" He
shrugged. "I didn't know what to think. There isn't a reason
I know of why he'd be following me around. I know one
thing, I wasn't any threat to him. I've been out of the Army
for better than a year and I was pretty anonymous when I was
in it. So if it's a grudge fight you've been considering, that's
out. I don't know the score, Captain Harrod." After all, it was
true, and it sounded true. "I'd like to know it."

"Tustin wasn't drunk last night."

Jose gave him a quick curious glance.

"He didn't die from rolling down an embankment. He died
from a knife in his back. He didn't bleed much but he didn't
bleed at all down there in the river."

Jose smiled dubiously. "If it's necessary, I'll say I didn't kill
him. I hope it isn't necessary."

"It isn't." Harrod didn't sound doubtful at all. "But you're
a link, Aragon, the only link we have. Now, I admit he could
have been knifed for a perfectly normal reason. In a drunken
brawl or by some poor devil who wanted his fine clothes bad
enough to break two commandments for them."

"But he hadn't been drinking," Jose said thoughtfully. "And
he was wearing a wrinkled seersucker like every second tour-

ist in Juarez. And he could have been flashing a roll but he wasn't flashy, he was a quiet worker."

"That's the way I figure it. If it had been an ordinary knifing, he wouldn't have been tossed into the river. He wasn't dragged there, Aragon. I figure he was moved by taxi."

Jose hoped his impassivity equalled Pablo's. It didn't at Harrod's next question.

"Have you any connection with Las Alamos?"

"None at all," he said when he'd got his breath. "I have some friends up there but you mean a tie-up? None."

"I'm guessing," Harrod admitted. "Jumping around. If it isn't for money or a fight, the border comes into it."

Jose was silent.

"We have a peaceful border and we're grateful for it. But that doesn't mean we don't get some ugly customers. I don't know an easier way for a fellow to get into this country than to walk across the bridge after a night in Juarez. We can't spot everyone who isn't returning from a night over there. Not if he has the look of a Norte Americano." Harrod cleared his throat. "Thirty years ago spies were something in an Oppenheim book. Something you'd expect to find if you moseyed around the Balkans or the Middle East. Now we've got atomic research up your way. We're the gate, the pass to the north. And you're thinking I'm an old fool with an imagination that works overtime."

"I'm not thinking that." Jose was honest. He was wishing Harrod would go and let him open the package that smelled.

"If you can think of any reason why Tustin followed you, I want to know. No matter how farfetched it seems to you."

Such as: because a ritzy blonde spoke to me at high noon. He must have smiled although he hadn't meant to. Because Harrod said slowly, "You young fellows haven't much patience with old ducks. You've concentrated so much experience into so few years, you think you're the only ones who can make the world go round. Maybe you're right, I wouldn't know. But I've been on the border thirty years, Aragon. Ever since I came out of my war. There isn't much I don't know about what goes on in my cabbage patch. What I don't know I generally find out."

Jose asked it then. "What about Praxiteles?"

It threw Harrod off center, not far off but enough for the silence to seem long. "Do you think he's mixed up with Tustin's death?" The milk voice wasn't deceiving. Jose himself had used that same trick too often.

"I'm not thinking. I don't know the border. But there are two men the people aren't talking about over there, and those are the two." He reached for a cigarette from Lou's box, his hand deliberately edging the package aside. There was no reaction from Harrod. Jose struck a match. "I've always believed the people are smarter quicker than the experts."

Harrod seemed about ready to go. Not satisfied, but he'd made a start. "My experience has been much the same. That's why I always call first on Senor el Greco when something goes wrong. The people are always sure his fine hand is somewhere in the muck." He stood up. "So far he's always managed to scour his hands before I show up."

Jose rose quickly to his feet. Not alone out of courtesy. It was essential to know what Praxiteles had mentioned of this business. Jose's attempt to dissemble was undoubtedly apparent to the trained officer but he asked with what he hoped would appear simple curiosity, "And the Senor knows nothing of Tustin?"

"As little as you." That was pointed. "He does not believe he ever set eyes on the man. Although with so many turistas coming to his poor shop, of that he cannot be certain." The imitation was strangely good, particularly so in that Harrod would have made four of the shriveled old man, and that the open face had no resemblance to the Senor's crafty, shuttered one. Harrod knew el Greco well indeed.

He ambled to the door. "When you planning to start home, Aragon?"

"Tonight."

"Driving?"

"I don't have a car down here. I'm hoping to catch a ride."

"I might hear of one." El Pasoans were hell on speeding the parting guest.

"Something will turn up. If not I'll fly up in the morning."

He bowed Harrod out, closed the door, but he didn't run for the package. He let it sit while he made a do at packing his bags. He let it sit until he was sure Harrod wasn't waiting around outside to surprise him.

II

When he'd waited long enough, Jose carried the package into the bedroom. As casually as if he were under observation. He very carefully maneuvered the cord off the green wrapping, neither cutting nor untying the knots. Sometimes the way a cord was tied had meaning. The green paper he unfolded. It was there, just what he expected. A bottle of La Rosa del Amor, in appearance differing not at all from the substitute bottle he'd sent north with Beach. But something else was there, something he couldn't have known about in the short time he'd been in possession of the wrapped package. It didn't seem important. It was a small box of cactus candy, made in Juarez, distributed by Praxiteles and Company. A *pilon* from the Senor?

He didn't think so. The Senor would give nothing for free. The box fit against the cardboard box holding the bottle so neatly that it was little wonder he hadn't guessed about it. He weighed it on his hand; it would seem to contain what the label read, candy. He couldn't open it unless he wished this fact known, it was machine-sealed cellophane, the way most candy boxes were sealed these days.

Candy for the candy kid. The diminutive of her name on the box, *Dulce*. His fingers tensed. There was meaning to it, of that he was certain. Again he rejected the temptation to rip

103

off the paper. First he must meet Dulcy again, find out what she had to say about the substitution. It would be pleasant to hop a plane now, be in Santa Fe in time for dinner with the lovely Miss Farrar. Very pleasant indeed if there were no packages involved, merely a tree-tall, dark-blond, summer visitor.

He didn't have to stay here any longer, he reminded himself, as he continued his packing. The string he tucked into a pocket of one suitcase; the wrapping paper, folded in its own particular grooves, into another. The perfume he wrapped in a discarded shirt before packing it. The unfinished business was finished, the package had been returned to him. Just in case of difficulties, he packed the box of candy in the other suitcase. The smell of perfume clung to it. He could check out right now and make happy such varied persons as Lou Chenoweth, Captain Harrod, and undoubtedly the interesting Miss Dulcy. "It is regrettable, Senor Aragon," Jose told himself, "that you have overdeveloped your sense of curiosity." Because if he departed now he wouldn't know any more about the *sorbita* than he knew right now. And he wouldn't know why Tustin had had to die. Somehow it didn't satisfy him to have the seersucker suit written off as a drunk who fell into the dregs of the Rio Grande.

He took a quick shower, changed to a light gabardine suit, and closed his bags. It was a good idea to check out, no matter in what direction he planned to move. It was always a good idea to act for the happiness of the greatest number. He called the switchboard and asked for a boy.

It was Pablo who came. Jose had expected him; he'd hoped for him. He waited for Pablo to say something but the boy stood there mute, masked. It was up to Jose.

"You brought up a package?"

"Yes, Senor."

"Where did it come from?"

"It was deliver to you."

"Who delivered it?"

The boy hesitated. He fell back on the familiar, "I do not know this."

Jose considered the mask. "How did you get it?"

Again there was the hesitation and a happy solution. "Jaime, he is the one who give it to me. He is so dumb, he will not remember who deliver it."

Jose accepted the warning. Jaime wouldn't remember, Pablo would make sure of that. Pablo ran things here. "I'm checking out," Jose announced. He wasn't sure whether or not it was good news to this one. "Before I leave, there's someone I want to talk to. You live in Juarez?"

Pablo was uncertain. But anyone who knew Miss Chenoweth well enough to live in her apartment could find out the truth. "Sometimes I live there, yes."

"You know a man they call Senor el Greco?"

The boy's breath hissed. "This one I do not know."

"You know who he is. Perhaps also you know a small girl who is called Francisca, who is *una nieta* to this man."

Pablo muttered in Spanish under his breath, too rapid and too silent to be understood.

"What do you say?" Jose demanded.

"This one I do not know," Pablo repeated humbly.

Jose's annoyance flared. "What about the man who died last night? What about the police all over the hotel? What would they say to you if they knew you delivered a package Mr. Tosteen was seeking?"

The boy's slender brown fingers held tightly to the blue smock. "I do not know about these things."

"I wish to see the small one. I'll be at Herrera's for dinner. You know the cafe of Senora Herrera?"

He knew it as well as the face reflected from his mirror but he continued to look blank. You learned early on the border to admit nothing. If you did not speak, who could accuse you of having spoken? This simply was silence made a virtue when young, a habit when older.

Jose accompanied Pablo and the bags to the desk. Lou's lifted face was hopeful. "You're going home?"

"After dinner. I trust. If your damn planes flew after sundown, I'd be sure. Dig me up a ride, Lou. I'll leave the bags here ready for action. Okay?"

She said dubiously, "The Mintons plan to start back at ten."

"Oh Lord," Jose breathed. "She gabbles."

"It's better than nothing, my fine beggar."

"Your words of wisdom I will treasure, dulcita—" He wasn't certain whether his endearment was accidental or an urge.

Lou was quick. "Jo, was the blonde, Farrar, part of this business?"

He answered slowly the same old way. "I don't know." His hand touched hers. "There is so little I know, Lou. Believe me."

"What you tell me, I believe." She sighed. "But you don't tell me much."

"This too you can believe. I'm coming for my suitcases myself. If Aleman or Truman or even Adam should say I sent for them, he's lying."

"What's in them? Isotopes?"

"Dirty laundry." He was firm. "But I am particular that no one but myself shall handle my dirty laundry."

He was the elegant Jose Aragon and he was welcomed as such by Senora Herrera. She regretted that he was alone; it was *triste, triste,* that a fine young man must dine alone on a summer evening. He helped her lead him to a corner table where his back was protected by the brilliance of tropical blossoms painted on the wall. He didn't say anything about Francisca. Nor did she. Together they selected a dinner, and only when the Senora started away to supervise its preparations did he remember that he had no cigarettes. To be sure he had the Philip Morris, but of the sweet native tobacco, he had none. If she would be so kind as to send to him the cigarette girl with her basket of supplies?

"But certainly, Senor. At once."

Francisca wasn't selling cigarettes tonight. The girl who balanced the large shallow basket was a plump and pretty child of the Herreras.

Jose said, "I'll bet a peso your name is Rosie."

She giggled richly. "Pay me, Senor. I am Lupe. Rosie she is over there."

Formally he presented her with *un peso*. She tucked it into a pocket of her ruffled skirt. "They teach you many things in the Army of the United States," she flirted.

"Meaning what?"

"The way to find out with a peso the name of a girl?"

He laughed with her. "Don't tell your *abuelita*."

"What she does not know will not hurt her," Lupe quoted pertly.

"You've learned many things from the Army of the United States," he commented. "My sympathies are with the *abuelita*." He was examining various brands of Mexican cigarettes, selecting from them. He hoped he could slide in the next question without her recognizing its importance. "Where is the *ninita* who sold me cigarettes last night?"

She didn't seem to understand whom he meant.

"She is called Francisca?"

"That one!" She was scornful. "She is so dumb, that one. She is fired."

"It is sad."

"But why?"

He shrugged. "It is always sad to be fired. No work, no money." He brightened. "Or is it she has found her a better job?"

Lupe obviously didn't care. "She is too dumb." She giggled daringly. "She is even too dumb to work in el Calle de la Luz Roja."

He too could be daring. "Is that why her *abuelo* sent her to work for Senora Herrera?"

107

"Who knows?" she shrugged cheerfully. "Who cares?" She flaunted her skirts away to another table.

He enjoyed his dinner fully, even to the *dulce* with which it came to an end. A gentleman lingered over coffee and a spicy cigarillo, so did he. Before he visited Senor el Greco tonight he would be well entrenched in the modes and manners of a fine gentleman.

He paid the bill to Senora Herrera herself, complimenting her on the excellent food, on the comfort of her cafe, on her business ability and her personal charms. He regretted the necessity of returning to his home so far from these many attractions. She was politely interested, no more. She wasn't in on what had transpired, she didn't care if he returned home or remained on the border. It was what he had believed but now he was sure. "If anyone should inquire for me," he told her as an afterthought, "I am paying a visit to Senor Praxiteles before setting out for home."

In this she was interested. She scowled. "The less one has to do with that one, the happier one will be."

He sighed. "This I know, Senora. It is not for myself that I visit this scoundrel, it is in the service of a friend."

She measured him shrewdly. "You will do well to consider all things when you choose a friend."

He agreed and took himself into the night. He crossed the warm, gentle patio with a jaunty step, let himself through the tinkling gate into the lane outside. A harmless lane with a few turista couples strolling toward their dinner. No one blocked the exit to the Avenida. The Avenida, too, was harmless, the usual crowd of early evening visitors milling into the stores, dallying at the street tiendas; the usual bands blaring through the loud-speakers of the big cafes, the usual under-tinkle of the street musicians.

He could have taken the short cut to Praxiteles, he knew the way by now. But for no particular reason, no more than a whim to repeat a previous pattern, and to remain on the lighted thoroughfare, he moved on down the Avenue toward the Plaza. At the end of the block he spied Canario, a lively gesticulating Canario, coaxing centavos by a trill of music, biding his time until later when the centavos would become pesos or preferably dollars. As Jose moved in his direction, the music stopped in a splash of cymbals, ceased abruptly and wasn't followed by a monkey grin and a sombrero outthrust to catch the copper pieces. Canario was gone before Jose could reach the place where he stood. Vanished.

Jose's own grin split his face from ear to ear. So tonight he was not to be welcomed by the band, tonight he was poison. It wasn't important enough to spy out the *burlero's* hiding place. He already knew he was poison. He couldn't have cared less.

He continued on to the Plaza. It was the same as it had been last night, the street urchins chasing their tails, the old men selling their watermelon or roasting ears or cheap sweets, the dogs scratching their flea-bitten ears, the girls flirting their shoulders at the young men, the old women visiting the house of God. The few strangers who had wandered this far from the Avenida were too conscious of their strangeness, eager to return to the safety of their own kind. Jose wandered into the native group as if he belonged there, struck a light to a sweet cigarillo and with a grand caballero sweep of his hand, waved away the urchins who came begging.

The street wasn't uneasy tonight. The business of Tustin had been disposed of, it had probably been disposed of before Harrod visited Jose. Without being told, he knew what the verdict had been. A man had come to accidental death through a drunken fall; most fortunate, he had fallen on the American side of the river. There was no reason for Jose to hang around, there was nothing to learn.

He was ready to move on when he saw her. It was so unexpected that he found himself gawking like the most stupid tourist. She wasn't one of the girls who sallied arm and arm in the vicinity of the young men, baiting her attractions with giggles. She wasn't one concerning whom the young men exchanged undertones or emitted Norte American wolfish whistles. She was with a swarm of kids playing in the street, a game of their own devising which might have been tag or shinny or kick the can, a bunch of kids, mostly boys, yelling and dodging and shouting slanderous epithets at the occasional car which dared interrupt their game. His gawking was of value in one respect, he was sure it was she although she wore dirty jeans and a faded polo shirt instead of ruffles, although the stone mask of her face was alive now with frenzied play. He knew the size of her and the shape of her eyes and the way her brittle black hair streamed away from her shoulders as she darted in and out of the crowd. He didn't need the dangle of her earrings for identification.

He caught her on one of those darts, his hand grasped her shoulder as earlier today it had grasped Canario. "Let go!" She whirled on him angrily but his hand didn't release its clench. When she saw who he was, fear crept around her mouth. She covered it with greater fury. "Take your hands off from me. Leave me alone. If you do not leave me alone, I will call the police." She and her grandfather. They talked bold.

The shoulder was too slippery. He moved his fingers down her firm arm for a tighter grip. "You call the police and I will tell them you are a thief," he replied.

"I am not a thief!" She began to whine in street-urchin fashion, "I swear by the Holy Mother I have never stolen nothing from you." It wasn't any more real in her mouth than in theirs. It was no more than a play for time before the kicking, the biting, the scrounging began anew. "Let go of me. I will scream for help."

He held on.

The gang she had been playing with didn't interfere. Unobtrusively they were moving the game as far away as possible. It was every man for himself. There were police who did not wear uniforms, the plain-clothes men. It was evident that this was a new one, sent to investigate their behavior. They would be lucky if only one of their group was interrogated.

She screamed abuse on him, she spattered him with obscene argot, she damned his soul but he held on. "When you are tired of making that noise," he said calmly, "I will tell you what it is I want from you." This he repeated every time she was forced to pause and refill her lungs.

She would get tired. It took a little time but she did. She went limp suddenly; he'd been expecting it and he didn't relax his grasp, he tightened it. "What is it you want?" she muttered sullenly.

"I want some information. I will pay you for it. Where can we talk this over?"

The suggestion of payment alerted her ears as he knew it would. She'd been pretending that she would fight him no more, waiting for the moment he dropped his guard. Now there was no pretense, she stopped the fight. But she warned him, more sullen, "I will not go to your room."

"I don't have a room. I wish to talk now, here in Juarez. Any place you say. But it must be where no one else will be listening."

Either she had no ideas or she didn't understand.

He shook her slightly. "Where? To the house of your *abuelo*?"

"No," she spat at him quickly. Her eyes remained on his face, trying to understand what it was he wanted. They didn't find out.

"Come," she decided. Not pleasantly. He didn't know what to expect, there'd been a glint which boded him ill. She led, his grasp still tight on her arm, toward the Avenida. She didn't go that far, only far enough to be away from the Plaza crowd. She gestured to the curbstone.

"My house is yours, Senor," she mocked.

Together they sat down in the dust.

III

She was a quiet hostess. She said, "You can let go my arm. I will not run away."

"If you do, I will trip you."

He released her and took from his pocket his cigarettes. He needed a drink after this hyena; temporarily he'd have to settle for a smoke. You didn't take kids into bars.

She stopped rubbing her arm and held out her hand. "Gimme cigarette." It was automatic.

"You're too young to smoke."

She didn't understand. On the Plaza they smoked before they could talk. He lit hers and his own. He was curious. "How old are you?"

She shrugged. "I don't know."

It could be true if you had el Greco for a grandfather. But he turned on her with a scowl. "I am going to ask you certain questions. You are going to answer them. If you lie, I will know you are lying. If you do not tell me the truth, I will give you to the police for stealing."

"I have stolen nothing," she screamed, and then her voice diminished to an undertone. She looked at him with hatred. "You have received what I took from you."

"And if I have?" He exaggerated the shrug. "It was none the less stolen. How do I know it is the same package which was returned to me? How do I know what was removed from the package while it was in the hands of a thief?"

Fury trembled her thin body. She found it hard to make words. They came out choked, "The package was not opened. It was put in a safe place until it could be delivered to you—"

"Who told you to take the package from me?"

She didn't answer him. She kept her eyes on him while she tried to think of an answer he would accept. Finally she said, "No one told me."

He jumped her words, "Then why did you do it?"

"Because I hate him," she answered with venom.

"Hate who?"

"El Greco."

Jose snorted. "A *nieta* does not hate her *abuelito*."

She was fierce. "I am no *nieta* of this devil."

"The *abuelo* is not the *abuelito*," he realized. He'd been right the first time, she was from the country. "Then why do you live in his house?"

She turned her head and looked at him. "Each time I run away, he pays someone to find me."

"What's he got on you?" he asked bluntly. "If he isn't your *abuelito*, you don't have to go back to him. Why don't you go home? Or is it you like better the lights of Juarez?"

"I hate Juarez," she cursed.

"Then why not go home to your family instead of living with that swine?"

"My family sold me to him."

His eyes stretched wide. She wasn't making it up; it was a simple and bitter statement of fact. "But—" He stammered. "But they can't do that. You can't sell human beings. It's against the law—of God and government."

"Many poor families sell their children."

"To him?"

"Sometimes to him."

He felt physically ill. He knew why. He didn't look at her. "How did you escape them?" It wasn't because she was too young.

Her lips pulled away from her teeth. "I kick them. No one will pay money for me. They are afraid of me. He beat me and I hurt them more. Unless he kill me, I will always hurt them."

"Why didn't he kill you?"

"Perhaps it is because he pay much money for me. Now I must be a servant in his house." She made a sound that could have been laughter. "I have run away again."

113

"You haven't run far. Why don't you go home?"

"They would sell me again."

She didn't say it but she had figured it out. Better to battle against an enemy she already knew. He took a breath of clean air before commencing again. "All right. You took the package because you wanted it. But what were you doing at the Cafe Herrera? You tried to stop me from going to el Greco. When you couldn't stop me, you ran out and waited for me. You can't expect me to believe that you did all this because you hate him. Somebody had to tell you that I'd be at the cafe and that I was planning to pick up that package. Somebody who knew these things."

Again there was the waiting period while she figured out what to say. "I will tell you how it is," she spoke resignedly. "I listen. Always I listen. While I am scrubbing his dirty floors. While I wash the filth of his clothes. I know there is an important package to be delivered. Always I know this. Because I listen, I know that the name of the one who will come for this package is Jose Aragon." She wasn't glib, she told it as if it were being pulled from her tongue, bit by bit. Lie by lie.

"One moment. How do you know the name? How is it you hear this?"

"It is in the afternoon," she remembered, lidding her eyes. "He is in the shop selling his stolen goods to turistas and the name is told to him."

"Who tells it to him? And what are you doing in the shop while you are scrubbing floors and washing clothes?"

She had to think a long time to dream up an answer to that. "I do not know who tells it to him. I am not in the shop. I am telling you the truth," she insisted. "I am in the kitchen when he is very angry over the telephone. The telephone he pretends he does not have but it is in a cupboard."

"So he's on the phone and who's he talking to?"

"To Ramirez." She was surprised at his stupidity.

"Ramirez is his hatchet-man? His *major-domo*?"

"His *agente*."

"Same thing. And Ramirez was one of those goons waiting for me last night?"

"Goons? I do not know this. Ramirez and his cousin are waiting for you. This you know but you go to meet them."

"I was safe. I didn't have the package. You'd snitched it. Let's get back on the phone. What was he telling Ramirez?"

Her lids lifted slowly. "He is telling him to follow you."

"Why?"

She was impatient with his ignorance. "To make certain you deliver the package to the Senorita. He does not trust you."

There were gaps in her story but part of it would be true. She might know even more. "Why is that perfume so important to the Senorita?"

"This I do not know."

If she'd answered, *"Quien sabe?"* he wouldn't have believed her. But she made a solemn statement of her ignorance.

"Didn't you ever listen in on her?"

"How can I? She comes to the shop, a turista. I am not permitted in the shop."

He pounced on it. "The boy, he who works in the shop. What did he tell you of her conversation?"

She seemed discouraged. "He did not hear what she says to the old man. Only that her package will be ready for her last night."

"And why were you at the Cafe Herrera?" he asked again. It could only be that someone had placed her there, with purpose, to watch for Jose Aragon.

She slanted her eyes at the richness of his suit. "To earn a little money, Senor," she began in a sing-song, beggar whine. "To buy for myself a new dress of silk—"

He clipped her wrist before she could move. "Suppose I tell you what really happened."

"It is true." She tried to twist away. "Every word I have spoken is true. I swear it by—"

"There are words you haven't spoken. You haven't said one

word about a certain Senor Tosteen who was found this morning in that trickle of water we call the Rio Grande. Dead as a doornail."

She was so still he would have thought she'd got away save for her fluttering wrist beneath his clamped hand.

"Senor Tosteen was most interested in Senorita Farrar's business. So interested that once she had spoken to me he included me in that interest. Now I hardly think he was fascinated by my beauty or even hers. I think it was the package." He shot the question. "How much did he pay you to get it for him?"

"It is not true!" she cried out. "I have not seen this man you speak of. I do not know him."

"You saw him all right. He spotted you and he hired you. He sent you to the cafe to keep an eye on me, to warn him when I was finishing my dinner. But I didn't finish dinner and you had to play sick, make a quick dash to pass the word. Was it then he decided to let you get the package from me? I hope he paid you in advance. Because he didn't show up to collect the package. He couldn't. He was dead."

"I didn't kill him!" she vowed. "I know nothing of this."

"I'm not saying you killed him." His hand tightened. "But when you learned he was dead, you were as scared as if you had. Because you were sure el Greco had had him killed, which may be true, and you didn't know how much the old spider had found out about your doings with Tosteen. That's why you didn't go home last night. And that's why you returned the package to me, it was too hot for you to hang on to. With a dead man's touch on it, it was even too hot for you to try to sell it. You had to get rid of it fast. How you got it across the bridge without any papers, I don't even care. I suspect that dumb Jaime or that smart Pablo had something to do with it. I suppose el Greco buys boys too and that they hate him almost as much as you do. There's one thing I do know. If the old man should find out your part in this, he'd kill you no matter how much money he paid for you." And he didn't know what he could do to help her.

She muttered defiance. "I am not afraid of him. I have run away from him."

"He'll find you. He'll pay to find you. Just as you said."

"He will not find me this time. I have many place to hide." And then she began to tremble. "You will not tell him you have seen me?"

"I wouldn't tell him the right time."

She was puzzled at the words but she accepted them as good. It was then he made the mistake of releasing her wrist. Only to reach for his wallet, to give her enough to help her until he could think of some way to get her out of this dirty business. But the minute his hand moved, she ran, fleet as a deer, fleet as an Indian.

As quickly as he was on his feet, calling, "Wait!" she had already disappeared into the street crowd. And by the time he reached the corner, she had vanished as completely as if she had never existed.

There was no particular reason to call upon Senor Praxiteles now. It was nothing but bravado leading him away from the street of lights into the dark byways. El Greco would tell him nothing new. Yet here he was, the dirt of the curbing brushed from his gabardine suit, his shoulders squared in Norte American style, stubbornly looking for trouble.

The shadows grew deeper, the sounds of human life fainter, as he approached the Calle de la Burrita. With nightfall, it was again deserted, silent, terrifying in its emptiness. Jose walked proudly, daring to whistle a tune, daring to intrude the red circle of a cigarette tip into the dark. He walked direct to el Greco's door, he pulled the bell, and impatiently pounded on the stout, ancient wood. There was someone on the premises, he had noted the ghost flame of light as he passed the shop window.

It did not appear that his pounding was to be attended, and for that neglect he hammered harder and rejangled the bell rope. He didn't intend to give up, not if he waked the dead who might be cowering behind the walls of the other houses

117

on this shabby street. He was beginning to doubt the virtue of boldness before the door was jerked open. "What you want ringing the bells, knocking down the door?" An old voice quavered, "You can not come in. Senor Praxiteles is not open."

Jose did not allow the door to be closed on him. He pushed into the vestibule while the old woman was speaking. In the near darkness he could discern only that she was very small and very old. The smell of her, too, was old, musky. "Tell the Senor that Jose Aragon is here to see him," he directed imperiously. He strode on into the shop.

She followed on small, protesting feet. "He is gone to bed. You come back tomorrow." Her shoes were scuffed, the black of her dress rusty. It was too heavy a dress for a hot night but she was too old to feel heat, her skin was dry as her bones. On the top of her head was a little skirl of gray hair, her scalp gleamed yellow beneath it.

He swaggered, "He saw me last night; he will see me tonight. Tell him—Jose Aragon."

She went away only because she hadn't the strength to eject him personally. She might deliver the message; she might summon the goons. But he didn't believe the goons were in residence. Praxiteles wouldn't trust strong-arm men to dwell in his house. It would be too easy for them to take advantage of a man who was fragile as a dried pea pod.

He was not too surprised that Praxiteles appeared. Curiosity would fetch him. Not fear, fear wouldn't figure in it; the old man was too rich, too important to be afraid. The shuffle of his carpet slippers had whispered his approach. He might have been in bed, he was robed in wine-colored velvet brocade as ancient as he. Fifty years ago it must have been a handsome piece. "What is it you want?" he inquired harshly. "Did not the Senora tell you, the shop is closed at night?"

"She told me, certainly," Jose answered insolently. He accented his words Spanish fashion. "But it is true that last night I received here a bottle of perfume. I have come for another bottle of the same perfume."

118

"I do not sell perfume," Praxiteles began, and his eyes narrowed. It was the first time he realized that Jose and the lout who inquired for perfume this afternoon were one and the same. His voice grated. "Did I not tell you this?"

Jose curled his lip. "Does it matter what you tell me? Last night I came for perfume. You supplied it."

The old one was trying to ferret out Jose's purpose in making the request. Searching through his endless channels of memory for a like demand. He couldn't find one. He said, "It was a favor, no more. I do not sell perfume."

"A favor for a young lady?" Jose was flippant. "For a most sweet young lady—*muy dulce.*" He shrugged. "That is why you must *por favor* supply me with an identical bottle." He smiled angelically at the ugly old man and then drew down the corners of his mouth in grief. "The first one I have lost."

He had timed the revelation for shock purposes; he was happy with the result. Praxiteles didn't quiver, he shrank deeper into his shrunken skin. His lizard eyes alone were alive, balefully alive. "You lost it!" He didn't believe it; he believed what Jose said but it was too incredible for belief.

"It is most sad," Jose agreed cheerfully. "So careless of me. You understand how it is, Senor. I stop at a bar here, and a bar there, I meet a few friends, somewhere I set down the package and forget it until this morning." He laughed at how amusing was his carelessness. "Today I return to look for the package but no one remembers it. It is not strange. Someone has found it, some boy who will perhaps make a few centavos selling it to a turista."

The old man was becoming more and more rigid. Jose felt that if he should poke a forefinger at him, he would disintegrate into dust. Jose continued, "The young lady paid well to have the package delivered to her. No doubt she had exhausted her quota of purchases for the month, this perfume someone else must carry across the bridge for her?"

The voice scraped from the scrawny throat. "You have told her it is lost?"

"How could I, Senor? She has gone north this morning."

"Without the package?"

"But how could she carry with her the package when I have lost it?"

Praxiteles trembled with fury. "You were to deliver the package to her last night. She would know last night you have lost it."

Jose smiled slyly. "She does not know. Last night she does not want the package. She asks that I deliver it to her in Santa Fe."

This was news to Praxiteles, news that shattered him further.

"It is quite natural therefore that I do not tell her it is lost but plan to search for it today." He sighed, "But I do not find it," and then he smiled again. "You understand now why it is essential you supply me with an identical bottle?"

Praxiteles said nothing for too long a time. He might have died standing there. Finally he whispered, "How is it you know what is in the package?"

Jose's nose wrinkled. "I smell what is in it. That smell, never would I forget it!" He added gratuitously, "I do not understand why such a lovely girl as Miss Farrar, one who could buy Chanel by the bucket, would select such a perfume." His nose repeated its distaste.

Again he waited for Praxiteles to speak. When it came it was too agreeable. "Wait here. I will get another bottle of perfume for you."

Jose waited until he could no longer hear the shuffling slippers. No longer than that. Holding the bells silent while he opened the door, he quietly let himself out of the shop, so quietly that he did not bother to close the door behind him. He was not such a fool as to remain until the Senor could summon his henchmen to do away with one who knew too much and too little.

Nor was he foolish enough to linger longer in the border city. The Juarez curtain had fallen, the next act would be played in Santa Fe. He took himself back to the Avenida as fast as possible and across the bridge. He was lucky enough on the Norte side to request a taxi-sharing with a plump, respectable couple who could only be from Wichita, Kansas. He was wrong, they were from Topeka, but they were naturally staying at the Chenoweth. They always stayed at a Chenoweth hotel in any town which boasted one. He did not exchange names with them, only his gratefulness for the ride.

He hadn't expected to find Lou behind the desk, she didn't take night duty. But she was there, and some of the anxiety went out of her face when he came in. He knew then with a welling of gratefulness that she'd been waiting for him. He further knew she hadn't expected him back so soon or in one piece.

He waited until the Topekans had collected their key and made for the elevator. Then he came grinning to her. "It wasn't so tough, after all, was it?"

She rallied. "No bullets, no knife cuts?"

"Not even a skinned knuckle. Juarez is highly overrated, Missy Lou."

"Don't be so smart. You tempted fate and won—this time."

"I never avoid temptation." He remembered his private debate of the day before. It seemed years ago. "That is for weaklings. What about the Mintons?"

She looked at the clock. "They'll be here at ten-thirty. They went out to dinner." She touched the call bell. The bellhop was neither Pablo nor Jaime. An old man, disinterested. "Take Mr. Aragon's bags. When the car comes, let us know." She waited until he had ambled to the street door. "Captain Harrod went through your stuff."

His head snapped away from the bellhop. She must have misread the expression on his face for anger because she defended herself hotly, "I couldn't stop him. He's the law."

"I hope he enjoyed his trip through my dirty laundry. Did he find what he was looking for?"

"I don't know what he was looking for. He took nothing. I stayed with him the whole time."

The old fellow was limping back to the desk. "The car, it is here now."

Jose tipped him.

Lou said, "Goodbye, Jo. Nice to have had you." While they clasped hands, curiosity broke. "Where did you get that stinking perfume? And why?"

"It's for old Juana, our cook. Her favorite brand. 'Bye, Lou. Thanks for everything."

"My best to your mother. Invite her to come see me when she gets back from Europe. And tell Adam I'm through with him. He didn't even come in to say goodbye before he went back to Santa Fe."

The car, a faded sedan, was humming at the curb, the door half-open for him. Jose's hand had pulled the door wide before he saw that the driver was not old Minton. It was Captain Harrod.

FOUR

HE DIDN'T HAVE TO GET IN. BUT HE DID. IT wasn't important who drove him to Santa Fe. The important thing was to get there. There was no reason for him to avoid the law even if it were possible. Let Harrod pry; the Spanish could gab the while they held their tongues.

But resentment burned at the betrayer as he slammed the door behind him. "Lou—"

"Doesn't know," Harrod said. "I fixed it for the Mintons to be delayed over dinner. That's the good part of living in a neighborly town. You can always fix things." He added dryly, "Should think I'm better company than that yawping Minton female."

"Could be." Jose offered a cigarette.

"I never smoke after ten at night," Harrod said as if he'd invented self-control.

Jose lit up. "Where you headed for?"

"Santa Fe."

"On business?"

"Yes, business." Now that he'd settled the car on the road, Harrod didn't seem to care about being good company.

Jose persisted. "I shouldn't think you could take off in the middle of an international murder."

A secret smile touched Harrod's mouth. "That one's over."

Jose's surprise echoed. "Over!"

"Yes."

"Who knifed him?"

"Oh." Harrod was surprised that Jose could be so ignorant. "It wasn't murder. Just another drunk in the river."

Jose eyed him to see if he meant it. He did. "So that's the way it's going to be."

"That's the way it is," Harrod corrected.

Jose gave a short laugh. "If I ever want to get rid of a guy, I'll know how to do it. And where."

Harrod was mild. "Did you ever kill anyone, Aragon?"

"Plenty." He jutted his chin. "It was that easy, too. I got medals for doing it."

"How did you make it right with your conscience? Don't tell me you haven't a conscience. You learned the Commandments just like everyone else."

"War doesn't have much to do with what any of us learned. It has its own commandments. Like kill or be killed."

"So you killed. Sure. Only it's a little different, isn't it, in the CIC? You aren't just a guy with a gun in your hand standing up against a guy with a gun in his hand who happens to speak a different language. In the CIC sometimes you have to go looking for guys to kill, don't you? Part of the time you're lucky. They don't know about you until you've stuck them in the back."

"So what?"

"So what does your conscience say about that one?"

"Look," Jose began, "if you still think I slipped a knife into Tustin because I didn't like his face or because I was conditioned to the black commandment of killing someone who stood in my way—if that's what you think, why didn't you arrest me this afternoon? Why this buggy ride?"

"I'm talking about something else," Harrod said calmly. "I'm talking about conscience."

"My conscience."

"Your conscience and mine. What did yours say when you killed some defenseless guy whose only mistake was to believe his side was right? Did you say like a lot of the losers are saying now: It was orders! I did not do this because I wanted to do it; I obeyed my orders and my conscience is clear; those who gave the orders are the guilty ones."

"One thing I'm not," Jose said precisely. "I am not a coward."

"What answer did you give to yourself?"

"I believe I know what you want me to say." Jose spoke slowly. "And for all I know it may be as dishonest a rationalization as the other one. But I'll say it, I've said it plenty of times to myself. In war one man's little life isn't as important as the lives of one man multiplied by thousands, perhaps millions. I killed one man to save many men from being killed. That's what you want, isn't it?"

"That's the way I've had to figure sometimes."

"Are you trying to tell me you killed Tustin?" Jose's laugh was sardonic.

Harrod's was amused. "Good gravy, no!"

"I didn't think so." Jose laughed freely now. "But you were building up a pretty good case for yourself."

"You know what I'm trying to say. It's better to write off Tustin's death as an accident. So far as I'm concerned it was accidental. If I'd had any idea, I wouldn't have let it happen. I was figuring on talking to him."

"Procrastination," Jose warned.

"Maybe. I knew he was on the border but he wasn't in my bailiwick until he crossed the bridge to our side. When he did, he registered at the Chenoweth just as if he was what he claimed to be, a Detroit business man. He was from Detroit even if he hasn't been there much in the last twenty years. Still has folks there, pretty proud of their globe-trotting brother. You call it procrastination. I call it waiting. Until I found out what he was after. He wasn't hard to keep an eye on. All he did was sit in a hotel rocker and read the newspapers. Maybe he was on vacation, how do I know? Until it's too late."

"Who was he?"

There was again that modicum of surprise in Harrod's answer. "He was a man for hire." He shook his head gently. "I'm surprised you didn't run into him in Germany. He was pretty busy there the same time you were."

"Or in Cairo or Panama City or maybe Lisbon?"

"He got around."

For moments they rode in silence, each thinking his own thoughts. Harrod broke the interlude, thinking aloud, "He caused plenty of accidents in his time. He came to the end of his road so often he must have thought it would take a silver bullet to do him in. He wouldn't figure on getting a grubby knife in his back in a dirty little border town. When you've beaten big danger you don't expect the little stuff to beat you."

"Is that another lesson of the day?"

"Could be. It pays to be as careful of mosquitoes as of elephants. Sometimes they're more deadly."

With this Jose agreed but he kept it to himself. He closed his eyes. There was a long trip ahead. Whatever rest he could get now would help out tomorrow. And the tomorrows thereafter until he was out of this. He must have slept; he came to as Harrod pulled up at a roadside truck stand.

"I'm for coffee," Harrod was saying.

"I'll join you."

They stretched in the warm starry dark of early morning. They were in New Mexico now. The night man at the stand knew Harrod. Like Adam, Harrod would know everyone up and down the highway. The two talked baseball and let Jose alone. He woke up on coffee and a hamburger; Harrod stowed away two hamburgers and a piece of pie. When they went back to the car, Jose offered, "I'll take over if you like. Unless you think I might try a break."

"What for?" Harrod was mild. He yawned. "Maybe I can catch a nap." He was snoring before they passed the second *pinon*.

Harrod woke in Albuquerque. The sky was paling for dawn, the far stars were already gone, as magically as sparks from a skyrocket. He was talkative again, "I suppose you'll be seeing the blonde."

"What blonde?"

"The one Tustin was trailing." Harrod was smart. He'd saved important talk until he'd had his nap. Until he was rested.

"You think she stuck him?"

Harrod drawled, Texas-style, "You're forgetting. He was just another drunk."

"So it doesn't matter who he was trailing or why."

"I haven't figured," Harrod said.

Jose's smile was wide. "If I chase blondes, it's because they're blondes." The air smelled good out here on the Santa Fe highway. A mountain chill in it. He drew in a lungful. The unrelieved heat of the southland sapped a man's confidence; he'd needed this. "And you know something? I prefer blondes to drunks who fall in the Rio Grande. You can have Tustin, I'll take the Candy Kid."

He'd talked too fast, the confident air had gone to his head. But Harrod didn't pick it up. He said only, "Glad to hear it, Jo."

It was breaking daylight when they entered the still-sleeping town. "I can drop off at La Fonda," Jose said.

"You stopping there?"

"I live here. I'm going home."

Harrod said, "Then go on home. I'll find my way back to the hotel."

Jose circled the Plaza, passed the Cathedral, and went on to the bridge, over the hill to home. The gates of the old Spanish wall stood open. He didn't drive in. He said, "Thanks, Harrod." He hauled out his bags.

"Be seeing you," Harrod said.

Jose was sure of it. He watched the car turn and start down the hill before he shouldered his bags. He entered quietly into the big, silent house. He would have preferred bed to Beach. But his cousin was yawning in the doorway of the guest bedroom. It wasn't usual; Beach must have slept with Jose heavy on his mind.

"You got a ride?"

"Yeah."

Beach followed into Jose's bedroom.

"I might as well tell you. You'll find out soon enough. With the chief of the border Feds."

"You don't say." Beach yawned wider. "What's he after you for?"

"Smuggling, murder, and who cares?"

"Speaking of smuggling, Dulcy wants to see you." Beach wasn't feigning boredom now. And he wasn't half asleep, his eyes were hard and bright.

Jose tried to kid it. "You've made progress." Because he didn't want to talk.

Beach wasn't having any. "Not much." He sat down on the edge of the bed. "I didn't get in until dinner time. Dropped the package at the hotel after I'd cleaned up. Mission accomplished, I decided to stick around a while, make sure it was picked up."

"Not because of blondes? Or beer in the Cantina?"

"Beer in the Cantina it was. Particularly since Tim and Rags were established there."

Jose said sharply, "Skip to Dulcy."

"She came in later. I gave her a big play, as if I were half in the kegs, but she was interested only in your whereabouts."

"Nothing about the package?"

"Not a word. Nor did I."

Jose had his clothes off. He shoved into bed. Beach stretched to his feet, looked down at him. "You're welcome to your harmless smuggling, Jo—but what's a Fed got to do with a bottle of perfume?"

Jose grunted, "That's what I want to find out."

"That's why you stayed behind today."

"Yeah. But I didn't find out."

Beach went slowly to the door. "I thought between the war

and the occupation you'd had yourself enough trouble to last a lifetime. I thought you went civvie to live out your years in peace."

"I thought so too," Jose sighed.

He was asleep almost before the door was shut.

II

The house wasn't silent when he woke. Old Juana was yelling at the granddaughters she'd brought along to do the work; yelling above a nasal Spanish singer squalling from the radio, turned loud to a local disk-jockey show. These natural disturbances hadn't waked him, rather it was the protracted jangling of the phone bell.

He pulled on his bathrobe, opened his door, and shouted above the clamor, "Somebody get that phone." He saw by his watch it was near noon. The phone had stopped ringing and he waited for a report. It came in a moment out of Nancita's head, poked around the corner. "There is nobody on the line," she announced with pleasure.

It wasn't important. If it were, the caller would try again. He said, "How about rustling some breakfast? I'll be out in about two minutes and I'm a hungry man."

The girl giggled and ran away.

He wasn't rested but he hadn't time for more sleep today. Not until he'd seen Dulcinda Farrar. He was washing up when the phone began jangling again. He listened and it was silent. Nancita didn't bother to knock on his door, she walked in. "Jo," she announced with the familiarity of one who had attended on the Aragon family from before her birth, "this time it is for you."

His bedroom slippers slopping along the polished brick corridor remembered old Praxiteles. He didn't want to think about el Greco. Let Harrod take care of the old one, it was his job. But the voice on the phone brought the Senor even closer to hand. He knew who it was when she spoke, before she said, "This is Dulcinda Farrar."

He recalled in time that with her he must be the Spanish-American playboy, nothing more. "Well," he caroled, "you don't waste any time, do you, Carita?"

"Will you have lunch with me?"

"Is it lunch time so soon?"

"It will be by the time you reach the hotel."

He gave a low laugh. "I'm not that far away." His performance wasn't going over; her voice continued to be clipped to business. But he wasn't going to know anything about that business. "Be patient, Dulce, I will be with you before you can order a Cantina punch."

"I will be waiting."

Nancita and her sister were standing near in big-eyed approbation of his charms. He hung up the phone, gave them a wink. "The food—you must eat it yourselves. I have a date." They giggled. Always they giggled.

He dressed fast. He mustn't keep Dulcy waiting. She might change her mind about talking; he took it for granted that she wouldn't have called unless she had something to say to him. He knew he was playing a danger game in dealing with her. He knew he ought to turn the contents of her damn package over to Harrod right now, along with his pittance of knowledge. Let the professional take over. He'd been a professional once; without the authority and machinery that went with the office, he was as helpless as the most inexperienced tyro.

And why wasn't he going to turn it over to Harrod? Because he was a stubborn Spanish fool, *un bobo,* that was why. Because he'd never yet left a job unfinished; because his curiosity was greater than his caution; because it was agreeable to have the charming Dulcinda whistling to him? Or because of a small, dark mestiza who had risked returning the package to him?

Before he went out he'd have to find a hiding place for his mementos of Juarez. He hadn't done anything about the stuff last night, it was still in his unpacked bags. He'd been too tired to care. But an empty house was an invitation to search; Juana and the girls would go home after lunch; Beach wouldn't be wasting his holiday hanging around. It was too much to hope that the phony package hadn't been spotted by now.

The cord and paper were easy, he put them under his pajamas in the lower bureau drawer. They probably didn't mean a thing. Where could you hide perfume where your nose wouldn't find it? Everything in his suitcase stunk of love roses. Where could you hide a box of candy where Nancita's sweet tooth wouldn't unearth it? She was a good girl, she wouldn't touch a battered penny but candy was something else again. She would have no compunctions about breaking through the sealed cellophane. Again his fingers itched to open that box. Nothing less than diamonds or pigeon's blood rubies must be smuggled in it; when death was part of the game, the stakes had to be large. Candy was an easy disguise. But there wasn't time now to investigate.

He wasn't too satisfied but the old credenza in his mother's room was the best hiding place for the moment. There was the usual secret drawer in the heart of it. Moreover, with his mother away, her room was entered but once a week, for cleaning, and another moreover, the girls stood sufficiently in awe of Senora Aragon not to snoop through her things. He draped a pajama top over the stuff in case any of the Juana outfit should be in the corridor. They weren't. He closed himself within his mother's room; on second thought, dropped the bolt on the door. The secret compartment was empty. It surprised him until he remembered that Mama Mia would have put her heirloom jewels in Tio Francisco's vaults as always when out of town.

The perfume first. The candy box was a close fit but he wedged it in, replaced the secret panel. He left the room as unobserved as he'd entered it. And now to join Dulcy. He picked up his wallet on the run, cut through the kitchen to ask the kids, "Where's Beach?"

They didn't know. Beach had left early.

"In my car?"

They giggled yes. As his mother's vintage motor was tucked away for the duration as carefully as her jewels, he was left to hoof it. To wait for a taxi would take twice as long.

The sky was a turquoise blaze, the noon sun was hot but the mountains were in it, none of that sticky border heat. He loped down the hill and had crossed the Garcia bridge before a familiar rattle and yell, "Hi, Santa Fe!" stopped him. The vacationing Fernandez brothers in their beaten truck. He climbed in. They'd started this whole thing with the foolish tag they'd given him. They now delivered him over to her again, straight to the door of the hotel: Foolish Gentleman arrives in style to lunch with Sinister Young Blonde.

She didn't look at all sinister. The yellow-and-brown shine of her hair, the unembellished yellow linen dress, the tanned clean skin, the modern mouth, bold and red. She was lovely, but it wasn't her loveliness alone that his pulses recognized. It was the girl beneath the beauty.

She'd staked out a couch in the smaller but more popular room of the Cantina. Two of Bob's special punches were already on the table. How she'd managed to keep away the Cantina *lobos*, Jose didn't know. They eyed him with loathsome envy as he established himself.

He didn't want to play games, he wanted to know her. But he said in a nice loud coo, "Hello, sweet."

Her yellow-brown eyes weren't those of a lovely young hotel guest, they were as stone cold as those of the *sorbita*. She said, "I would prefer you didn't call me that."

"But it's your name. *Dulce* is sweet, sweet is Dulce. Sweet as candy." He took a sip of the punch and saluted its creator presiding behind the bar. "Sweet as La Rosa del Amor."

She wasted no more time. "What did you do with the package?"

He was as distressed as Juana would have been at an accusation. "You didn't receive it?"

132

"You didn't deliver it."

"My cousin delivered it. The very first thing I checked on when I returned last night."

She said quietly, "It wasn't the right package."

He was voluble. "The package you sent me to pick up contained a bottle of perfume. True? The perfume was La Rosa del Amor. True? A bottle of La Rosa del Amor was delivered to you at the desk last night? Also true?" He pretended to be quite proud of his logic.

She repeated, "It wasn't the right package. What did you do with the original one?"

"Sweet," he began and at her faint frown, apologized, "Sorry. It goes better in Spanish, yes? Dulce—"

"The name is Dulcy."

"My pronunciation she is not so good?" he protested with as heavy an accent as Jaime could have offered.

"Stop playing games. What did you do with the package you picked up for me at Senor Praxiteles'?"

"I lost it."

She didn't believe him. She was nearing anger. "That isn't true. You opened it."

"Dulce!"

"If you hadn't, you wouldn't have known what was in the package. You wouldn't have known what to substitute."

"Dulce!" he explained simply, "I have a nose!" His grimace underlined it. "I didn't find it difficult at all. That smell one could never forget." He laughed. "It is very popular with the girls of Juarez."

She hadn't mentioned the candy; if she believed him ever so slightly, she wasn't going to. Nor was he. The *dulce* was the important part of it.

"I did not open your package," he continued with dignity. "I merely lost it." As if confessing a humiliation, he added, "I believed you would not know the difference if I replaced it."

While she thought it over, he beckoned a waitress. "Another punch?"

Dulcy shook her head.

"Then we'll order."

She barely waited for the attendant to leave the table. "Where did you lose it?"

"In Juarez."

"Where?"

"Look, chiqua, you don't really want me to give you the old gag, do you?"

Annoyed, she bit the corner of her lip. "You had it at the Cock. You left the Cock, crossed the bridge, took a cab to the hotel."

He lifted his eyebrows. "You used binoculars."

She was stonily silent.

"Or X-ray eyes," he proceeded blithely. "Or," he smiled, "you had a little talk with Canario."

She neither affirmed nor denied. She didn't care. She said, "I must have that package, Mr. Aragon."

"I did my best, Miss Farrar," he imitated. "I even went so far as to return to Praxiteles' filthy hole and ask him for a re-fill."

"You did what?" She wasn't the icily controlled Miss Farrar now. A part of her reaction came from anger, a part from incredulity—that he had confessed to Praxiteles and lived to tell the tale?—and a part, undeniably, was from fear.

"He tried to tell me that he didn't sell perfume."

Lunch intruded. He began to eat at once. She looked at her plate but not as if she was seeing it. She said, "It is important that I find the original package."

"Might not be easy," he decided, eating heartily. "Lot of petty thievery in a border town. Borders always attract scum for a good many reasons. But then there's always informers, if you can pay. Take Canario, for example."

She broke in, "You aren't a fool, Mr. Aragon. Maybe I am. I didn't know who you were when I asked you to get the package for me. I did know when I asked you to bring it here, but I believed you were honorable." An honorable sucker. She began to eat without tasting. "You didn't lose that package. For some reason you have decided to keep it for yourself."

"Why is it so important to you?" he asked.

She put down the fork as if she'd made a decision to speak frankly. "Because it wasn't for me, Mr. Aragon, it was for a friend. One who had done a favor for me. I was returning the favor. You can imagine how I felt when it was the wrong package."

"And how did you know it was the wrong one?"

"He knew," she said. She began to eat again as if she'd talked too much.

Jose leaned across the table. "Don't look now but just entering is a long, tall fellow with that weather-beaten Texas look all over his face. I wouldn't mention him only he happens to be an El Paso cop."

She tried to put on the what-is-it-to-me expression but it wasn't good.

"He drove me to Santa Fe last night. Before that he'd searched my bags."

She didn't try to hide the start that one gave her.

"And before that he'd asked me a lot of questions about certain events that had to do with your precious package. In particular about the death of a man named Tustin."

She was finishing-school polite about the way she buttered her bread.

"Let's both stop playing games. Tustin was after you until you transferred the responsibility of safe delivery of the package to me. You were scared of him, that's why you hired what you believed was a Mexican punk to pick up that package. Maybe you thought no one would suspect the punk, I'll credit you with that much, but at the same time you were thinking if there was any real trouble brewing, he was expendable and you weren't."

"You are insulting, Mr. Aragon."

"Let's cut out the Mr. Aragon business. We're going to see a lot of each other while you're hanging around these parts and I'm not risking my reputation as a caballero by having a babe like you handle me with ice tongs. You can save your own face by reminding yourself that the hired man is called by his front name, none of this mister stuff. And I'm still your hired man. Until I hand the package over to you."

"You did find it then?" she asked quickly.

"I didn't lose it. It was lifted from me. I'll get it for you. May take a little time but I'll get it."

"You know who took it."

"Yeah, I know who took it. And I'm not telling that to you or to your dear brother or to that cop over by the bar. Us hirelings stick together. There's two parties after that original bottle of perfume to say nothing of the cops." He laughed. "Might be remunerative to set them bidding against each other."

She said bluntly, "You need money like I need more men tagging after me. You're the Spanish-grant Aragon." Her lips curled. "Yes, I looked you up quite completely after my initial error. What is it you really want?"

He considered the question. "I want to talk to the man for whom the package was intended."

"That's all?"

"That's all."

"And you'll turn it over to him?"

"Dulcita, carita, bobita!" he laughed. He simmered down. "I will tell him where he can find it."

He didn't mention that Harrod was approaching the table. That Harrod had kept an eye on them all the while he stood at the bar. She didn't know about the cop until he was speaking over her head to Jose.

"Hello, Jo. None the worse for your late journey?"

Jose played it surprised. "Good afternoon, sir. I'm fine. You too?" He didn't make introductions.

Not that it bothered Harrod. "I'd like to meet your friend." It was demand not request.

136

Jose smiled. "I ought to insist you find your own friends. Miss Farrar, Captain Harrod."

"Do you mind if I sit down?" He pushed in by Dulcinda without waiting for a reply. "I missed talking to you in El Paso."

"Yes?" she replied uncuriously.

"You were at the Chenoweth the same time that Tustin was there."

She seemed exasperated at what could have been an insinuation. "I wasn't with him, whoever he is. I didn't know anyone at the hotel."

"Except Beach and me," Jose supplied blandly.

She was precise. "Your cousin joined my table in a Juarez cafe. He'd had a little too much to drink and felt flirtatious. Later you joined us. I had no idea that either of you was staying at the Chenoweth until your cousin mentioned it. I had not noticed either of you there." It was full statement, for Harrod not for Jose.

"You were at the hotel about a week." Harrod pushed at a bread crumb.

"Yes." The monosyllable was tentative.

"Why?" At the lift of her eyebrows, Harrod continued. He was exploring the same vein Jose had wondered about when he first met her. "We've got a nice little city, Miss Farrar, I'm not saying anything against it. But even the Chamber of Commerce knows it's no summer resort. A lot of folks come through in the summer, sure, on their way east or west. And a lot of folks have to come down on business. And there's some who come visiting friends or their folks. But I don't know anybody who'd spend a week there in August for no good reason."

She spoke with chilly amusement. "I never thought I'd have to account to the police in this country for my spending a week in any city I chose. I had a very good reason for being there, Captain Harrod. I was waiting for my brother and a friend to arrive."

"From Mexico?" He slid it in so easily that she'd said, "Yes," before she knew it.

"They got delayed?"

Her eyes were quick. "No," she denied. "I didn't know exactly when they would arrive. I was ahead of schedule."

"Were they motoring?"

"Really!" she murmured. "You'd better ask them about their trip. They may have traveled by train or plane or motor or burro, I didn't ask."

"They must have covered a lot of territory," Harrod mused. "You were in Mexico too, weren't you?"

"I've been there."

"I didn't exactly mean that," he said quietly. "What I meant was you were all down there together only you came back first. You flew to El Paso and waited for the others to catch up."

She was seething. But it was an act. Beneath, she was frightened. "Really, Captain, why do you bother to question me? You seem to know everything there is to know about my business."

"Not everything," he corrected.

She let herself get mad now, the way a person would who had nothing to hide. "I can't see that it's any of your business if I travel in Mexico or Patagonia or stay at a hotel in El Paso or Paris."

"Now, maybe I'm too curious," Harrod mused.

"Maybe you are," she said shortly. She wanted to get up and leave but she was boxed in by the two men and by the low table pushed against her knees. She couldn't move until one of them helped her.

"But it's hard not to be curious when somebody spends a week in August in El Paso."

"I told you—"

"Yeah. I didn't know you were waiting to meet someone. Kind of surprising you didn't pick out another meeting place

138

but then I guess you folks wouldn't know about our climate in the summer." He cleared his throat. "Then I'm kind of curious about you coming in from Mexico and Mr. Tustin coming right after you."

She tried to push the table away. It didn't budge. "Captain Harrod, I am quite certain there must be many people who come from Mexico to your city. It's a direct route to the States. As for this man you speak of, I assure you I know nothing about him." She implied that she didn't care to.

Harrod went on just as if she hadn't interrupted, "And both of you hanging around instead of going about your business the way other folks do when they're heading north."

"I've explained—"

"But this fellow waited too. Funny you didn't meet him, he kept following you around."

"Very funny," she commented. She added, "I'd have gone to the police had I known I was followed."

"Too bad you didn't know," Harrod said. "He might be alive today if you had."

"You mean this man is dead?" She couldn't have sounded more honestly astounded.

"Yes, he's dead now." They were two experts playing each other. But she was scared. Jose watched one and then the other. Silently. She murmured something that might have meant she was sorry to hear it even if it meant nothing to her. Harrod said, "Happened the night your brother got in."

She ignored the reference to her brother. She clutched her purse and gloves. "I'm sorry, Captain Harrod. I didn't know this man existed."

Adam was just coming into the Cantina. Jose gesticulated but the big fellow didn't see him. Harrod and Dulcinda each gave Jose a disapproving glint. "Sorry," he murmured.

"I'm sure my brother knows as little about him," she concluded.

"Might as well ask him. Where can I find him?"

All at once she was sweet as candy. "Mr. Aragon's cousin,

Beach Aragon, drove him and Mr. Ragsdale up to Los Alamos today."

Jose was alert. "You didn't tell me that!"

"Didn't you know? We planned it last night. I'm afraid I overslept." She smiled apology. "I'll have to go another time. They say it's quite interesting."

Harrod's only answer was a vague "Mmm." He shoved out the table as if needing to let off steam. "I'll talk to him later. I'm sure you'll tell him what I'm after." His stork legs carried him out of the bar.

Dulcinda watched until he was out of sight. Her voice came disturbed. "Why didn't you warn me?"

"Warn you of what?"

She shook her head, shaking away whatever was churning there. "He isn't interested in the package. He's interested in that man you were talking about—what's the name—Tustin?"

She didn't need to fumble for the name, it was easy to remember.

"What do you care? You didn't know him. You didn't know he existed." He pushed out the table. They rose together.

"You doubt it?"

"No more than Harrod does." Their eyes met, unsmiling.

But he didn't want it to break up this way. Whether she was innocently involved in an unsavory mess or whether she was in it up to her eyes, didn't matter right now. It was important not to lose her. His hand touched her arm. "Come on, let's forget it. Have a liqueur and meet Adam."

She removed the hand as if it were a bug. She said nothing, walked away. The laughter from the near tables wasn't accidental. Nor the jeers. He ignored both, sidling through the aisle to reach Adam at the bar.

"What you doing with that outfit, son?"

"That's my blonde," he responded. Not happily.

Adam rumbled, "Give him a Bromo, Bob. He's got a headache." He laid a sympathetic paw on Jose's shoulder. "I was referring to the cowpuncher."

"He's border patrol."

"What the hell's he doing so far from the border?"

Bob made it a beer not a Bromo.

"He's trying to pin a murder on me."

Adam waited for the punch line. When there wasn't any, he began to snicker. "Who'd you murder? Her husband? You ought to be careful about these things, Jo. Always knew you'd get caught some day."

"Bail out," Jose advised dourly.

"You mean to tell me you are mixed up in a murder?"

"Finish your drink," Jose directed. "Let's go to the house. I'll tell you the whole sad story."

"I can't. I've got a date." He shook his head. "No blonde. Business. Come out for dinner at my place."

Jose hesitated.

"Bring her along," Adam urged.

"I'll bring Beach," Jose said. "I'm off women."

"If I know you, sonny, that won't last till dinner time."

Jose left him there at the bar and took himself out to the Plaza. It didn't differ in appearance from any Saturday afternoon. The usual shoppers ambling on the streets, the usual flower-skirted and faded-jeaned teenagers blocking the door of the Botica, the usual battered cars squaring the park where black-eyed children played and the old men, their faces made browner by their white heads, nodded under the shade trees. It didn't differ much in appearance from Juarez or any Mexican town. It was a little patch of Mexico or old Spain here in the United States. He lifted his eyes to the blank windows of Tio Francisco's office across the narrow street. He had a report to turn in on the ranch; Uncle Frank was away on a South American junket during the congressional holiday but the office was fully staffed. Not on a Saturday afternoon. He sighed faintly. Work with clean mathematical figures would have driven away the megrims. He started to plod homeward, following the road past the Archbishop's garden.

He felt lost, the way a man did after he'd been away and

before he was again settled in routine. He could have sunned himself on the tiled rim of half a dozen swimming pools; he could have called a dozen fellows, worked up a game of tennis or golf, made plans for the evening with as many charming senoritas, all of whom would be delighted to hear that Jose Aragon was returned from the ranch and in need of friendship. He didn't want any of it. It wasn't wholly because of a nagging anxiety over the hiding place of perfume and candy. He was headed home because he was too troubled in mind to face the town's summer trivia.

He saw no one he knew after leaving the Plaza; he saw no one at all after he began to climb el Camino de la Casa. On the shallow slope where the small adobe houses pricked the sandy waste, there were sounds of children and dogs; here on the hillside only the silence of the big places. Even in a town as small as this one, it would be simple to cause a man to disappear, much too simple. He picked up a bit more speed. This was not the hour to be walking abroad, this was the solitude time of siesta.

The blazing white thunderheads which accumulated daily at noon over the Sangre de Cristos had not yet piled high enough to discharge the coming storm. The blue blaze of sky, the white blaze of clouds gave a peculiar intensity of heat to the yellow-brown earth. Yellow-brown like Dulcy's hair.

When he reached the gate he saw that Juana and the girls had gone for the day. They always left the gate standing open. He closed it after him and walked around to the back patio. None of the family except great-aunts ever used the formal front door.

He was overheated from the climb and dropped into a canopied swing to cool off. He set it stirring. The only thing wrong with this picture of a patio dappled in sunlight and cottonwood shade was that he'd have to fetch his own beer. If Beach hadn't got stuck with those two characters, they could toss for it. And he admitted that a good part of his gloom was apprehension over Beach being with them. Visitor restrictions at

Los Alamos had been tightened again this summer. He didn't understand why Beach would plan to take the Farrar up there. Except that they'd manipulated it without Beach being aware. That didn't hold water; Beach was keen. Despite it increasing his apprehension, Jose faced the fact that Beach had acted deliberately and for a reason. Placed in juxtaposition with Harrod's cryptic remarks about the border and the hill, Jose didn't like any part of it. What he wanted to do was get in his car and start for Los Alamos right now, find Beach, and remove him from the picture. The trouble was that he didn't have his car; Beach had it on the Hill.

He bolted upright. Against the screen of the door, a shadow had formed. "Who's there?" There was no answer and it took a moment looking from sun into house shade to realize that it was one of the girls. "Nan? Rosie?" he called. "How about bringing me a beer?"

For once, whichever one it was didn't giggle at him. She merely slurred a *"Si"* and disappeared into the depths of the house. Luck had slanted a bit in his direction. He'd wished for a beer and a beer was coming. He settled himself full length in the swing, pushing the cushions under his head. If he could prevail upon Rosie or Nannie to stick around this afternoon to answer the phone or warn of approaching callers, he'd know the saints were with him. He might be able to make up some lost sleep while waiting for Beach to return.

It was the first time he'd been peaceful for forty-eight hours. He closed his eyes, wallowing in the gentle cradle of the swing, until he heard the door open and the girl announce in her accent, "Here is the beer."

For the second time he sat bolt upright. She was holding out to him the bottle of *Tecate* he'd expected but she wasn't the girl he'd expected. She was the *sorbita*.

"What the hell are you doing here?" Automatically he grabbed the bottle from her. He needed it.

She wasn't insulted or hurt by his lack of welcome. She wasn't angry. She wasn't anything. She stood there with that impassive blankness on her face, looking at him out of those unblinking black stone eyes. "I come to see you," she announced.

"My God, don't I have enough troubles?" He drank a third of the bottle in lieu of answer. "How did you get here?"

"I hitch-hike." She'd evidently enjoyed that. She became almost cheerful.

"How did you get across the bridge? Do you have a work permit, a visitor's permit—"

"I do not come across the bridge. I come another way."

He'd known it, he needn't have bothered to ask. She'd come wetback. There wasn't a kid in Juarez who didn't know a dozen ways to cross the border without squandering centavos at the barrier. They crossed whenever they pleased, for any reason, to go to the movies or a parade or merely to behold the magic of the Five-and-Ten. It didn't worry anyone; it had nothing to do with the economics of immigration.

But Francisca was something else again. If it were known that she'd skipped over the border, there'd be trouble. Senor Praxiteles was her *abuelo*.

"Are you crazy?" he asked. "Do you know what they can do to you for that?"

"I know. Deport me."

They could throw her in the juzgado but he didn't bring it up. She'd know well enough that she wouldn't go to jail unless Praxiteles so demanded. She might prefer jail to his house.

"But first they must find me," she stated. She didn't bother to add that he wouldn't give her away. She knew darn well he wouldn't. He was one of those foolish Norte Americanos who had kindness in their hearts for poor people.

"It's going to make you very happy to know that Captain Harrod is already here."

She swaggered, "Who is this Captain Harrod?" but she knew the answer. She began to back toward the house.

"He isn't right here but he's in town. And he doesn't know you're here unless somebody down below talked." He was pretty sure that no one down below would know her where-abouts; she wasn't one for idle chatter. "He came up with me last night."

She didn't like the implication. She said, "What do you want with that one?"

"What does he want with me is a better way to put it. And the answer to that one is easy. It's the dead man in the river."

"This is all over," she said.

"That's what you think," Jose muttered. "You can't bury some guys deep enough." He finished the beer. "Your turn now. You came to see me. Why?"

She must have discarded a dozen reasons, it took her that long to answer. She finally announced, "I have come to help you."

"A big help," Jose said. "The border patrol is already hounding me. Now they've got a real reason. Hiding out a Mexican national."

"You will not hide me. I will hide myself."

"And how are you going to help me?"

She stated, "You are in danger of death, Senor."

It wasn't news, although it did sound a little startling to hear it cold, against the dapple of sunshine and shadow, against the mild creak of the swing, against the hum of bees in the climbing roses, and the flavor of chilled beer on the tongue. "Who has decided I must die? The *abuelo*?"

She nodded. The brittle black hair swung away from her shoulders. Her levis and her ragged T-shirt were filthy, her bare feet encrusted with layers of dirt.

"You went back home and he told you," he said sarcastically.

"I hear it in the street."

"You hear it in the street," he mimicked. "So you hitch-hike three hundred miles, after sneaking across the border, to tell me something you hear on the street. Without finding out if it's true."

"It is true."

145

"I'm not doubting it. But you didn't have to hitch to Santa Fe to tell me. I knew it when I was in Juarez. You knew I knew it. What's the true reason you came here?"

Again she was silent. Finally she muttered, "I hate him."

"I know that too. Did he send you up here to get back the stuff?"

The first rumble of thunder came from the castellated white clouds. She looked at the sky curiously and then she shivered.

"It's the rainy season," he informed her. "It rains every afternoon."

She didn't appear to have heard him. She said, "I am afraid of him. He will kill me if he finds me."

Reluctantly he climbed out of the comfortable swing. "Come on." Maybe el Greco had sent her to get the stuff, and maybe she'd come running here because for her there were no more hiding places on the border. One thing sure, he wouldn't turn her over either to the old man or to the patrol. He'd give her a chance.

He headed to the house. A second growl of thunder went with him. She continued to stand motionless staring up at the sky. "Come on," he repeated. "If you're going to hide, you'll have to look like a Norte Americano."

There was no way to hide her except openly. The first thing was to get the jungle dirt off. He led her to his sister's room. "Take a bath, use a lot of soap," he directed. He opened the door of the clothes closet, grabbed a handful of peasant skirts and blouses. In the bureau he rummaged for underclothes. He flung all on the bed. She stood warily half-in, half-out of the room, watching him. "Take a bath," he repeated. "Wash your hair, you'll find shampoo. When you're clean, get dressed. By then I hope I'll have figured out what we're going to do with you."

He left her there, hoping she understood shampoo. The sky was darkening fast; a first fork of lightning stabbed at it and the thunder repeated. Time for the usual afternoon routine of closing windows and doors before the downpour. The first large splatters of rain hit the patio outside. He speeded up the casements, the downpour was in full force before he'd made the rounds. The thunder no longer muttered, it roared with deafening impact after each white-hot jab of lightning. The weather makers were putting on a real show today.

He hadn't heard a car stop, it was a wonder he heard the hammering at the front of the house, the shouting with it. Even without the thunder, the violent rain eliminated most sound. He lifted the iron bolt, tugged open the heavy door, and began to laugh.

The size of Adam made him appear twice as soaked as an ordinary guy. He was like a half-drowned whale. "Laugh, damn you," he bubbled, pushing in and dripping all over the polished tiles of the hallway.

"Did you swim up from the hotel?"

"I thought I could make it before the storm broke. Knew I couldn't get out home in time. If you didn't keep your goddam gates closed, I could have driven in."

"Mother likes it neat."

"Don't you tell me. She's told me often enough." He was peeling off his sodden jacket.

Jose mused, "If I had a tent, I'd offer it while you dry out. I might supply you with a blanket. You could make like an Indian."

"Make like a barman and get me a drink." Adam dropped the jacket and squushed to the dining room. He poured himself a straight one while Jose loaded a tray of ice, seltzer, bottle, and glasses. "Got to ward off pneumonia, don't I?" Adam glowered.

They returned to the comfort of the library. The electricity was muttering out of the air, the rain was slashing steadily now, the temperature had dropped at least fifteen degrees. Jose put a match to the kindling crisscrossed under the pinon logs in the fireplace. "Try that on your pneumonia. Want to shack up here tonight?"

"You're coming to dinner at my place, remember?"

147

"Not if the arroyos are running. Catch me pushing your truck and you out of the mud."

"What's the matter with driving your own swell car?"

"Beach has it at Los Alamos."

Adam scowled. "Crazy bastard. What'd he want to go up there for? In rainy season yet."

He wouldn't pass on his alarm. Beach knew what he was doing. "He's conducting a tour for the Farrars." He managed to smile. "Only the one he wanted pulled a swiftie and he drew the brother and his pal. You haven't met the men in the party yet, have you?"

"I haven't even met the dame," Adam grunted.

"They're probably both wanted items."

Adam squinted into his glass. "Have you tipped off our *Jefe*?"

Jose shrugged. "Why bother our police? When Harrod wants them picked up, he'll do it. A smart operator, Harrod. You can bet Tim Farrar and his boy friend are loose for one reason only, they aren't important enough. Harrod's on a trail."

"Great God!" Adam exclaimed softly. But it wasn't for Jose's dissertation. He was gazing at the doorway. "Didn't know you had company."

Francisca had materialized, a small, silent, clean ghost. The clothes were somewhat large but not enough to notice. Her hair was wet and shining, as if she'd just run in out of the rain.

Jose said, "I brought her up from the ranch." He could have told Adam the truth but he didn't want Francisca to think he was selling her out. It was a good time to try out the story. "She'll go to the Academy this winter and help Mother after school." His mother had educated plenty of country girls. No one should suspect that Francisca wasn't another of them. While he was talking, she faded out as silently as she had appeared.

"Spooky," Adam decided. "Buy her some *guaraches*. Give

you warning before she shows up. She might embarrass you some night."

It should have been comfortable sitting here, listening to Adam tell old tales while the rain rained and fire colored the fireplace. But Jose could not rest in the quiet pool of peace; his thoughts muddied the waters. If Adam had asked what he was thinking of he couldn't have told. A blond girl and a dark child, cheap perfume and a musky old man, a man for hire whose wrinkled seersucker suit was his shroud, an immigration officer who was troubled about atoms, and Beach who was too curious. If he could have made words from it, he would have unburdened himself to Adam. Instead he listened to the tall tales and the rain.

At four it was over. The gray of the sky became blue; a few white clouds, harmless as cotton, hung above the horizon. Adam said, "Got to go home." He urged, "Come along with me."

Jose said, "I'll wait for Beach." He couldn't go anywhere until he'd had a report of the day. "See you about seven."

"See you." They returned to the hallway. The wet jacket wasn't on the floor, it was hung properly from the back of a chair. The way a woman would hang it.

Jose watched Adam avoid the biggest puddles on the bricked courtyard, like an elephant trying to be dainty. Adam was a funny guy. You'd think he'd have something better to do than sit around here killing a rainy afternoon, even if it was sitting in the Cantina where he could have a bigger audience. Adam liked a lot of people around him. Maybe that was why he'd never married, maybe he was afraid a wife would try to close him in. Lou would make him a good wife; she wasn't that dedicated to being a hotel career woman that she wouldn't leave it if he said the word. So Adam was dedicated to prowling Mexico on the trail of hoary ollas or herb-dyed weaving or hammered silver? It wasn't good enough. After twelve and more years of it, you'd think he'd know it wasn't good enough.

And it wasn't that Adam wasn't aware of Lou's yearning, it was rather that he refused to know it.

Oddly enough, good friends as they were, it was something José had never talked over with Adam. Not so odd when you got down to it, the cupboard of Adam's personal life had always been labeled Do Not Open. He'd never mentioned his family, not even in the midst of the abundance of Aragon family. It might be there was a wife in the background, trouble he didn't want to remember. Before the war it wasn't surprising he wouldn't talk to the Aragon kids of anything but his travels, with a touch of the Munchausen which made the kids his faithful followers. But the space of years which separated them had closed up with the war. It was man to man now, equal footing, but still no reminiscences of the past, never a hint of the man's own troubles.

It was a damn shame, whatever it was that kept Lou and Adam separate instead of bedded comfortably under the same roof. He was a homey man, hadn't he even built himself a little house on a secluded road outside of town, a homey little house? A house that lacked nothing for comfort but a woman? To be sure, Lou wasn't as young as she once was but neither was the old Adam. They deserved to be together and, by the grace of God, once José got himself over this hump with the Candy Kid, he was going to give Adam a real shove. It was high time Adam stopped being a shy guy.

José stood on the threshold sniffing the rain-sweetened afternoon until he heard the last faint echoes of the truck motor down the hill. When he turned back into the hallway, Francisca was watching him. She ought to be belled.

III

Francisca's eyebrows were black as thunder. "What did you tell that man?"

"You heard me. I brought you here from the ranch to go

to school. That's what I'm going to tell everyone." He headed for the library. She walked on silent feet after him. "There's only one hurdle to jump. You *sabe* hurdle?"

She didn't say whether she did or not but he didn't bother to explain.

"There's an old woman who comes in every morning to clean. Old Juana. She's a privileged character, used to be the cook. Don't let her know anything about you, just stick to the ranch. And the same goes for her *nietas*—she brings them along to help out. You do what Juana tells you but don't talk. No talk." Actually he was wasting his words, no one could be less talkative. "If I buy you some *guaraches,* will you wear them?"

"I do not like shoes," she frowned.

"I did not ask if you liked them." He capped the bottles. As he started out of the library, she was again behind him. He turned on her. "I'm going to have a shower and get dressed for dinner. I go out to dinner." It was like speaking to a block of wood. He said it plainly, "Don't follow me. Go out in the kitchen and feed yourself. Go in your room and take a nap. Go play the radio. But don't follow me!"

He almost ran for it. Twice crossing to the bedroom wing, he looked over his shoulder, fast. As if he'd catch her slinking behind him. He didn't. He locked the door of his bedroom. She'd probably be curled up on the floor outside when he emerged.

He didn't believe for one minute that she'd come here to warn him he was in danger. Whoever took Tustin's place in the quadrille had undoubtedly offered her another handful of pesos to get the package again. Tustin's failure meant little. There were hundreds of Tustins ready to carry on. Too many men were for hire, you had to know no more than what would tempt them, a place in the sun, or dollars, vengeance or a dream or a few pesos. Jose could buy Francisca to his side. But only until a better offer came along. She'd had too much experience to respect a bargain.

It wasn't safe to keep the candy and perfume in the house

now. Tomorrow he'd move them to Tio Francisco's vaults. Sunday or no, he'd have the vaults opened. For tonight the credenza would have to do, not that anyone entering his mother's room wouldn't know the perfume was there. What to do with Francisca tonight was the problem. He'd be damned if he'd take her along to Adam's, like a dowager lugging a pet poodle. Preferably he'd take along Dulcinda's souvenirs. Or skip the dinner. He was tired enough for bed. If Beach were late, he'd have a legitimate excuse to offer Adam.

He was just finishing his shave when he heard the phone. He ran for it, pushing the bolt and opening his door in one move. For her own safety she shouldn't answer it. She wasn't on his doorstep but he almost ran over her in the gloom of the corridor. He said, "I'll get it," not that it deterred her. She was in the doorway when he spoke, "Hello." The voice on the other end was that of the Chief of the State Police, Danny Moreno.

At first he didn't understand, half of his mind was on the *sorbita,* watching him, listening. He had to ask a repetition, to repeat dully, ". . . Hill road . . . accident. . . ." When he hung up, he remained there, clenching the phone, not believing it. Refusing to believe it. Beach. Beach wasn't dead. Beach was alive, the most alive person he knew. She came into focus again, she and her watchful eyes. "Accident," he said. And shouted it, "Accident!"

He pushed her out of the way. Blindly he made for his room, buttoning his shirt as he ran from the house, struggling into the jacket as he plunged down the muddy hill. At Canyon Road he picked up a ride with a kid, one of Marcelino's, headed for Saturday night fun on the Plaza. He could have asked the kid to take him to Danny Moreno but he didn't want conversation about it. He dropped off at the Museum, cut across to Jack's taxi stand, and caught one just coming in. He didn't wait for the driver to check with the office; he said, "State cops," and maybe it was his destination that eliminated argument. The driver bumped through traffic to the highway,

deposited him too soon at the handsome adobe-colored building. Its apron of grass smelled wet and sweet after the rain.

Jose walked in. "Danny here?"

He didn't see the fellow he asked. The officer said, "Yes.
Gee, Jo, I'm sorry—" Something must have cut him off, something in Jose's face. His hand finished the sentence aimlessly,
"—he's in his office."

Jose walked past and opened the door marked *Capt. Dan
Moreno*. Danny got off the desk. He, too, began, "Jo, I am so
sorry—"

Jose said, "I want to go out there."

"He won't be there, Jo. They're bringing him back now."

"They can't bring him back. He's dead," Jose said cruelly.
"I want to go out there."

"There's no use, Jo. The boys have a full report on it."

"Will you take me?"

Danny was a little man, he didn't look like the head of the
state cops. He looked like a half-pint pinon-picker. His eyes
pitied.

"I'm going out there." Jose was grim. "Will you take me or
do I call a cab?"

Danny decided, "I'll take you." He nodded to the other of-
ficer; Jose hadn't known he'd come in the room. "Take over,
Ike." He picked up his cap, set it just right on his black head.
"Come on, Jo."

Danny didn't try to offer conversation as they headed
through town and out the Espanola road. Not until they passed
Tesuque did he begin to talk about it. "That road's bad enough
without a cloudburst."

"Beach knew how to drive a car."

"He skidded, it happens plenty times."

"What about the other men?"

"What others? He was by himself."

"He wasn't when he went up there this morning. The only
reason he went was because some tourists wanted to go."

Danny said, "They must have stayed on the Hill."

"Why? Because they knew Beach was going to have a wreck?"

"Listen, Jo," the cop's voice was mildly surprised. "Are you trying to tell me this was not an accident?" He reassured himself. "It was an accident. My boys they gave me a full report over the phone. The car skidded and went off the road. You know these mountain roads."

"Beach flew fighters in the war."

"Many times it happens this way. A man does dangerous things and is safe. He slips on a cake of soap or falls from a ladder. . . ."

"Who called in first?" He had to keep talking. He mustn't hear the scream of an ambulance passing; he mustn't notice a pile of junk being hauled in to the graveyard.

"Some fellows who work on the Hill. On their way home."

"I want to talk to them."

"Sure, Jo. They will come in and tell me personally about it. You may listen to what they say."

"Where did they call from?"

"Maybe it was Espanola. Maybe they live in Espanola." Danny didn't care. He was turning off the highway, beginning to climb the Hill road. It was past sundown, passing twilight, almost dark. The days were growing shorter. Danny said so. The clouds were mushrooming again over the northern horizon. They were pearl gray, not black or white. Little shivers of lightning ran through them.

The after-work traffic from Los Alamos was gone. Only occasional pinpoints of light pricked from above, to materialize later as descending cars. Off to a Saturday night party in town or a party in the Valley. He should have called Adam. It wasn't important, Adam would know the Aragon cousins weren't coming to dinner. Someone would have called him, Adam was always the first person in the Valley to be told about things. Jose didn't want to see even Adam tonight.

He said, "It isn't very slick."

"It was earlier, Jo. It hadn't stopped raining up here. It was slick then."

Danny pulled off to the side of the road. This was where it had to happen, where it was steep enough for an overturned car to mean certain death. The mud was churned by cars and boots and curiosity. Jose got out of the car and walked to the wide smudge on the rim. Yes, it was steep enough. He came back to the car and climbed in.

"You see how it was, Jo." Danny was gentle.

"I want to go on up."

"But, Jo!" He pleaded. "Why?"

"I want to go up there while it's hot. While everyone who saw Beach today or spoke to him remembers. I want to know everything he did. And I want to know where Tim Farrar and Rags Ragsdale are now."

Silently Danny slid the car forward. "All right, Jo," he agreed, still gently. He knew that a man stricken with grief was a man not himself. And he knew the Spanish people grieved more deeply than others because they loved more deeply.

From town the Hill of Los Alamos was a lovely coronet of golden lights suspended in the darkness. From the road the entrance lights were blinding white, a part of security. There was no trouble about passing the security officers at the entrance. Not with Captain Dan Moreno at the wheel and him requesting a pass for Jose Aragon.

"Up here about that accident?" the young officer at the desk queried, and then he noticed the name he was writing. His eyes slid up to Jose's face.

"Yes," Danny said hesitantly.

Jose asked, "Do you remember when he left?"

"I wasn't on duty." The young fellow thought back. "Staub and MacReady would have been on before six."

Danny took over. "Where do we find them?"

"Ask at the barracks. Mac was going to the dance but it's early."

Danny pulled the car along. They were lucky. They located the two who'd been on duty. Young officers and keen but they didn't remember. "At five o'clock everybody's leaving the Hill." Mac rumpled his hair. "It was wet." They'd collected passes but that was routine. They didn't remember a certain convertible. It wouldn't look convertible anyway, closed by the rain. No one would have noticed if Beach was alone or accompanied.

When they proceeded on into the town, Danny insisted, "He was alone, Jo."

"When you found him he was."

The cop asked his first real question, instinctively knowing the answer: "What are you trying to prove?"

Jose said, "Murder."

Danny sighed. "There is no reason for this."

Jose didn't argue. "Stop at the Center, Danny. While I'm phoning, see what they're saying around the bowling alley and the cafe."

"Who do you phone?"

"Everybody I've ever met who lives up here," Jose said savagely. "I'm going through the book." In the drugstore he changed dollars to nickles, took the phone book into the booth with him. He began with the A's.

It was almost an hour before he emerged. He hadn't learned much and only one piece of information held any promise. He found Danny at the cafe counter patiently sucking at a strawberry soda.

"You through?" Danny asked hopefully.

He ordered a coke. "I haven't found Farrar and Ragsdale. Have you?"

Danny shook his head. "No one knows their names."

"Did anyone see them with Beach?"

"But yes. They were regular tourists, they visited everything from the super-market to the radio station. Every place they are permitted to visit. They walked about the town."

"They took off in the car for a look at the rest of it?"

"That's right."

Jose recited what he had learned. "Beach was full of high spirits. The way he always was." He swallowed. "The other two were their customary nasty selves. The three eventually landed at a cocktail party at Dr. Troop's. They were there during the storm. Farrar was in a hurry to leave. Beach wasn't; he always had fun wherever he was. He wanted to wait until the rain ceased. Rags had nothing to say as usual."

Danny was thinking that a cocktail party and a storm and the Hill road didn't mix well. Jose knew what he was thinking. He said coldly, "A fellow who works in the lab, Alvin Struyker, is the one who took them to Troop's. I don't know Struyker, I don't think Beach knew him. I can't get him on the phone. He was in a hurry to leave too, he had a dinner date."

"I'll talk to him," Danny promised. "I'll get in touch with him tomorrow."

"I want to go up to his house now," Jose said stubbornly. "I have the address."

"I can't break into his house," Danny pleaded. "You know I cannot do that."

"I know." It didn't change his mind. "I'll leave you out of it, Danny."

The cop sucked the last of the pink foam. He was resigned. "Let's go." He took the wheel. "You have directions? I don't think I know so well the residential part of Los Alamos." He'd prefer to get lost.

Jose said, "I have them. He has a room with a young couple. They've got a kid. I'm hoping they're home."

"Maybe you know they're not home. Maybe you think there's a baby sitter."

"Maybe," Jose agreed.

He directed to the small house, a typical Los Alamos bungalow with overhanging blackout roof over the entrance. A blue light made small illumination.

"We visit the baby sitter?" Danny asked sadly. "What can she possibly know?"

Jose opened the door on his side. "You stay in the car. Your uniform might scare her. I won't be long." At Danny's hesitation, he continued heatedly, "I'm not going to hurt her."

Danny pulled out cigarettes. "Okay," he sighed.

Jose made footprints on the wet gravel path. He heard the doorbell chime behind the closed Venetian blinds. The breaks were with him; it was a baby sitter, she was Spanish, and she was hardly in her teens. He managed a smile as he pushed inside. "Is Mr. Struyker home yet?"

"He is not here."

"My cousin left his jacket this afternoon. Which is Mr. Struyker's room?"

She didn't question his asking. She led him to the door. He knew the moment the door was opened; he smelled it. La Rosa del Amor. The bottle was on the desk. Beach had seen it there. And Beach was curious. Blindly Jose quit the room.

The girl said, "The jacket?"

"He must have left it some other place," he managed to say. Blindly he left the house, climbed in beside Danny.

"Where to now?"

It wasn't his voice. "Santa Fe."

Danny gave a small whisper of relief.

Jose said, "Beach was murdered."

Danny kept asking why. Not why Beach had been murdered. Why Jose called it murder. Danny was tops of the State Police. He had a right to ask questions. But Jose didn't have any answers to give him. Not who had done it, not why. Not that it was a colossal blunder for a lab employee to hang on to a wrong bottle of cheap perfume. Not that it was a worse bonehead play for someone to get panicky when Beach asked a quick question about it. The lab man didn't have to know anything about the bottle, someone could have given it to him or he could have picked it out of a trash can. But he did know something or Beach wouldn't be dead.

Jose let Danny ask questions, let him sputter, get mad, simmer down, come to patient resignation. Jose kept the cork in the bottle of his increasing hate. He had killed Beach. When he left that bottle on the seat of the truck, he killed Beach. There was no justification, not even the bitter one of sacrifice. Beach hadn't died in Jose's place, he'd just been a gadfly who buzzed in for a moment's irritation and had been swatted.

Danny was still talking as they pulled over the Tesuque crest and saw the careless spill of lights, yellow and white and neon pink, which were Santa Fe. Still confident that his reason and logic had convinced Jose.

Jose said, "Let me out at the Plaza."

Danny was dubious. "Sure. But don't you think you should go home? Or to your Aunt's house? The family is probably all now at your Aunt Caterina's."

"Tell them I'll be there later." He let himself out at the Museum corner while the car was still moving. He said, "Thank you, Danny. *Mil gracias.*"

"Drop in tomorrow."

"You'll be seeing me."

He waited on the corner, under the dark beamed portales, until the tail lights circled the Plaza and disappeared. Danny might hide out around the corner to see where Jose was heading and he might not. There wasn't anything to do except stand on the corner or go to La Fonda. Jose walked past the fancy stores, past the dark, paper-strewn staircase which by day led to Tio Francisco's, past the flower store and the bank and the windows of exquisite Indian jewelry, past the ticket office and across to the hotel. He didn't meet anyone.

The lobby was busy enough on a Saturday night, there was laughter and yak from the doors of the Cantina, the restaurant was filled, stringed music came from the New Mexican room beyond. He didn't speak to anyone; if they spoke first, he nodded. The ones who knew Beach was dead would understand why he wasn't friendly; when the others heard about it, they'd understand too. They probably all knew, even the tourists; in a small town everyone knew everything. Or thought they did. They didn't have anything to do with their minds except probe their neighbors' affairs.

He went directly to the desk. "What's the number of Tim Farrar's room?" He knew the clerk but not well, new men had come in during his years away. His face stopped any sympathy, he couldn't take sympathy tonight.

The clerk told him. Because it was a small town and a small hotel, the clerk knew Jose wasn't asking the number in order to go up and rifle the room. Jose picked up the house phone and gave the number. He didn't have to wait long. She answered it.

He didn't want her to know his voice. It didn't sound much like his, it was tight, as if he were coming down with quinsy. "Tim Farrar in?"

She said, "No, he isn't. Who is calling?"

He didn't know whether she sounded uneasy or not. He said, "Moreno," and hung up before she could ask any further questions. He took the long way to the elevators. As if he were going to the New Mexican room to dance. But no one cared where he was going or why.

Five hundred was the big suite, the best in the house. The living room was as big as the Cantina. You paid plenty for Five hundred. He knocked, waited, had his knuckles up to knock again when the door opened. His knuckles nearly shoved her face.

She said, "Oh?" and then, "Oh!" She wasn't expecting him. Her hair was ruffled, as if she'd been lying down, and she had on a pink chiffon thing, made innocent with a little high round collar trimmed in baby lace and smocking; his sister had worn a dress like that when she was seven. Baby lace ruffled the wrists. Innocent, only you could see through chiffon like through a windowpane. She was ready for bed, she had on a pink ruffly thing underneath the chiffon, more like an evening than a night dress.

His hate of her was bile in his mouth. And yet hating her, he wanted to take her in his arms, to hold her until she became warm, until he could forget.

She backed away as he slammed the door. Fright was a quivering hand passing over her face.

He said, "Where's your brother? Where's Tim?"

"I don't know."

He took a step toward her and she said hurriedly, "I don't know! He and Rags are having dinner with some friend in the Valley."

"With Alvin Struyker?"

"No ... I don't know.... Perhaps ..."

"Why didn't they have dinner with him on the Hill? Why come down to the Valley for dinner?" He wouldn't have known he was moving in on her only she kept backing away.

"I don't know," she cried again. "I only know they called me that they wouldn't be here for dinner." She had backed to the windows, the opened casements that looked down on the patio. She couldn't move further except out those windows.

He stood in front of her. He said, "You killed Beach."

Her mouth and eyes widened.

He repeated through clenched teeth, "You killed Beach." His hands were on her arms, her shoulders, biting into the pink chiffon, clawing toward her throat.

She fought back, whispering, "No," over and again. Her mouth was a machine, it could make only that husky sound. He might have killed her if the screaming laughter hadn't sounded from the patio below. Someone who pointed out the figures in the lighted window, some dopes who thought they were witnessing a rape scene. And someone yelled the inevitable, "Hey, Jo!" before remembering it couldn't be Jose Aragon up there with Beach dead.

His hands went limp at his sides and he walked over to the low couch, dropped there. He buried his face in those same hands. Not until then did he know what he had been about to do. She came to him, he could smell her standing there above him. She didn't use cheap perfume, hers was the best.

He felt her touch on his shaking shoulder. He snarled, "Keep your hands off me!" He heard her walk away; he didn't move.

After a moment she was in front of him again. She said without expression, "Drink this."

He let his hands fall and he looked up at her. He didn't know why but his hands and face were wet. She held out a glass of brandy. "Drink it."

He drank it in one swallow.

She took the glass from him and she returned to the bar on the other side of the room. He was all right now. He could leave.

She brought another glass, a tall one this time. She handed it to him and she sat down across from him in a squat armchair. "I didn't know your cousin was dead," she said quietly.

"Didn't Tim tell you?" His voice was ugly. "He called you about dinner arrangements. Didn't he tell you Beach wouldn't be there?"

She still had fear of him although he was well behaved now, almost like any man having a social glass with a woman. She could sit there quietly talking with him, almost like any woman with a man, but the fear was there, beneath the pink chiffon, beneath her clean tan skin, beneath her quietness.

"He didn't mention Beach."

"And you didn't," he said sardonically.

"No, I didn't. I took it for granted they were together. Or that Beach was returning to town." At the look he gave her, she said with a spurt of anger, "I didn't think of him at all. I wasn't accustomed to taking care of him." She broke off. Her fingers clenched together. "What happened to Beach?"

"He was in an accident," he said. "His car went over a cliff."

He watched the fear go out of her like smoke out of a cigarette. He didn't understand.

162

"Oh," she said. And realized she should say more. "I'm sorry."

He cut off her sympathy. "An accident," he stressed.

It didn't seem to mean anything to her. "I'm terribly sorry. If we hadn't wanted to see Los Alamos—"

He cut in again. "You didn't go."

Her eyes winged to his face.

"You planned the trip but you didn't go."

"What are you trying to say?" Her voice was as taut as his.

"You killed him. Not with your fine hands, you wouldn't want to spoil them. But you arranged for him to die."

She hated him as much as he hated her. She said, "You're crazy."

He took another drink of the highball, to show her how well controlled he was. "Why didn't you go on the trip today? Don't give me the overslept routine."

"I won't. I didn't go because Tim didn't want me to go. He was so thoroughly nasty about it that I didn't want to go. If you don't believe that, ask Rags."

She spoke with such heat that he almost believed her.

"Why didn't Tim want you to go?"

"Ask Rags," she said with set lips. "Or ask Tim. He'd tell you." She laughed, just once. The sound of it was bitter.

"Do you know Alvin Struyker?"

"I've met him. Once."

"He's a friend of your brother's."

"Tim met him when I did."

"When he came for the perfume?"

She glanced at him quickly, wondering what he knew. She nodded.

"A friend of Rags?"

"Rags met him for the first time when we did."

"Where does Rags stand in your trio? Who is he?"

"He is Tim's"—she hesitated, found a word—"companion."

He supplied another word. "Or bodyguard."

Her fingers tightened together.

And another, "Or gunsel."

She said, "Fix yourself another drink. Fix one for me, too."

He took his empty glass across the room. "You told me you brought the perfume to Santa Fe for a friend. If you just met Struyker, he isn't the friend. Yet he has the perfume." He fizzed soda into two glasses, carried them back across the room. "There's a discrepancy."

"No. The friend lives in Mexico. He asked me to bring the package from el Greco's to Mr. Struyker. I didn't know Mr. Struyker."

"You know what Struyker's job is?"

"I believe he has something to do with research at Los Alamos."

"He has," Jose said. "He's in the Lab." He eyed her. "No connection?"

From the open curiosity in her face, to her there wasn't.

"Harrod thinks there is. He thought so after Tustin's accident. Way down on the border. He's going to think so again now that Beach has had an accident on the Los Alamos road." He couldn't keep it easy when Beach came into it.

She said, "I don't understand."

"I'm going to ask you something straight." He implied that he didn't expect a straight answer. He didn't. "Did you know what you were bringing across the border?"

Slowly she shook her head.

He probed, "This friend didn't tell you? He simply asked you to bring it across, he didn't explain anything?"

"That's right."

"And you were willing," he scorned.

"He did me a great favor. I was willing to do him a small one," she defended herself. "It wasn't smuggling. He assured me of that."

"Then why didn't you do it yourself?" he pounced. "Why did you hire me?"

She took it carefully. "I was afraid." At the droop of his lip, she was defensive again. "I didn't think there was anything wrong in what I was doing. It wasn't that at all. It was meeting that horrible old man, the one they call el Greco, the way he looked at me." She didn't shiver, she was only very still for a moment. "I didn't want to go back to his shop again. I—I couldn't. And the other man, the one who was following me. The one you call Tustin. Yes, I knew he was following me," she admitted impatiently. She pleaded, "Don't you understand? I couldn't let anything happen to that package. The favor had already been done. I had to get it here safely. I didn't think they'd know about you."

"You didn't know Tustin?"

Her eyes widened. "No. He never spoke to me. I didn't actually know he was following me. But wherever I went that week, I'd see him. Even when I went to—to el Greco's shop, I saw him waiting across the street. I knew it must be the package."

It was a long shot but he took it. Her defenses were down. "What was the great favor?"

Fear sprang to her face anew.

"Passport trouble?" He was close. He could tell that.

She kept her face averted. She said, "I'm an American. A citizen. I didn't need a passport to come in from Mexico."

"But Tim was in a mess." He'd come closer. She wasn't going to say anything. Her lips were tight. It was Tim, her part was protecting that—cagajon. And suddenly he knew. Hunch, yes, but he knew. Because he'd once been in the business of finding out things without having anything but hunch to start with. Tim was a killer. Her fear tonight was that Tim had struck again. He said, "Murder is a mess."

She began to cry. Without warning, without sound, huddled there in the big, rich chair. She wouldn't cry easily, she probably hadn't cried in front of anyone since she was a very little girl. All the tensions, all the fears, the actual fear tonight of death at Jose's hands; these things and the din of his questions, crowned by his hunch, had broken her.

He let her alone. He took her glass from the table and his

own, fixed them fresh, returned and held hers to her. "Drink this," he echoed. Again he sat opposite her.

When she could, she took a swallow. "How did you know?"

He didn't answer her. He said, "It's not going to help anyone now to keep it bottled. The circle's closing. Beach's death was a mistake, you can't protect Tim any longer."

"He didn't kill Beach," she begged. "It was an accident. You said it was."

"It wasn't good enough," he said. She had to do the talking or she'd find out how little he knew. He was impatient. "Why do you want to protect him?"

She shook her head. "He's my brother." It was a whimper. "My little brother." Some spirit returned. "He didn't have a chance to grow up right." Again she hated Jose. "You probably grew up with love. We didn't. No one cared about us. I can't count how many stepfathers and stepmothers we had—new ones every six months. We had doctors and lawyers and Frauleins and tutors and schools, everything money could buy. But nobody cared. Did you ever hear of the Maquis?" She didn't wait for his nod. "He went underground with them when he was still a boy. Not that he cared about them but he wouldn't leave his tutor. A man who was good to him."

"You were in Paris during the occupation?"

"I was taken out in time. To Switzerland. But Tim had disappeared. He learned to kill. He killed—I don't know how many. When he was a boy."

He said harshly, "That was war. In war you kill in self-defense."

"What does a boy know about ethical rationalizations?" she asked with equal harshness. "He killed those he hated. He killed those who were in his way. He killed because he wanted to kill."

"He's not a boy now, he's responsible for what he does. You can't excuse him now. You can't excuse killing."

She negated his words. "You excuse it in war. You and all

the rest of the world. You can't breed killers and expect them to turn off the impulse when you want them to."

He didn't argue it. There was too much to be said; it would take a Socrates to come up with any answers. He said, "When it's kill or be killed, a man will kill. That doesn't mean he's a murderer. I'll grant you that Tim didn't have all the breaks but there isn't any man who has had them. He had a lot more than plenty of men I know, right here in this little town. And one thing he did have, one thing that every man has is the choice between right or wrong. It's the ones who choose wrong who whine the excuses." He softened, "You can't excuse him any longer, Dulce. You can't protect him much longer. I'm sorry for you, I know what it means. Beach was like a brother to me, a little brother." The tears for the slayer would be more harsh than those for the slain. He got up from the couch. "You can warn him if you like. But he can't run far enough away this time."

He wanted to touch her shining head, gently, with compassion. He couldn't. He walked out of the room and left her huddled there. She didn't move, she didn't say goodbye.

IV

Saturday night was in full swing when he reached the first floor. It overflowed the dancing and drinking rooms into the open portales and the cool darkened patio. Saturday night at La Fonda was a tradition, it was possible that Tim Farrar and his friends had returned here to complete their gala day.

Crossing the lounge, he stepped over to the open French doorway and looked out into the patio. From the spills of light slanting from the surrounding portales, he recognized a few town faces among the hotel summer guests. Tim Farrar's beard wasn't visible.

"Looking for me?" The voice came from behind him. He

wasn't. Not yet. "You were up there a long time. Find out anything?"

He turned a weary face to Harrod. "I guess so. Tim Farrar ran out on a murder in Mexico."

"He tell you that?"

Jose said, "His sister didn't deny it. I'm looking for him. There was another accident today."

"I heard about it." Harrod didn't say he was sorry, he had more appreciation of the fitness of things.

"I went up there. With Dan Moreno of the state cops."

"I've talked with Moreno. He thinks you are suffering from shock. I told him you might be."

"What else did you tell him?"

"To keep an eye on you. Was the wrong Aragon killed?"

"No, it wasn't that. It was a bottle of perfume."

"A bottle of perfume," Harrod repeated. "From el Greco's."

He had seen it in Jose's luggage. And left it there. Timing things his own way. If an innocent bystander or so got hurt, Harrod couldn't let it matter to him. He had to move on to the predetermined conclusion. Maybe he knew, maybe not, that there were two bottles.

Jose said, "The wrong bottle. Beach must have asked the wrong questions." It wasn't jagged any more. It was a dull stone he'd have to carry inside of him for a long time.

"And you're looking for Tim Farrar," Harrod said.

"He's a killer. Don't you know that?"

"I've had reports from Mexico. He might have killed a girl. Or an old man. Or a shoeshine boy. She was beaten to death. The *viejo* was hit and run. The boy knifed. Those are three unsolved cases about the time Tim went traveling."

"What about Ragsdale?"

"He's hung around Chapala for years. Never has cared who supported him so long as he was supported. They took him on there."

"They?"

"The Farrars. She left Tim with him and went back to Mexico City alone. She stayed on another month."

"Who was her friend?"

"Plenty of them. She belonged to the smart set, the international set as the society reporters call it."

She would. And Tim would be safe with a tutor, he liked tutors. Until she could arrange to get him out of the country.

The shape of it wasn't sharp the way he had seen it when it started. He'd found that out tonight from her, now from Harrod. Harrod had tried to tell him before but he'd insisted on her being the focal point. She was no more than a smudge on the edges of the pattern. An instrument, as Jose had been. Because he'd seen it wrong, Beach was dead. And he didn't know whether underneath everything it had only been because he'd wanted to hang on to her; he couldn't even now be that honest with himself.

He said to Harrod, "I've got the right bottle."

"How do you know which is the right one?"

He couldn't go through anything more tonight. He was dried up. He said, "I have the clue." The jangle of the music and the yapping and the laughter, drunk and sober, were like a knife in his head. He said, "Do you want to come up to the house and get it?"

Harrod must have seen he was ready to fold. He said, "If it's kept this long, it'll keep till morning, won't it? I'll come then."

Jose moved from the door.

Harrod said, "Go home and sleep. Don't look any further for Tim Farrar tonight. He'll keep too."

He said, "All right." When reaction gave you the rabbit punch, there wasn't anything else to do. He went out into the night. The Plaza was quiet now, everything dark but the hotel. The quietness of the mountain sky, the clean stab of stars was good. The chill of night was good. He wasn't physically tired, he was only tired of thinking and feeling. He couldn't face being shut into a gritty taxi.

It was good to walk, to be alone in the emptiness of the night. It would be good to keep walking, on and on into the dark mountains fringing the horizon. But he had to go home. He had to be there in the morning to do all the things that must be done. He had to go home because he couldn't leave Francisca alone there all night.

She'd had too long a time now to search if that was why she had come to him. She'd had time to find the stuff and hitch halfway back to the border. Without realizing, he was striding faster; he knew he was climbing the Camino when his breathing grew heavy. He tried to slow down, to tell himself he didn't care, that Harrod could handle her along with all the rest of it. It wasn't true, he did care. One decent thing had to come out of this. The *sorbita* had to be given a chance. She couldn't be allowed to turn into an animal like Tim Farrar.

The house was dark. Habit took him around the back way. He hurried across the patio. Before he could open the door, he heard her speak from a distance in the dark corridor. "You have come back." She had the eyes of a cat.

He said, "Why didn't you turn on the lights?"

She didn't answer him. Maybe she didn't know how.

He switched on a lamp in the library. She was still dressed in the skirt and blouse he'd given her. The small hearts quivered from her ears. He questioned again, almost angrily, "Why did you wait up? Why didn't you go to bed?"

She didn't seem to know any answers. She stood there quietly, like a servant. "You can go to bed now," he dismissed her.

"Where do I go to bed?"

He was angered. Not with her, with himself, with the world of men. "In the room I gave you. Where did you think?" It wasn't her fault she was what she was. He said more kindly, "Good night, Quica."

She said, "Good night," but she didn't move. She was wanting to say more. He waited until it came.

"The phone, it rang very much."

170

"Did you answer it?"

"Yes, Senor."

"What did you tell them?"

"I say you are not here."

"That's right." There was no use asking who had called. Even if she knew enough to take the names, she wouldn't be able to write them. The family council, the family friends, the curious and the shocked and the kindly. The phone would have rung very much. It rang again now, a shrill prolonged sound. He didn't want to answer but he couldn't stand the sound.

It was Adam. "Where have you been, Jo? I've called and called—I've called every place I could think of."

"Thanks, Adam." He told part of the truth. "I've been with the police."

"That's one spot I missed." Adam was like Harrod, a sense of fitness. He didn't say anything about Beach. "Do you need me?"

He said no, and thanks again. "I'm too tired. I'm going to bed."

"Anything I can do, you know."

"I know, Adam." He rang off.

She was still hanging around. "That man came back," she said.

"What man?"

"The big one."

"Oh." Yes, Adam would have made a trip in when he couldn't locate Jose by phone. "That was he just now."

"He waited for you."

"He's my friend," Jose told her. A man had so few friends. "Go to bed now."

It looked as if she weren't going but finally, reluctantly, she left him. He gave her time to get there and then he went to his room. He bolted his door.

FIVE

DROWNED IN SLEEP, HE COULD HEAR THE POUND-
ing without responding to it. Until it grew more thunderous,
until his name came over the booming, and the wave of it
washed him awake.

Adam was thumping on the door, shouting, "Jo! Are you
in there, Jo? Wake up, Jo!" It was as if he'd been at it a long
time, there was a rumble of alarm.

"I'm awake. Hold on." He came slowly out of bed to open
the door.

"Why the barricade?" Adam's shaggy brows lifted.

He couldn't say why. "Maybe I didn't want to be disturbed."

"Sorry to be the one. But you have company."

"Captain Harrod?"

"Yes. He was waiting in the patio. I just got here."

"Keep him company," Jose requested. "Tell the kid to fix
some coffee for all of us."

"Haven't seen her."

Of course he hadn't. She'd hide out with Harrod around.

"Juana and her tribe are just arriving."

"What time is it?"

"After nine."

"Ask Rosie to fix the breakfast. She makes the best coffee.
I won't be long."

He was fully awake after he sloshed cold water on his face.
He'd had enough sleep, more than usual. Only the emotional

weight of last night had kept him under. A cotton pullover, slacks, guaraches, and he was dressed. He joined Adam and Harrod in the patio.

"I didn't want to wake you," Harrod apologized.

He said, "I should have been up. It'll be a heavy day."

"I figured it would. That's why I came early."

Nancita was bringing a tray. She was subdued, more by the strange man in the patio than by death in the Aragon house. Death was no stranger. She whispered, "Rosie say what else you want, Jose?"

There was orange juice and coffee. "More cups. You'll join me?" he asked the others.

Nan was in a hurry to get away. She brought two more cups and scuttled.

Harrod said, "I'm seeing the Farrars at eleven."

"Tim?"

"Yes."

"I want to go with you." Jose's jaw set.

Adam pursed his mouth. "What good will it do, Jo?"

He was as stubborn as he'd been with Dan Moreno. "I want to."

Harrod humored him, "Okay, okay. If you have time for it."

"I have time for it." The coffee wasn't bitter, the others were drinking it. "Will Struyker be there?"

"He's gone fishing." Harrod was annoyed. With himself. "Sunday, I forgot. I called Los Alamos early but he'd gone earlier."

Adam asked, "You mean Struyker at the Lab? What do you want with him?"

Jose had forgotten how little Adam knew. Adam had left Juarez too early, before things started. Better that he remain ignorant for the present, Adam's temper was slow to rise but it was powerful. Some day when this was over and done with, Jose would tell him the whole story.

He said, "Beach was with him yesterday. He was the friend Tim Farrar wanted to visit on the Hill."

Adam said laconically, "You're putting yourself through a lot of grief, Jo."

Only then did he flare. "I'm looking for it. I want to carry it with me as long as I live." Because deliberately he had involved Beach. Factually, he stated, "Beach was with Struyker before he started home. He was with him at a cocktail party. He was in his room."

Adam didn't say anything more. He, too, humored.

"I'll get you the perfume," Jose nodded to Harrod. At any other time he'd have laughed at the expression that burst on Adam's big face. Adam was baffled, knocked for a loop. It did sound peculiar without a background; Harrod, the border patrol bloodhound, getting up early for a bottle of perfume.

Harrod didn't make a point of it but he was accompanying Jose. Adam's curiosity brought him along.

Jose said, "I stashed it in my mother's room."

"In the secret drawer, I bet," Adam rumbled.

"Sure." Jose had to smile.

Adam explained to Harrod, "Jose's mother is so tickled with that secret drawer of hers, she shows it to everyone."

"Uh-uh," Jose denied. "Only to friends. And not all of them —only to friends she can trust. Unless you know the way to open it," he told Harrod, "it is secret." He was talking up, in case the *sorbita* was in the corridor; she could hide herself before they entered the wing. No one was in sight when they appeared.

He opened the door into his mother's room.

"That's a fine credenza," Harrod said. He was close behind Jose.

"I guess it's safe for you to know the secret. Nothing any safer than the police." But like his mother, even when she displayed the drawer to the most thrustworthy of friends, his fingers hid the secret. The panel moved and there was a sweet familiar smell before he opened the drawer. The smell was there; the drawer was empty.

He was the one who made the groan of disbelief. The others

peered silently over his shoulder into the emptiness. "God—"
He broke the curse, shoved the drawer at Harrod, and ran for
his sister's room. It was neat and clean and empty as the drawer.

Adam and Harrod had followed. They watched him as if
he'd gone berserk.

"What gives?" Adam demanded.

Not even now could he give her away. She'd explain when
she came out of hiding, when he got rid of Harrod. She'd
explain if he had to chase her back across the border and beat
it out of her. His face tightened and Adam repeated sharply,
"What gives?"

She was just a kid. She could have been hiding in the shadows
watching when he secreted the stuff. She didn't know right
from wrong, she'd never had a chance to find out. He said to
Harrod, "I'll get it for you." It was a vow. "I'll get it."

Harrod had learned patience. He said, "All right. You get
it." He left the room first. At the front door he stopped. "Meet
me at the hotel around eleven if you still want to talk to Tim."

He'd be there. He and Adam returned in silence to the
patio. The coffee was yet hot enough, standing in the sun in a
silver pot. Jose poured for both of them.

"You think the kid you brought from the ranch has light
fingers," Adam remarked.

He didn't say yes or no. Although it wouldn't mean anything to Adam without the background, he said it. "She's not
from the ranch. She's from Juarez. One of the Praxiteles
girls."

Adam's face again exploded. "You mean old el Greco?"

"Yeah."

"My God." He slopped his coffee as he came to his feet.
"My God, you turned one of those girls loose in your house!
With something important—" He broke off. "I take it this per-
fume was important?"

"Yeah."

Adam paced. He stopped at Jose's chair. "Where is she?"

"How the hell do I know?" Jose flared back. It hurt. Not

that it hadn't occurred to him she'd steal the stuff but because he'd believed, last night he'd believed it, that she'd wanted the kindness he was offering. Or because he'd been fool enough to think she couldn't find the hiding place. "Maybe she's gone back to the boss."

Adam subsided in the swing. "Praxiteles is a mean character. What are you mixed up with, Jo?"

He attempted a smile, his thanks for Adam's concern. "It's too long a story to go into now. I'm an innocent bystander." The smile went away. Beach was the innocent one. He said, "Beach was murdered."

It hit Adam between the eyes. "For God's sake, Jo!" Maybe he was certain now that Jose was off his rocker. "Beach was in a car accident."

"Beach was murdered," he repeated. "I don't know how it was worked—there are plenty of ways. Moreno doesn't believe it. Perhaps Harrod does." He'd had enough coffee. "Tim Farrar may know. Or this Struyker. Or Tim's friend from Chapala. I'm going to find out." He stood up. "Give me a lift to town? It won't take me a minute to change."

Adam said, "What about the perfume? And the girl?"

"I haven't forgotten. One thing at a time."

He changed to Sunday clothes and returned through the kitchen. Juana mourned, *"El pobrecito! El pobrecito,* Beechee. Oh, la madre, pobrecita. . . ."

She would have gone through the whole family, poor one by poor one, but he cut her off. "You needn't stay around. I don't know when I'll get back." He smiled at the girls, touched Juana's thin old shoulder. He didn't want them in Francisca's way if she decided to return.

Adam led to the truck. "I'm going with you."

"No," Jose said fast. He wasn't bringing anyone else into this. "Harrod might object."

"The hell with Harrod."

"Look, Adam, you want to help me, don't you?"

"Sure."

"Then go up to Aunt Cat's. The clan will be there. Tell them I'll be along as soon as I can. Explain how it is."

"How is it?"

Jose hesitated. "The police—" At the quick angle of Adam's head, he said, "Not this business. Just Danny Moreno and the accident. So much to be done. You can fix it."

"I'll take care of it while you're at church. I want to hear what this Farrar has to say."

Jose sighed. Maybe Harrod wouldn't permit it. It was a foolish hope. No one unmade Adam's mind. Harrod didn't say a word when they found him in the hotel lounge. He merely rose to meet them and headed for the elevator. As if he thought Jose had brought Adam for support.

"Does he know we're coming?" The palms of Jose's hands had begun to sweat. Not because of Tim; because he had to wring her again. She wouldn't let baby brother be tackled alone.

"I called early and suggested he be here." Harrod rapped on the door, a sharp, demanding rap.

"Is Danny Moreno coming?"

"He's busy."

It was she who opened the door. She was surprised, not pleasantly, when she saw that Harrod wasn't alone. She hadn't slept much, there were purple swatches under her eyes. She was wearing the same checkered suit she'd worn that first morning in El Paso. She could be dressed for traveling.

She said, "Good morning, Captain Harrod," and nothing more.

Tim was sprawled in the best chair, he didn't bother to get to his feet. Rags stood in the farthest corner. The boys were dressed for tennis, it was a wonder they weren't holding the rackets in their hands. They made it that clear how little time they intended to give to this intrusion.

No one offered hospitality. Dulcy had retreated to the windows, then quickly away from them to the other side of the room. Harrod stood firm. "Tim Farrar?"

Tim said insolently, "Captain Harrod, I presume."

Adam made deliberate tracks across the rug and sank down on the couch. He said, "Have a chair, Captain. Sit down, Jo." His voice was disgusted.

Harrod said, "Thanks." He pulled up a chair to a position where he could observe all of the faces. Jose didn't accept the invitation. He stood behind Harrod. He too wanted the faces.

Harrod continued, "I am here for Captain Moreno of the State Police, investigating the accident in which Beach Aragon was killed yesterday."

Disinterest was the only response.

"What do you know about it?" he directed to Tim.

"Nothing at all," Tim said idly.

"The car was in good condition when you drove up to Los Alamos?"

Tim fingered a yawn. "Really, I have no idea. I'm not a mechanic."

Harrod's lips thinned. He nodded to Rags. "What about it?"

Rags wasn't insolent, nor was he glib. "We got there all right. No trouble." He thought of something and added it, "It wasn't raining then." He thought of something else and added it quick, "He drove pretty fast." He'd been coached; he was pleased with his performance.

Jose couldn't hold his tongue. "The car was in perfect condition. I keep it that way." Beach drove fast but he was a good driver. He wouldn't take chances on a slick hill in a rainstorm.

Harrod took over again. "All right, you got there. No trouble. Then what did you do?" His eyes fixed on Tim.

"Beg pardon?" Tim was bored.

Dulcinda said coaxingly, "Captain Harrod wants to know what you did up there?"

"How ridiculous," Tim sneered at her.

"That's what I mean," Harrod said sharply.

Tim stroked his decadent beard. "Nothing interesting, I assure you, my dear Captain. We sight-saw. All the dull routine, and we dutifully murmured, 'How interesting.' The compleat tourists, weren't we, Rags?"

Rags said nothing. His knuckles were at his mouth.

"Decidedly dull," Tim repeated, "although it's considered quite a historical monument, you know. It's where they created the atomic gadget."

Harrod said briefly, "I know." After a long moment he continued the questions. It was slow going but he got through lunch, the meeting with various Los Alamosans, the impending storm, and the drive to Struyker's house.

"He simply insisted we stay over for someone's cocktail party. Quite tedious people, I can't remember who they were. Then the storm. It was electric and so were the drinks. Cheap liquor is so potent. It was then that Alvie—Alvie Struyker, our host—decided he'd take us to dinner. We didn't have anything to say about it, actually! He wanted us to meet a perfect character, Adamsson was the name—" He glinted a nasty smile.

Adam burst, "So you're what he wanted to bring to dinner!" He explained to Harrod and to Jose, "This Struyker called and asked if he could bring some friends to dinner. I told him no." He addressed Jose alone, "I was expecting you and Beach, you remember?"

"He invited Beach too," Tim inserted loftily.

Harrod said to Adam, "You know Struyker?"

"I've met him a couple of times, someone brought him to my place for a drink. We're informal in the Valley. He must have got the idea I kept open house." He was burning with rage.

Jose knew the type, party parasites, Santa Fe was full of them as well as the Valley. They insinuated themselves into your house, bumming drinks, brazening friendship. But it might have been something else. Someone might have known that the Aragons were having dinner at Adam's; someone might have planned to get rid of both of them. Two nosy Aragons.

Tim was bored. "Beach embraced the idea. He claimed to be a great friend of this Adamsson."

"He was my friend," Adam thundered.

The golden eyebrows lifted at him. "Your friend insisted he must drive back to town for my sister. For some reason or other, he wanted her to join us for dinner."

Jose gritted, "Which one of you went with him?"

"My dear!" Tim exclaimed softly. "Did you think the rest of us were insane?"

Harrod quieted Jose with a glance. "You mean he went alone?"

"Quite."

"Was he drunk?"

Jose's hands tightened.

Tim sighed hopelessly at Ragsdale. Rags said, "Everybody was drinking plenty. It was a cocktail party."

"And you'd had drinks at Struyker's before you went to the party?"

Tim said, "But naturally. That is how one entertains in this country, is it not?"

Jose cried out, "Are you trying to say Beach was drunk and ran off the road?"

"We're trying not to say it," Tim said. "But isn't it obvious?"

"No, it isn't!" Jose denied. "What about the bottle?"

"Bottle?" Tim frowned from Ragsdale to his sister. Rags kept his knuckles in his mouth; Dulcinda was a ramrod. Tim looked to Adam and to Harrod. They were waiting silently.

"The bottle of perfume," Jose said flatly.

"Oh!" Tim began to titter. "That bottle." He tittered into a vacuum. He apologized, "It was really amusing."

"In what way?" Harrod asked too quietly.

"Because it was such dreadful perfume. Mexican, you know. And Beach kept twittering, 'Bottle, bottle, who's got the bottle?' And that poor chap, Struyker, trying to explain that it was a present he'd bought for his mother."

"After that you went to the cocktail party and then to dinner?" Harrod's voice beat relentlessly. "But Beach left the party to go for your sister? You let him go although he was drunk and there wasn't to be any dinner party?"

"We didn't know that yet," Tim said haughtily. "All of us were rather spiffed. Rather."

"I see," Harrod said.

"You don't see," Jose cried. "It didn't happen that way."

"I know it didn't," Harrod agreed.

Wrath twisted Tim's simpering face. No one else stirred.

"All of you left the cocktail party together. Beach Aragon was alone only after he went through the exit gate. And the steering wheel on his car was defective." He got to his feet. "Captain Moreno has gone to bring in Mr. Struyker. We'll all get together later." He touched Jose's arm.

At the door they waited for Adam. The big man towered for a moment over the three who sat there, holding his strength leashed. Then, still silent, he lumbered to where Jose and Harrod waited.

The Cathedral bells were ringing the noon mass as Jose reached the street.

II

When Jose came out of church, there was the gauntlet of sympathy to run. He made the correct responses but he didn't know to whom he was making them. Under the old cottonwood tree in the churchyard Dulcinda was waiting. She was patient. She waited while he was proper; she waited while he convinced a brace of cousins that he couldn't go with them to Aunt Caterina's. He didn't want to join in family mourning; his grief was his own. He didn't want to have anything to do with plans to send Beach home to California in a wooden box. What was left wasn't Beach. What was Beach was gone forever.

He couldn't remain there any longer arguing, he moved down the walk with the cousins. When they came opposite the tree, Dulcy put out her white-gloved hand in a restraining gesture. The cousins didn't notice. He could have continued on down the steps with them; he could have made it harder for her. But he didn't. He didn't care what they thought. He needed to know what she had to say.

He murmured, "Excuse me," to the boys, not watching the disapproval which would follow him. He walked to her.

"I've been waiting for you."

"How did you know where I was?"

She said, "Your friend, Mr. Adamsson, was in the lobby when I came down. I asked him."

Adam must have made Jose's excuses to the family by phone. He wouldn't want to be weighted by their mourning either.

Jose said, "Well, I'm here. Now what?"

"I must talk with you."

"Go ahead."

She turned her eyes about the barren churchyard. "Not here."

"What's the matter? Afraid you might get religion?"

She flushed slightly. "I'd rather be more comfortable."

He dropped his glance to her tall heels, raised it slowly up the tailored suit of small checks to her proud head. Her cold, proud head. "Very well," he agreed. "I'll take you to lunch."

She drew back. "Not the hotel. I want to be private."

Deliberately he curled his lip. "This is so sudden, sweet."

The expression on her face slapped him. And then she set her short white glove on his arm. "If that's the way you want it, Jo." If she weren't mixed up in God alone knew what, if this weren't strictly phony, he'd have set to leaping. As it was, he felt nothing but pity. Until she asked, "What about your house?"

He could have saved her the trip. He could have told her the stuff was no longer there. But he picked up her words, "If that's the way you want it."

The Sunday strollers watched them descend the eroded concrete steps. Across the way, under the beamed portales of the postoffice, the idlers watched them. All over town it would be whispered that Jose Aragon was dating a sleek blonde instead of weeping with his family. He couldn't say that he didn't care; it angered him to know that his old aunts and uncles would be given the additional burden of gossip to bear. But he didn't care enough to relinquish a private conversation with her.

He said, "I don't have a car. It got broken." They walked on the opposite side from the hotel. "If it weren't Sunday, I could buy another one," he said sardonically. Obviously her heels weren't designed for walking. "We'll taxi, which will leave you stranded with me in the country."

She said, "I don't mind."

There didn't seem to be anyone watching from the hotel. By now, Tim would know that his sister would be successful in what she set out to do. It wasn't her fault that the package hadn't been delivered as ordered. Outside of that one mischance, everything was on schedule. Tim was safely out of Mexico.

They rounded the ticket-office corner and advanced toward Jack's stand. Nothing like strolling through the center of village life, let everyone have a good look. The girl on duty in the booth-like taxi office said, "There'll be one here any minute now." They always said that.

Jose ignored Dulcy's nervousness. He leaned against the outside wall and asked, "Cigarette?"

"No, thanks." She wanted to hide inside that crowded, smelly booth but there wasn't any excuse for it. Not on a perfect August morning.

"I hope you can cook," Jose told her. "Lunch will be on us." She didn't look as if she could so much as open a can or that she had ever tried. Or that she cared to try.

She tried to smile, keeping her back turned to the street. She wasn't such a professional, after all. Or she wasn't afraid. Yet she was afraid; when the cab drove up, she was in it before it braked.

Only when they were at the gates of the casa did he let

himself think of the *sorbita*. She wouldn't be hanging around; she had what she wanted. Because he hoped for her to come back, wouldn't change that cold fact. Juana and the girls had gone, the gates were open. He touched Dulcinda's arm, guided her up the gravel path. "You don't mind the back door, do you, sweet? Only my friends use it." He helped her through the patio entrance.

"Does that make me a friend?"

They stood close together, too close. Because of the heels, her tilted head was where it should be, the right height. She'd go this far and farther for her lousy brother.

He answered her question bluntly. "No."

She turned, walked to the swing, and sat down. Her eyes were averted. From her white pouch she took cigarettes and a lighter. He let her service her own smoke.

"I'm getting myself a beer," he told her. "Do you want one?"

"If you please."

The white clouds were fluffing over the blue horizon. In less than an hour they'd be unmasked as thunderheads, at the moment they were innocently decorative. He built a couple of bulky cold-beef sandwiches, hot with sauce, carried them out with the beer. "Hors d'oeuvres." There'd been no sound of Francisca within.

She smiled briefly. "Thank you."

He pulled a canopied chair nearer the swing. With a mouthful he said, "Go on, talk."

She lifted her lashes. "I need help."

"And you come to me?"

"I don't know where else to turn."

"You're in a poor way." Again she seemed lost. "If you have to depend on me for help, you're licked before you start." He wouldn't be stirred by her; it was an act, nothing more. "I don't like you. Or your brother. Or his friends."

"I know that," she said. "But I believe that you are too honest to permit a person to be what you call framed." She

184

looked into his skeptical eyes. "My brother had nothing to do with Beach's death."

"Oh, no!" he said wearily.

"It's true! You must believe me. I know it's true. After you left, he went over and over it with Rags, trying to figure out when and how it could have been done."

"They're going to frame Struyker, is that it?"

"It must have been Struyker! All of them had been drinking too much. It's true that they did leave the cocktail party together. They went back to Struyker's house. Tim figures Struyker must have tinkered with the car there."

"Why did they go back to Struyker's?"

"Tim can't remember. But don't you see, Struyker must have arranged it that way." She stressed, "They're not trying to make up a story, they're trying to figure it out. That's why I know that Tim didn't do it; if he had, he'd have an excuse." Her voice was thin. "He always has an excuse."

He waited for her to continue.

"They remember that Struyker said he'd ride down as far as the gate with Beach to show him the way. He'd pick up his own car where he'd left it in town. They remember this because both Tim and Rags suggested going along but Struyker insisted they wait at the house. Because of the heavy rain."

"What about the couple he lives with?"

"They were still at the cocktail party. The baby and the nursemaid were the only ones at home. She was getting the baby ready for bed."

"Go on."

"That's all. Tim and Rags waited until Struyker returned and then they all sat around about an hour longer. To give Beach time to call for me and return to meet them. It wasn't until they left the house that Struyker told them they weren't having dinner with Mr. Adamsson but would go to a restaurant in Tesuque."

"You told me last night that Tim called you he wouldn't be home to dinner."

"That was earlier. Before any of these arrangements were made." Without expression, she said, "Tim is careful to avoid being saddled with me."

He said, "They must have noticed the accident when they went down the hill."

"They did. But they didn't know who it was or what. They didn't stop, a person doesn't. The police were there."

"You want me to save Struyker from this frame?"

"You must understand!" she cried. "It's Tim who's being framed, I tell you. Struyker must be the guilty one. But he'll let Tim take the blame, because of Tim's . . . mistakes."

"Struyker knows about Tim's . . . mistakes?"

She said quietly, "I'm terribly afraid that he does. It was he who came for the package."

The clouds were mounting higher. You could see the darkness in them. He said, "Begin at the beginning, Dulce. You were in Mexico and Tim made a mistake. Whom did he kill, the girl or the boy? Or was it the old man?"

She shook her head, "I don't know—"

"Don't start that. He said a him or a her."

"It was the girl. But he doesn't remember." Her voice was under her breath. "He doesn't know what he did that night."

"He says. You decided to get him out of it." He didn't try to keep the contempt from his voice. "Because he was your little brother. How did you know what to do? You picked a sucker and said, 'I need help'?"

She didn't defend herself. She said flatly, "Tim had a friend. He worked in the office of one of the big export companies. He knew what to do."

"Who was he?"

"The name would mean nothing to you."

"What is the name?"

"Luis de Vaca." The heat before the storm was oppressive. She pushed her hair away from her face. "Luis told me to take Tim to Chapala, to a friend of his there. Ragsdale. I was to leave Tim with Rags who would see him to the border."

"Then what?"

"Then I went back to the city and waited until Luis could make the arrangements for Tim to cross the border safely."

"How much did the arrangements cost you?"

"He wanted five thousand dollars. I couldn't raise that much." She remembered the hopelessness. "He agreed to arrange it for one thousand if I would carry a package across the border for a friend of his." She said defiantly, "I suspected it was smuggling but I didn't care. I had to help Tim."

"A murderer."

"I don't know. He doesn't know. How could I let him go to prison?" She believed she was right. Tim was her blind spot.

"Then you picked a dumb Mexican to do the dirty work."

She had the grace to flush. Or it was the heat. "Only because I was afraid to go back to that dreadful Senor Praxiteles. That is the truth. No harm could have come to the Mexican. He could have proved he was hired for an errand."

"He might have had a rough time. But okay, he didn't. And you told the truth as far as it went. He wasn't smuggling the package across the border, he had a receipt. He was only smuggling what was in the package. What was it?"

"I don't know." It was truth or he didn't recognize truth.

"Let's get on with it." As he spoke thunder quivered in the sky.

"Mr. Struyker called me the afternoon I arrived. He was pleasant. He said he understood I had a package for him and he'd pick it up after dinner. That was agreeable. But I was worried. Because the package hadn't arrived. I didn't know what had happened to you. But it worked out all right. The package was there by seven. When Mr. Struyker came for it, I gave it to him." A blast of thunder split the yellowing sky.

He said, "We'd better move inside. It's coming fast." The first drops were falling as they ran toward the house. "I have to see to the windows. The library's there."

"Let me go with you."

"Afraid of storms? Or just afraid?"

She didn't answer but she followed him. If Francisca were near, the clat of Dulcinda's heels was an advance warning. He thought he saw a shadow in the bedroom corridor but it was no more than a trick contrived by a half-opened door.

"Now that the hatches are battened, I'll get more beer and we'll carry on." Again she followed him. Almost as if she were the *sorbita*. The kitchen door had blown open; it banged in the wind and the rain laid wet fingers across the floor. He made it fast. "Maybe you're afraid accidents come in threes." He uncapped two bottles, brought out fresh glasses. The others were outside in the rain. "You needn't be afraid for yourself. You're on the safe side of this. Now, it's different with me." He led her back to the library. "I'm next. Only I'm not superstitious."

He put her in the big leather chair. It fit Adam yesterday; she was slight in it. The world outside had darkened under the lowering sky and sheeted rain; the room was twilit. Too dark to watch her face. He turned on a mellow lamp.

She said, "You have a nice home."

"Yes. I like it."

"Have you always lived here? When you were a little boy?"

"I was born here."

"I suppose you had a sandpile when you were a little boy. I always wanted a sandpile. I read about one in a book once. We used to go to the seashore some summers but that was different. A sandpile would be something you could hold, something small and your very own." A touch of smile came to her lips. "Do you know what Tim always wanted? A red wagon. There's no room for a wagon in an apartment. That was when we lived in New York. We were very young. In Paris we lived in a hotel. When we weren't at school."

He was brusque. "You gave Struyker the package?"

"Yes." Again she pushed back her hair although there was no heat in the air now. It was chill as death. "He called me from the lobby and I came down and gave it to him. He thanked me and went away. In about an hour he returned. I had joined Tim and Rags in the Cantina."

"Where were they when you gave Struyker the package?"

"They'd gone down earlier. They didn't know why I was waiting upstairs."

He leaned toward her, not believing. "You mean they don't know about the package?"

"No. I didn't tell Tim that part of it. I didn't want him to know. He had enough to worry about."

If this were true, Tim would have had no reason to kill Beach. Nor would Rags. It left only Struyker or an accident. "You joined them in the Cantina," he reminded her.

"Yes. And Beach was there and a lot of his friends kept coming and going from the table." She was trying to remember the sequence. "And then Mr. Struyker came back. That was when he met my brother and the others. And invited all of us to visit Los Alamos today. When he had an opportunity to speak privately to me, he told me it was the wrong package. He seemed quite disturbed."

He'd taken the package and gone away. It was an hour before he returned, "quite disturbed." Struyker wasn't the end of the trail. He was just another of the messenger boys. It didn't take an hour to open a package and find it wrong. But to deliver it to someone who would know its wrongness, and to return, would consume an hour. He couldn't very well have made it to Los Alamos and back in that time. But he'd driven somewhere, checked with someone.

"You know the rest," she said. "Now will you give me the right package?"

For a moment they sat there in silence while the rain slashed the windows. Silently studying each other.

"What good will it do you?"

She said, "I want to give it to Captain Harrod."

He was half out of his chair. "What?"

"What else is there to do?" She argued in desperation, "I tried to save Tim. I'd do it again. I was afraid he'd killed that

Mexican girl because he'd killed before. He was afraid too. Now I don't believe he did. I believe we were both being used to carry something into this country, something so dangerous that murder means nothing to those behind it. You asked me if I was afraid. I'm terribly afraid. For myself and for Tim and" —there was an imperceptible catch of breath—"for you. If Beach, who had nothing to do with this package, was killed, what chance have the rest of us? I want to put it in Captain Harrod's hands and tell him everything. Will you give it to me?"

The crash was like a bomb, the white heat of lightning flared in the room. She was out of the chair in momentary panic, he met her halfway with the strength of his arms. He held her quietly for a long moment. Until she stopped trembling and drew away from him.

"I'm sorry," she said. She sat down in the chair again, quietly, but her hands were clenched so tight they ached. She tried a shaky laugh. "War nerves."

He didn't say anything. He could still feel the silkiness of her, still smell her fragrance. He didn't know what were lies and what was truth. He knew only that he hadn't wanted to let her go. The rain was frenzied. He said, "Do you like candy?"

Her eyes were bewildered. "Candy? Why, yes, sometimes."

"Cactus candy?"

The bewilderment increased. "I don't believe I've ever tasted it."

He laughed, a short, bitter laugh. At himself. Because he didn't know what she was and because at the moment he didn't care. He wanted only to know her. He said, "I can't give you the package. It was stolen from me last night."

She disbelieved. She cried, "You're lying."

"Ask Harrod. He came for it this morning. It was gone."

A wasteland of silence lay between them. Until she said wearily, "I'd better get back to the hotel."

"You can't go out in this storm."

"Before Tim and Rags get there."

"Where are they?"

"They went to find Struyker." She touched the telephone. "May I call for a cab?"

"But that's ridiculous," he pointed out. "The State Police had already gone after him."

She said quietly, "They didn't believe the police would find him. Actually he wasn't going fishing. Rags remembered him saying he was spending the week-end with a friend."

He was beginning to function. "When did Rags remember that one?"

"After you left."

The thoughts were coming more rapidly, more horribly. "When? Right after? Did he have a telephone call first?"

"What are you trying to say?" She began to tremble.

He went to her rapidly, laid his hand over hers. "Answer me."

"After he returned from buying some cigarettes in the lobby."

"And you let Tim go with him after Struyker?" He was incredulous.

"I couldn't have stopped Tim. I didn't know. I didn't dream." She pleaded, "They wouldn't do anything to Tim. He doesn't know anything!" And she broke off, remembering Beach. Remembering how much less Beach had known. She said frantically, "They wouldn't do anything to him. Not until I found the package for them."

"They know it's gone." His voice was flat. He took the phone from under her hand, called headquarters. Danny Moreno hadn't returned. They didn't know where Harrod was. He called the hotel. Harrod wasn't there. Neither was Tim nor Rags. Her face was gray as the world outside. The only thing alive was the color painted on her mouth. He called Jack's for a cab. There'd be an hour's wait. Every cab company said the same.

She said, "I can walk."

He was afraid to leave her here alone. Afraid someone would come for her. She'd be safe at the hotel. He said, "I'll get you a raincoat."

The rain was slackening after the outburst. He quoted irrelevantly, "The harder the shower, the quicker it's over." To say something that didn't count helped. The hill under its gravel was soft, sucking mud. Her heels sank into it. She took off her shoes. "I can walk faster."

He held her close by her arm. There were no offers of a ride today. When they were on pavement again, she still carried her shoes. Her nylons were caked with mud. The way the *sorbita's* feet had been. He was walking too fast for her but he couldn't help it. He was in a hurry.

As they neared the hotel, he said, "Wait for me in the lobby."

"I'll have to change."

She was right; you couldn't sit in La Fonda lobby bedraggled, rain-soaked, mud-splattered. In a world that pretended to be civilized, it was necessary to conform to the civilized pattern. No matter what hazards it entailed.

He said, "I'll go up with you."

There was no one in the suite. He made sure of it. He said, "Put the night latch on your door. Don't let anyone in. Not anyone at all."

"I won't." Her eyes were sharp with pain. "You'll find Tim?"

"I'll find Tim." Very gently he put his mouth to hers. In pity. Because they were the bunglers and because of them the innocent died. "Don't let anyone in," he repeated. He had to move fast before there were more accidents.

III

He walked to McAllister's garage. It was no longer raining, shards of blue splintered the moving clouds. He said, "I've got to have a car." He should have borrowed one sooner, he wouldn't have had to wait while they decided which one he could use. He said, "It'll have to take a beating. Be sure it's insured."

It didn't look like much but it ran. He eased it around the Plaza, up Washington, until he hit the Tesuque highway. Then he cut it loose. In less than fifteen minutes he'd reached Adam's place. The side road was rutted but the car pulled through.

The house seemed deserted. He pounded on the door, shouted, "Adam. Adam, it's Jo." When there was no answer, he tried the door. It was locked. He circled the house. The back door too was locked. The windows were closed against the rain. He prised out a kitchen screen, forced up the window behind it, and boosted himself in.

He went through the house, afraid of what he would find. He didn't find Adam. The man sprawled grotesquely by the front door had a golden beard. It wasn't an accident that he was lying there. His neck was broken.

Jose didn't touch him. He departed by the window, lowering it after him and replacing the screen. Let Tim be found in the locked house, the way it was planned. Only it didn't look as if this one had been planned, this was hurried.

No one had seen Jose come, no one saw him leave. Adam's house was hidden in its own little valley, there were no neighbors. There'd be no one to remember that Rags brought Tim here and left him here. The *gente* in the smaller house a half mile around the bend of the road might, if prodded, remember strange cars. That was for Danny Moreno to find out.

Jose drove back to town. He didn't stop there. He didn't go near the hotel. She'd find out soon enough, too soon. He could have stopped to telephone her. But he didn't want to speak with her, to answer her unanswerable questions. He wondered if he would ever see her again. Death was jealous of what could be between them. Three times he had struck them apart.

He by-passed the Plaza to the highway south. He took it easy past State Police headquarters; when he reached the airfield cutoff he set a speed of seventy and held it to Bajada. He had to take it easier there, the storm had left not only small lakes but boulders in the road. He didn't want to be a real accident over the side of this mountain. When he hit the plain at the foot of the hill, he returned the needle to seventy as far as Algodones.

From there on he lost time; Bernalillo was a trap and the highway in to Albuquerque too heavy with traffic after the storm. The rain had been heavy here too, sienna mud smeared the sides of the road. He forded two arroyos, they weren't too bad yet; the brunt of the storm was yet in the Sandias. He cut off the town, using the back road to the University, from there across to the airport. He was lucky there'd be a plane south at six. It gave him time to eat a sandwich at the airport lunch counter.

By six he was flying to El Paso. It was a rough passage, the plane was tossed in and out of storms, but he felt nothing. His body was as narcotized as his mind and spirit. He didn't want to think; he wouldn't let himself think. Only one thing was in focus, the need to reach Francisca before the others could.

They set down in the warm Texas night. He shared a cab into town with a business man from Denver and another from Raton. They got out at the Chenoweth. He didn't, he kept his face averted in the cab darkness while Jaime lifted their luggage. His destination was the border.

It hadn't changed. It was as it had been only a couple of nights ago when he and Beach and Adam had strolled across the bridge together for dinner in Juarez. The lights were a spangled fan across the dark sky. Music tinkled and music blared but they didn't set his heels to dancing. He walked heavily across the dark, dirty span, not looking at the trickle of the Rio Grande below. He spoke his piece to the American customs, dropped his pennies into the toll box, walked evenly on to the Mexican side. The heat and the stench and the sound and the color of the border pushed at him but he pushed back, winding his way through the delaying tourists.

He was safe enough here in the crowd. But once he left its cover, there was no more protection. He had no gun, no knife, only his two hands and they weren't worth much against hands which could break a man's neck like a brittle stick. Yet if he could reach the Plaza without being spotted by el Greco's men, his chances were good. He hadn't thought about arming himself when he set out, his thoughts were running deeper than protection of his own hide. It was just as well. There'd been too much killing, he wouldn't want to add to it.

His eyes watched the faces he passed, his ears were lifted for the sing-song of the *piada*. He knew there could be un-knowns set to watch for him, it was a chance he had to take. But he resembled too many others here to be easy to spot. Unless he were already known to the spotters.

He traversed the first two blocks and started into the third. It was then he heard the clink and tootle of Canario. The music came from within a raucous saloon. As Jose reached it, his luck splintered. The doors swung outward and with them Canario and his band. Jose took the full thudding impact of the small man and his clattering *instrumentos*. It was Jose who steadied him, kept him from falling.

Canario didn't say thank you. He didn't see Jose. He was shaking his fists at the roars of laughter behind the swaying doors. *"Borrachos! Asesions! Gringos!"* He spattered their habits and their ancestries with the mud of his imagination.

Jose could have slipped away but a motley group of *nativos* had gathered for the denunciation. On the outskirts were a sprinkling of tourists. He was caught in the center of the dou-ble circle. Only when Canario had lost breath, did he bend to retrieve his battered sombrero. And, in bending, saw Jose. For a moment Canario remained frozen in that crab-like position. Then he swooped up the hat, pulled it over his matted hair like a bowl, murmured a quick, *" 'Cias, Senor."* In another moment he would have crabbed out of the circle.

Jose didn't let him go. He flung his arm about the dirty little man's shoulder. "That's telling them, Senor Pajaro," he applauded. He might have been any *borrachito*—not *borracho*, *borrachito*—amused by the altercation. "They did not appreciate you, no? Come you shall play for one who does appreciate you." He couldn't let Canario run to inform. "A concert for the *ninos!* That is what we shall have from you, Senor Bird." He lurched Canario forward, holding him tightly. With his free hand, he fumbled in his inner pocket.

Canario whimpered, "Yes, Senor. I will go with you, Senor." His fear was stark, he thought his captor was reaching for a gun.

Jose muttered, "Walk right along. Make music!" He lifted his voice. *"Musica, musical!"* They weren't alone, they were tagged by the inevitable beggar boys. "Sing a merry song," he commanded.

His hand slid out with the wallet. Canario's voice quavered, "On Sunday night we are happy, we dance and we sing. . . ."

Jose dropped one step behind. Covering his wallet in his hand, he extracted a couple of bills. One he crumpled deep into his pocket, the other he folded with the numeral alone visible. At the present exchange on the peso, five dollars American was *mucho dinero*. He pushed close against Canario's shoulder. The musico's voice shrilled more lustily, "We are happy . . ."

Jose let Canario see the bill. "You will make a fine concert for me and I will repay you."

The voice became more happy. "My very good friend and I . . ." it sang.

"We are going to the Plaza. There you will make music for *los ninos de la calle*. You understand?"

Canario nodded to the words he was singing.

They wouldn't be looking for Jose yet, they wouldn't think he could get here so quickly. He doubted very much if they were expecting him. He would be presumed to be content to remain in Santa Fe, comforting Dulcy. If he could get to the *sorbita* before the word of his presence was whispered to Praxiteles, he'd take care of them for everything they'd done.

Canario wasn't one of them. Canario was no more than a street urchin grown old, picking up centavos where he could. He didn't want trouble with Jose or with el Greco or with the police; all he wanted was a little money with which to buy a little wine. Anybody's money was good. For five dollars American he would be on Jose's side for this little needed time.

They advanced toward the Plaza. Vespers were just ended, through the opened doors of the church the candles were being snuffed out, one by lonely one. The churchyard was lively as a fiesta, the old and the young and the little ones made a pattern of sound and movement. In the street below there was more sound and movement. Laughter hung over the warm night.

Jose halted Canario at the corner. "Play now," he ordered. "Play fine and strong, the old songs that all may sing with you. The lively tunes for dancing." Under his breath, he said fiercely, "Tell them you come to play for them. Make them happy to sing and dance. I will be watching." His hand gestured to his pocket.

Canario's head bobbed like a strawman's. He clanged the cymbals, he blew the cornet, he trilled the flute. The children were beginning to gather around him. Jose stepped back against the wall. No one would notice him. It would not be often that Canario left the tourists of an evening to play for the people of Juarez.

Jose waited until the circles widened about the songbird. He moved with the swiftness of a shadow. To the side of a boy. He whispered, "Five dollars American to speak with Francisca." The boy turned black stone eyes up at him. He darted away. Jose moved to another. "Five dollars American to speak with Francisca." He weaved in and out of the throng. Whispering where he thought it was wise. And not too unsafe. When he'd completed the circle he returned to the black shadow of the wall.

Canario wasn't frightened any longer. He was enjoying his art. Jose didn't have to prod him to continue the concert, he had forgotten the instigator. But it wouldn't go on forever. The old bones of the *viejos* would begin to ache for the bed. The little ones' eyes would hang heavy; the fathers and mothers would remember the work to be done tomorrow. The lovers would seek darker corners.

And Jose waited on against the dark wall. He was stricken with the hopelessness of it before a boy sidled to him. "What is it you want with Francisca?"

He restrained the surge of excitement. He spoke quietly, "Only to speak with her. Five dollars American. The same for her."

"You are not the police?" The boy was an innocent, a wise one would not have dared ask.

He said, "If I were the police, would I offer dollars? I would demand you take me to her. Five dollars," he tempted.

The boy couldn't refuse. "I will see if I can find her."

He could find her. He wouldn't have approached the stranger if he hadn't known where she was. But she would have more than one hiding place. If endangered, she would disappear into a deeper hole. Jose couldn't risk that. How to send word without speaking his name. It wasn't safe to speak it lest the whisper reach the Calle de la Burrita before he was ready. He hesitated. "Tell her it is one who needs her help."

He didn't know whether it would work. He didn't know why she'd run away. If, inconceivably, it had been because she was frightened of him, she'd be scarcely less frightened that he had followed her. If it had been because she had come to him for one purpose only, to steal the Praxiteles' package, she'd have a price on it. Unless she already had had her price. He had no facts, nothing but a mouthful of ifs. If she wanted to sell him out, he was here waiting for it, a sitting pigeon. Yet he dared not move to a safer spot. He must be waiting when the boy returned.

The merrymakers were still clustered about Canario but already they were dwindling. It wasn't heat that made Jose's shirt cling to his shoulders; after sundown it wasn't that hot.

No one seemed to be paying any attention to him but you could never tell. Others too could be hiding in shadow. To break the tension, he cupped a cigarette and lighted it.

He'd taken but a few draws when he spied the skulking boy. Whether the same one or not, he didn't know, even when the *muchacho* sidled against the wall toward him. It could have been the cigarette he desired. Jose dropped the cigarette and the boy swooped it up. But he muttered, "Come."

Jose didn't follow too closely. He thought he'd lost the kid as they edged through the crowd and then he saw the shape of him half a block ahead. He knew it was the right one from the little wraith of smoke wisping from his mouth. After another block Jose had lost him. He was alone, an open target in a part of the city which belonged to the people. Where he was an intrusion. And he heard the whisper from the deeper dark of an alley, "Come," saw again the small carmine circle in the dark.

He followed on, twisting through these hidden warrens as did the boy. He had no idea where he was, he could never find his way back to the square without a guide. No longer could he hear the faint tinkle of Canario. Overhead there was the clean dark of the sky and the whiteness of a million stars but these were too far away to light his path. When he came to a stop in the meanest of the alleys, it was because he had bumped into the boy. The *nino* didn't say, "Come," this time; he said, "Gimme."

For one sickening moment Jose called himself fool. The boy didn't care whether he led the way to Francisca. Why should he? A fool had five dollars to throw away; why shouldn't a *pobrecito* accept it? Or more, with a knife in a dark alley. The boy was young but no one was young who lived on the streets of a border city. Jose tensed himself, ready to spring, to strike, when her voice came to him. "What is it you want with me?"

He couldn't see her. She was somewhere in the deep darkness, somewhere beyond the boy.

The boy whined softly, "You say you will gimme five dollars."

Jose fumbled for the boy's hand. The child, suddenly ugly, said, "You give me paper."

"It's a five-dollar bill," Jose snapped. He turned the small shoulders to face the last curve they had made. "Wait for me back there." He mustn't lose his guide.

The child passed him on soft feet. Jose moved in the direction of Francisca's voice until he could see the shape of her against the crumbling wall. Until he could hear the muted tinkle of her earrings.

"Keep away from me," she whispered.

"I won't hurt you," he said angrily. "You don't want me to shout what I must say."

"Stay where you are," she insisted. But she moved a few steps closer, not too close. She was wearing the clothes he had given her.

"Why did you run away?"

She was sullen. "You do not want me. It is the *gringo* you want in your house."

"What *gringo*?"

"The one who comes to you at night. With the hair—*mantaquilla*—"

"Oh, no!" Jose breathed softly. The answer couldn't be that this guttersnipe was jealous of Dulcy. "Oh, no!" he repeated. It couldn't be for this that the pack had had to run full tilt for the border.

"It is not true?" she raged. "With my own eyes I see her. She say she will wait for you—"

He broke in. "Wait a minute. When did she come?"

"After you went away. When the accident happen. But she will not stay. Before your friend came, she was not there."

He was trying to make it fit. "You didn't skip out then. You were there when I got home."

Out of the silence came her smaller voice. "I did not know.

200

Until you sent me away that night. Because it was not me you wanted." She spat the words, "It was The Blonde!"

He sighed, *"Quica."* But he let it alone. He said, "You have the perfume. And the sweets."

She maintained sullen silence.

"You didn't take them because Dulcy came to my house. You had taken them before."

She muttered, "I didn't steal them."

"I didn't say you stole them. But you took them from me again. I know this is true. If any of the others had them, they wouldn't have had to come to the border to find you."

"They are seeking me?" She moved a little closer to him.

"They're seeking what you have. And they know you have it." He remembered briefly, without emotion, the men who lay dead. He said, "You don't matter any more to them than— than anyone else who's been in their way."

She blustered, "They will not find me." But fear whistled through the words.

"They'll find you. Senor el Greco will pay much to find you."

Again she shivered closer. They'd said all these words before, not so long ago, yet long ago. Then there had been time for words.

"Where is the perfume?"

"I hide it."

"It wouldn't take you long to find it, would it?" He didn't know how to appeal to her because he wasn't sure yet why she had taken the things. He had to ask, pleading a straight answer, "Why did you take them again, Francisca? Why?"

She said, "It was better that you do not keep these things."

"Because you knew they were dangerous to me?" He said, "I'm in worse danger now."

After a moment she whispered, "Go away. Go home."

"I can't. Unless I end this. Running away won't help. Death can run faster than I." He spaced the words evenly, as if he'd committed them to memory. He might have been discussing a piece of bread. "Before I visit Senor Praxiteles, I wish the perfume."

She whispered quickly, "You will not go there."

"I must. To make an end to all of this."

"An end to you."

"I don't think so." If he were wrong, he wouldn't care very much.

"You do not go there," she touched his sleeve. Most lightly. "Let the police take care of him."

"I wish I could." He meant it. "It isn't that easy. Not on the border." And there was a part of it that had to be his, that no one else could pay off. "Well?"

She said reluctantly, "I will give the perfume to you."

He didn't hear her leave him. He didn't know she had gone until he realized that he could not longer distinguish the rise and fall of her breath. He was alone in this ugly, hostile dark. He needed a cigarette to quell the beat of his nerves but he was afraid to make a light. He leaned away from the wall just enough to peer up to the bend of the narrow alley. The blur must be the boy who had led him here. The boy would hang around only as long as his patience permitted. He was missing the *cabalgata*. He already had more money in his jeans than he'd ever had at one time, even if he couldn't believe the piece of green paper was as good as silver cartwheels.

The night was warm, too warm for comfort. The minutes passed with sticky slowness. She might not return. She couldn't fail to realize the importance of what she held, not with everyone concerned shuttling back to the border after it. She could decide to hold it for a higher bid. And again, she might not return because she couldn't. There wouldn't be a kid on the Plaza who didn't know where she was hidden. Among them there could be one who would sell her out to Praxiteles, or let loose a foolish word. If she didn't return, Jose would have no idea where to search for her. He could search but he would never find. His nerves were unraveling when he felt her beside him.

"This is what you want?"

His hand fumbled for hers, closed over the roundness of the bottle, removed from the cheap cardboard box. The insidious scent was already filtering into his nostrils. "That's it." He slid it into his jacket pocket. "Thanks. There's one thing more, *ninita.*" He hoped he could put it across without making it sound important. "I want you to meet me on the other side. Later. Can you make it?"

"I can." She had no hesitation about the answer. But for him she was disturbed. "You will not be there."

"I'll be there," he vowed. "Go to the Chenoweth."

"They do not want me at the Chenoweth."

He repeated with emphasis, "Go to the Chenoweth. To Lou. Tell her I send you and that she's to keep you safe for me." He added, making it casual but definite, "Take the *dulce* with you. You will do this for me?"

Her answer came slowly. "Yes. I will do this."

"I'll meet you there." He glanced up the street. His small guide was still leaning against the corner house. He was no more than a shadow against the darkness but he was there. "Until later," Jose murmured. He started to move but her hand caught his sleeve.

"My five dollars," she demanded. "You tell this boy five dollars for him, five dollars for me, if I talk to you."

He'd forgotten. "Sure," he said. It was too dark to distinguish one bill from another. Just in case this was a signal of betrayal, he stooped to his haunches before he struck a light. He extinguished it almost at once. But there was no activity from any direction. He extracted the five he'd thumbed and passed it into her hand. "There'll be more," he said quietly, "if you bring the sweets to me at the Chenoweth."

She didn't respond. She had already faded away into the deep dark.

IV

There was no longer song and dance on the Plaza. No longer did Canario chirp his merry tune. Only a few quiet ones strolled together. Jose gave the guide a silver cartwheel, it made up for the disappointment of the piece of paper.

Canario would be searching for Jose. Because of the five dollars promised to him for the concert and yet unpaid. But the musico wouldn't be searching the back streets, he'd be again on the Avenida, collecting from the turistas while he watched for Jose. Canario could watch a bit longer.

Jose remained on the corner until long after the boy had disappeared. He didn't want to do what must be done. It wasn't that he was afraid. It was the sickness of his spirit which held him motionless.

It was necessary that he force himself to set out. No one followed. No one wondered why a solitary man was stumbling across the wide street. It would not be remembered that he had passed this way. He didn't approach the Street of the Little Burro in customary fashion. Tonight he would not wait politely outside to be admitted to Senor Praxiteles' humble shop. His entrance must be a surprise to those gathered there. He could move softly, so softly that the echo of music from the Avenida would muffle the impress of his foot.

This was the rear wall of the Senor's casa. He lifted the latch of the gate silently. The courtyard was open to starshine. He crossed it, made silent ejaculation to his patron saint as he touched the back door of the house. It wasn't like any Mexican to lock his doors against his neighbors. But no matter how much he owned of Ciudad Juarez, Praxiteles was not a Mejicano. Either luck held or the good saint had interceded with a heavenly key. The door opened under Jose's hand.

There was yet the risk of running into the old woman before finding the room in which the Senor entertained his guests. From the entryway, Jose could hear no voices. He padded the closing of the door with his hand, stood in house darkness. He felt his way through the kitchen to another door. It squealed faintly as he edged it open. He waited without breath but the sound evidently had not carried beyond his own ears. He was in a corridor now, without light, but he was moving in the right direction. He could hear the voices ahead of him. And after a few more steps, a mote of dusty illumination sifted into the hallway.

The door was ajar. He approached it, rubbing against the wall. He could smell over the perfume in his pocket, the sweetness of Mexican cigarettes and the sour-sweet of the Senor's cheap wine. Praxiteles croaked, "Do not be impatient, Senores. She will be found."

"When?" was the impatient demand. "We have other things to do besides hang around here all night. . . ."

If it had been expedient, Jose would have remained here listening. But his must be the offensive, there was too much risk of being discovered. He took a breath and showed himself in the doorway.

The three he expected were here. Senor el Greco, dressed for important company in his rusty black frock coat and carpet slippers, rocked in a chair as old as he. In the big sagging leather armchair was Adam. And in the corner was Rags. It was Adam whom Jose faced.

Jose said, "Hello." He was a surprise. He knew it from the frown that curdled Adam's eyebrows. Rags was quick on his feet. Adam gestured him back into the corner.

Praxiteles agitated, "How did you get in here? What do you want?"

Adam ordered, *"Quitate!"* and the old man hushed. But he rocked a little faster. To Jose, Adam said, "You knew before you came here?"

"Yes, I knew."

"Captain Harrod?"

"No. I figured it out." He didn't want to talk about it, he

wanted to hear the ranch bell clanging and wake up to another day of the cattle, to laugh this off as an evil dream. But he couldn't. "When I found Tim, I was sure."

"He asked for it," Rags snarled. "That little louse, trying to muscle in—"

Adam said, "Shut up. I'll do the talking." He turned his eyes again to Jose. "He was a louse. I lost my temper."

"I knew it happened that way with him. But not Tustin. Or Beach."

Adam opened his mouth, but Jose didn't give him a chance to speak. "I should have known sooner. You were the only one who could have taken care of Tustin. But I thought you'd really started home. I had a brush with him just before I went into the Cock that night. Rags and Tim were already at a table, they didn't leave until after I did. Tustin was dead by then. Senor el Greco wasn't strong enough to heave a body around. And he wouldn't have dared ride a dead man through customs. His reputation isn't good enough. It had to be someone like you." His smile was twisted. "And it never occurred to me that you weren't my best friend."

Adam said, "Tustin was a hired spy."

Jose didn't pay any attention. "You too had just come up from Mexico. But that didn't mean anything to me, you were always traveling back and forth on business. It didn't mean anything to me that you know everyone below the border the same as you know everyone above it. That you must have known Rags. No one suspects a big, easy-going, friendly guy of dirty business."

Adam's face looked as if Jose had struck him.

"You're the one who grabbed the chance of using Tim's trouble to smuggle something too hot for you to handle personally. You told that exporter's clerk what to do. With Rags on the spot to watch the Farrars, it must have looked foolproof. I was a mistake."

"Yes," Adam monotoned.

"You didn't know about me until you saw the Senor that

night, did you? After he'd given me the package. I didn't say anything to you or Beach because I didn't want you two to be involved in trouble. I knew it was trouble. I'd caught Tustin searching my room."

"Why didn't you drop it then?" Adam asked in the same monotone.

"I was curious. Beach and I were alike that way, curious." He probed, "You didn't know, did you, Adam? You didn't tell el Greco to set his goons on me that night?"

"I didn't know until after you had the package. I wasn't worried when I did know. I didn't expect anyone to be curious about a girl buying a perfume, a girl who would have used up her shopping quota the first day. I wasn't worried until I found out she'd asked you to bring the package to Santa Fe. And it was the wrong package."

"Yes," Jose said. He scowled. "I don't get why you tried to saddle me with Tustin's body. The police would have been curious about the package."

Adam's face darkened. "Fool!"

"You mean you didn't tell Rags to hire Canario to warn you when I was coming across the border?"

"That dirty bug," Rags began.

Jose said coldly, "Canario didn't give you away. He handed me a *piada* about Dulcinda planning it. Like you told him. But she couldn't have. She wouldn't know I'd make the bars looking for Beach. Adam was the only one who knew our habits."

Adam's anger had solidified. He didn't care how much Jose knew, it no longer was important. "The *piada* was to warn of your crossing. The Senor's men were to take the package from you because you might become curious. You left the Cock sooner than I thought Beach would permit, especially with the blonde there. I hadn't time to complete my job." His hands knotted. "That greedy fool. I paid that cabbie plenty but he couldn't miss an extra fare. He picked up you and Beach."

Jose waited for Adam's eyes to meet his. He said then, "You didn't have to kill Beach."

From the depths, Adam cried, "I didn't. . . ."

Jose cut him off. "Not with your hands. But you ordered it. When your bright boys got scared at his questions and telephoned you."

"I didn't mean he was to die."

"What did you tell them?" Jose asked bitterly. "To take care of him? What did you think they'd do, slap his wrist? You killed Beach. Afterwards you hoped it was an accident." His hand curled over the bottle in his pocket. He could smell it even if the smoke and wine kept it from their nostrils. "I don't know what's behind this. I don't have to know. Harrod will take care of that, he's close."

"I know," Adam said shortly.

Rags swung around. "Then why don't you do something besides gabbing?"

"Shut up," Adam grunted.

Rags couldn't shut up. "Let's get started. Do you want to sit here until Harrod walks in with those greaser cops and extradition paper?"

"You cannot leave without the diamonds," el Greco blinked. With his toe, he set the rocker creaking.

"Diamonds!" Rags glared. "Do you think we'd be hanging around here if it was diamonds?"

Senor Praxiteles stopped rocking. "It is not diamonds?" he quavered.

Rags put his back to the old man. He demanded of Adam, "What's more important, a damn list or our lives? I say, let's get out of here."

"Shut up," Adam roared. He returned his eyes curiously to Jose. "Why are you here, Jo?"

"I don't know," he admitted. "Maybe I had to hear it from you. Even knowing the way it must be." No one believed him. They were watching the shape of his hand clutched in his pocket. "You don't have to kill me, Adam. I've brought you what you're waiting for." They were on the edge of their chairs. "I don't have a gun," he smiled assurance. "Only this." He whipped out the bottle. "Catch," he said. He threw it toward Adam. It was a good catch.

Adam held the bottle but he didn't look at it. His eyes were on Jose. "Where's the rest of it? The candy?"

"But that was a *pilon?*" Innocently, he asked Praxiteles, "No?"

"Where is it?" Adam rumbled.

"I didn't keep it," Jose said.

"Francisca!" Adam glared at el Greco.

"Do not be disturbed," he whined. "She will be found. Even now Salvador and Ramirez—"

"He's been saying that for two hours," Rags shouted. "For Christ sake, how long do we have to wait?"

Adam looked over his scowl at Jose. "Francisca?"

Jose smiled. "She is just a child. Children like sweets." His smile became a taunt. "I wouldn't wait too long for her. I think she's safely across the border by now."

Adam and Rags were on their feet before he finished speaking. Praxiteles' chair became motionless. Adam's fists were knotty but Jose wasn't afraid. There was no time left for fear.

"You knew," Adam accused. "You knew all along." He realized he was clutching the perfume and with an angry gesture cast it away. The perfume meant nothing; it was identification only. As the glass broke, the smell was overpowering.

"Call it a hunch," Jose said. He threw his bluff, "I'd better get back to Harrod before he starts worrying about me."

Rags was alarmed. "You aren't letting him walk out of here?"

Adam said with cold deliberation, "No. I'm not letting him walk out of here."

Jose stood quietly. "Even I, Adam."

"There's no choice," Adam said.

The perfume was seeping on the floor like blood. Jose smiled arrogantly. "Without me you will never find Francisca and the *dulce.*"

A crash shattered the quietness. Praxiteles teetered to his feet. "It is the window," he screamed. "My show window."

Jose ran first, up the corridor from where the sound had come. The others were on his heels. But Praxiteles was between him and Adam, Rags was somewhere in the rear. Or skinning out the back way. Jose could outrun the old man and the big man. Only in passing did he note the jagged shop window. The vestibule door was open. He ducked through it, heard the whispered, "This way," and followed the fleet heels into the darkness.

The bullet spattered as he sprinted across the street. It was offside. Adam wouldn't want to kill him, not yet. Shooting was out of desperation; it would bring the police. Yet there'd be a sane story to tell them, thieves or hoodlums destroying el Greco's property.

Jose kept running because there was nothing else he could do. He didn't know whom he was following or where. He didn't hesitate to dart after the shadow into a burrow between two warehouses. He knew then they were on the river bank. The darkness was absolute. A hand touched his, a small hand. He whispered, "For God's sake, Francisca!"

"We go this way," she whispered.

"I told you to wait across the border."

"It was not safe that you go to Senor Praxiteles alone. He is a very bad man."

The passage narrowed. He crept after her. "Where were you?"

"I listen. When I hear them say you cannot leave, I go quickly and I throw a big rock." Her whisper was fierce. "Always I have wanted to throw a rock through his fine window."

He laughed silently. Then remembered, "The sweets! You have them?"

"No."

A stone dropped into the pit of his stomach. After all this. . . . He groaned, "What did you do with them?"

"I give them to Jaime. My *primo*. He will deliver them."

Somehow he believed it. They would be waiting at the Chenoweth. On the coffee table in Lou's room.

She had stopped moving. "When you go outside, you will slide down the bank into the river. It will be muddy but not very wet. You will run fast and climb up the other side. Then you are safe."

"Let's get going," he decided.

Her words were softer than a breath. "You do not need me with you now. You will be safe."

He felt for her in the darkness. His hands fell roughly on the thin blouse covering her shoulders. "Get going," he commanded. "If you think I'm going to let you stay here, you're crazy. After all I've gone through to keep you safe. *Anda!*"

She wriggled through the small aperture. He followed, sliding after her down the rough embankment. Before they hit bottom, the cries came from the top of the bank nearer the bridge. "*Alto!* Stop! *Alto!* We will fire!"

"It is the police who demands you stop!"

He shouted to her, "Keep going. We've got to get across to the other side."

She was running ahead of him. Lights were being played over the riverbed. The mud was thick, like gumbo. Adam wouldn't hold his fire, he'd have to stop them. But they were moving targets, zigzagging, crouching low. The first bullet whined past.

"Keep going," Jose shouted again.

They were across the dividing line. They plowed to the opposite bank. The Juarez police wouldn't fire on the North American side. It was Adam whose rage wouldn't permit him to cease.

She clambered the opposite bank like a mountain goat. He followed laboriously, scraping his hands, ripping the knees of his trousers. But he followed. And joined her at the top. He caught her hand and ran with her into the deep shadows of a protective building. "We made it," he panted. He caught her up in his arms and hugged her. "Baby," he exulted, "we made it."

V

Lou clutched her bathrobe around her as she opened the door of her suite. "For God's sake, what happened to you?"

They were a sorry mess to barge in on anyone at midnight. Muddy, bloody, but unbowed. They'd walked the back streets to the hotel. Not daring trust a cab. He held tight to Francisca's reluctant hand. "Fell in the river. Got a drink?" The box was on the table. In plain view, unwrapped. Cactus candy packed by Praxiteles and Company. Still holding on to Francisca, he reached for it.

Lou went to the bar, poured him a straight one. She watched him pick up the box. "Jaime brought it. Said to give it to you."

"Thanks." He took the drink. He released Francisca but was careful to stand between her and the door. Even now she might bolt. "Better give the kid a glass of wine. She's had it rugged."

Lou poured a glass. "That's what a girl gets messing with you. Trouble."

"Where's Harrod?"

"Should I know?" She refilled his glass.

"I was hoping you would." He was ready to fall on his face without the drink. Francisca ought to be keeling over. He said, "How about letting us wash up, Lou? So we can rest on your fancy chairs."

"Go on. Sit down."

"My mother raised me better. You go first, Baby," he told Francisca. "Bath, shower, get clean."

"Shampoo?" She touched her head.

"Yeah, the works. Lend her a robe, Lou."

212

Lou said, "You and your ideas," but she went to her bedroom, fetched the terry robe.

Jose wheeled Francisca to the guest room, pointed the door beyond. "Go on. Scrape off the mud." He closed the bedroom door on her. She couldn't skip out for a while now.

"Where did you find her?" Lou asked.

"At el Greco's. The old devil has some good stock." His fingernail was ripping at the cellophane of the candy box. "See if you can locate Harrod, Lou." She got on the phone. But she watched what he was doing. He lifted the lid from the shallow box. If he was expecting something fancy, this wasn't it. The rounds of cactus candy were packed neatly. He took one, bit it in two pieces, put it back in the box. It was nothing but candy. He started on the second piece.

"Hungry?" Lou wanted to know.

"Sweet tooth," he grimaced. The second piece was candy. He began on the third.

Lou replaced the phone. "Harrod isn't in. His wife says he's in Santa Fe. The office isn't that talkative. He's out." She gestured. "Sit down, Jo. Before you fall down. Dirt washes off."

He opened the evening paper, spread it on the couch, and rested gingerly on the edge of it.

"And pass the candy."

"Uh-uh. This is mine." He'd bit into something. He ripped the sticky sweet away from it. Microfilm. A minute roll. He pushed it into his pocket, picked up another sweet. The knock attacked the door before he could bite. "Don't answer it!"

"But, Jo—"

He caught her wrist. "You don't have visitors at this hour. Not unless they ring up from the desk." The knocking continued. "Ask who it is." Adam wouldn't dare cross the border. There was too much against him. He'd have to send someone after Jose.

Her voice was uneven. "Who is it? I'm in bed."

"It is the police." The voice was accented.

Jose dumped the candy into his pockets. He said under his

breath, "You haven't seen me. Stick close to the phone." He grabbed up the empty box and retreated to the guest room. The door remained open a hairline crack.

"Just a minute," Lou was saying. She was refolding the newspaper, placing it on the table, before she crossed to open the door.

They were very polite. They were so sorry to disturb her. Through the crack he could observe them. Two purple blue suits. And Senor Praxiteles. Yes, Praxiteles would dare come. He would know nothing but that he had delivered a package at the request of the *mas importante* Norte Americano, Senor Adamsson. Not for pay, *por favor,* Senor. No one had ever pinned anything on the wily old man. No one but St. Peter ever would.

He was saying, "I am most sorry to disturb you, Miss Chenoweth."

Lou was ironic. "Police?" The purple suits faded back.

Praxiteles bowed his sly head. "The plainclothes police like in the United States, no? Special deputies, you will see." His sharp elbow jabbed the nearer one who rustled a dirty paper from his pocket. "At my request, for my protection . . ." Praxiteles murmured.

Lou said, "I must say I don't understand this at all." She ignored the dirty paper. "There are certain house rules about allowing anyone to come to the rooms without a call first from the desk. And it seems to me there are certain international rules about your police crossing the border."

Senor Praxiteles said boldly, "I have permission to call upon you. My police prevailed upon your clerk to make no announcement. I am seeking a girl who has been tempted to run away with an evil character."

Jose had to turn away from Lou's hauteur. Francisca was emerging from the bath. He crossed to her swiftly, spoke into her ear, "Stay in there. Lock the door. El Greco is here."

It wasn't fright that turned her face to stone; it was hatred.

"Do as I say," Jose ordered with fury. He returned to his

peephole while Lou was concluding, "I fail to understand why you believe you'd find the runaway girl in my apartment?"

Senor Praxiteles bent down over the rug. "She is here." He was pointing to the footprints of mud. He folded his hands together piously. "You will tell her, her *abuelo* has come for her."

Lou couldn't go on with it. She didn't know enough. Jose opened the door just enough. He stood in the aperture.

El Greco was not surprised. *"Buenos noches,* Senor," he bowed. To Lou he said, "This is the man who has taken her away."

"Prove it," Jose swaggered.

The old man spat at his men, "He has hidden her. You will find her here."

Jose filled the doorway. "You won't find her here. Unless you're looking for trouble."

No one moved toward him. The goons might be brave in a dark alley but not in the Hotel Chenoweth. Not on the wrong side of their border.

"What do you want with her anyway?" Jose laughed at the old one. "She gives you nothing but trouble."

"She is a thief! I want what she has stolen!"

"This?" The empty box was still in his hand. He pitched it at the old man's feet. El Greco wasn't wearing the carpet slippers. For this foreign call he had taken the pains to change to black patent-leather oxfords, networked with cracks, salvaged from some ashcan long ago.

Jose knew Francisca could move without sound; he'd thought his angry command would keep her out of this. Until she slipped under his arm. She must have had the knife with her all this night. He caught her just in time, his arm swung her to safety. His right hand immobilized her wrist.

"I will kill him! I will kill him!" she screamed.

Praxiteles shrank between his protection. He rubbed his scrawny neck at the spot the knife point had touched.

"Let me kill him! I am no thief!"

Jose held her as fast as one could an eel.

It could have been Ramirez who asked dubiously, "This is the girl you want?" He hoped not.

"Go get her," Praxiteles croaked malignantly.

"You can't have her," Jose stated. "The American side wants her. You'll have to wait until Captain Harrod gets here." He appealed to Lou. "For God's sake, can't you run Harrod down?"

Lou swallowed. Again she picked up the phone. Her hand was shaking. She hung up at once. Her voice wouldn't sound. She finally forced it. "Harrod's just coming into the lobby."

Praxiteles said unctuously, "If Captain Harrod wishes this girl, I would not interfere." He began to bow himself toward the door. "I wish to make no trouble on the border. I am a peaceful man." His lidded eyes sought Jose. "You will not return my property to me?" He knew the answer. "I can wait, Senor. I can wait," he threatened softly.

Jose said to the goons, "Go with him. It isn't safe for el Greco to wander around by himself." He emphasized, "On either side of the bridge."

They were in a bigger hurry than el Greco. They crowded the old one out of the door.

For a brief respite they were alone, he holding fast the rigid girl, Lou slumped in the opposite chair.

Lou said, "You could have held them."

"What for? Harrod knows more than I do about the Greek. When he wants him, he'll take him." His voice was tired. "You'd better get out the brandy," he told her. "It isn't over yet."

The door was ajar. Harrod walked in, closed it. "What was el Greco doing here?"

"Does it matter? He's gone." He released Francisca now. She wouldn't run. Not until she was sure el Greco was across the border.

"You have the lists?"

216

Jose emptied his sticky pockets on the coffee table. "There's one. On film. You eat the rest of the stuff. There may be more. It's important?"

"Yes. We think so. The names of some troublemakers who have come over the bridge. And some who are planning to come." Harrod began to bite into the remaining pieces. "Adam was a stationmaster."

"Adam?" Lou's voice caught.

"Drink the brandy," Jose said sharply. To Harrod, "Where is he?"

"Headed south. I talked to him before he left. He knew I couldn't force him to cross the bridge. We may be a long time getting him. But it doesn't matter. He's no use any more."

"Rags?"

"He'd already skipped. He's not important. He didn't know anything. Just did odd jobs for Adam."

"Adam," Lou trembled again.

"Why, Harrod?" Jose cried. "Why did he do it?"

Harrod said heavily, "How do we know? How does any man know what motivates any other man? We keep our thoughts in secret places. Maybe he really believed his side was working for peace. Maybe by the time he found out different, he was in too deep. Or maybe he's never found out different." He'd bit on another roll of film. He spat it into his hand. He said, "Nice to have known you, Aragon. Any time you want to get into harness again, let me know."

"I don't want to," Jose returned quietly. "I hope to God it won't ever be necessary."

Harrod moved toward Lou. But he didn't say anything. The hand he lifted dropped. He went out.

Lou stirred at the closing door. She wore her years like a yoke. "You're staying tonight?"

He nodded. "I'll sleep on the couch. Let the kid have the bedroom." He went to her.

As if it were a compulsion, she repeated the name. "Adam."

"He killed Beach."

217

She didn't say anything else. She went slowly into her own bedroom, closed the door.

Jose turned to the *sorbita*. "You can go to bed now."

She glared at him. "I am not a thief. You will not give me to this policeman. I will run away."

"I didn't say Harrod wanted you. I said you were wanted on this side. You are. I'm taking you home with me."

"Why?"

He wondered himself. "I'm going to send you to school."

"I do not think I want to go to school."

"Well, you're going," he snapped. "That'll fix it with immigration. And Lord knows you can do with some polishing."

She was lost in the bathrobe. She came over to him, looked up into his face. Hers was thunderous. "You will put me in school and you will bring that blond *asquerosa* into your house. You will call her sweet names. You will put your arms around her. You will—"

"Listen!" He took her by the shoulders, held her firmly. "I'll probably have three dozen blondes before you grow up. But they won't mean a thing. If I wait for you . . . you'll snap your fingers at me and grab yourself a young guy."

"No," she said. The silver hearts in her ears quivered.

"No?" He grinned. "I wouldn't bet on it. Now go to bed . . . *querida*."

Reluctantly she went to the bedroom door. She turned there. "I am not a baby," she said.

He sighed and shook his head. *"Manana,"* he told her.

≫≫ If you've enjoyed this book and would like to discover more great vintage crime and thriller titles, as well as the most exciting crime and thriller authors writing today, visit: ≫≫

The Murder Room
Where Criminal Minds Meet

themurderroom.com

www.ingramcontent.com/pod-product-compliance
Ingram Content Group UK Ltd.
Pitfield, Milton Keynes, MK11 3LW, UK
UKHW022316280225
455674UK00004B/324

9 781471 917431